Just Pretend

R.R. BANKS

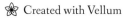

Just Pretend

"Just pretend to be my fiancée for Christmas."
Sure. What could go wrong?

The richest man in this city is an Adonis in the flesh.
So damn gorgeous, he can stop my heart with a single glance.
But he also happens to be my sworn enemy.
From his designer suits to his pompous air,
Colin encompasses every quality I hate.
If only I could stop fantasizing about him...

His hands, caressing every inch of me.
His mouth, pressing against mine.

Ugh, let me stop myself there.
He's the enemy. You don't bang your enemies.

That is 'til I broke my cardinal rule, _repeatedly._
Goodbye, virginity.

I fell into the "Just Pretend" trap with the most eligible
bachelor in the country.

Oh, did I mention I'm now carrying his baby?
How did I let this happen?!

Chapter One

Colin

"Oh shit," I mutter to myself.

I pull my car to a stop near the site and stare at the gathered crowd of protesters. It doesn't take me long to spot the ringleader – the one who always whips these degenerates up into a frenzy. With her raven-black hair, alabaster-colored skin, and seemingly boundless energy, she tends to stand out from the crowd – and piss me off.

Mason, the foreman on my project, opens the door of my BMW, his face taut with tension. He's clearly as annoyed as I am about the riff-raff cluttering up our construction site.

"They were here before we even showed up. Chained themselves to fences and the equipment," Mason says, his voice as tight as his face. "We haven't been able to do shit."

I grumble under my breath, feeling my irritation ratcheting up a few more notches. I'm really close to redlining already.

"Have you called the cops?" I ask, as I get out of my car.

Mason looks a little uncertain. "N – no, not yet," he stammers. "I wasn't sure if you'd want me to."

"Use your damn head, Mason," I snap. "I put you in charge here for a reason – I thought you could handle it and deal with bullshit like this. Was I wrong to believe that?"

He shakes his head vigorously. "No, Mr. Anderson," he says. "You're not wrong. I can do this –"

"Then go do it, damn it!" I roar. "Get someone out here to clear up this disturbance."

Mason scurries off to do as I command. I don't like coming down on him like that, but he needs to understand that you need to be hard when it comes to dealing with these sort of people. You can't afford to show any weakness. Like the old saying goes, give them an inch, they take a mile.

Nothing can be allowed to get in the way of business or progress. Period.

Knowing I need to put an end to this mess, I stride over to the ringleader – Bonnie, or Betty, or something. She sees me coming and turns on her heels, walking toward me with a determined look on her face, and a gleam in her eye. One thing I can say about her is that she's tough, and not easily intimidated.

But, she's also young. Naive. Idealistic. That sort of bright-eyed idealism and optimism would be cute, maybe even admirable, if it wasn't so goddamn annoying, and standing in the way of getting work done.

As she approaches me, boos and jeers rain down on me from the crowd behind her. They start chanting some ridiculous catch-phrase about gentrification they think sounds snappy and intellectual.

"Mr. Anderson," she says. "Lovely to see you again this morning."

"Wish I could say the same, Betty," I say, rolling the dice on getting her name right.

Her eyes narrow and a feral, dangerous smirk touches her lips. "It's Bailey," she says. "My name is Bailey."

"Right. Bailey," I say, and take a sip of my coffee. "Sorry. My bad."

"Has anybody ever told you that you're an arrogant, dismissive, condescending jerk?" she asks.

"Actually, yeah," I reply. "I think it was the last time I saw you, in fact."

She crosses her arms over her chest and glares at me. "You can remember a specific insult, but not something as simple as someone's name?"

I shrug. "Insults tend to stand out to me more," I respond with a smirk. "Especially the more creative ones."

Her grin is more amused than anything, but she tries to mask it behind an expression of righteous indignation. Bailey is a very pretty girl. Her midnight black hair – pulled back into a braid that reaches the middle of her back – seems to perfectly compliment her smooth, flawless, pale skin. There is a splash of freckles across the bridge of her nose, and her big, doe eyes are as dark and fathomless as her hair. Her body is soft, feminine, with generous curves in her hips, and full, round breasts.

I give my head a small shake, trying to pull my thoughts out of her panties, and put it back on the issue at hand. And that issue, of course, is the fact that her people are blocking access to my site. I've got dozens of men sitting around, being paid for nothing, because these goddamn social justice warriors won't get the hell out of the way.

"So, what's the issue today, Bailey?" I say, stressing her name for some added emphasis.

"The same thing it is every time we picket one of your evil, profits-over-people work sites," she says. "Your continued gentrification of this part of town is displacing a lot of people. Kicking them to the curb with nowhere to go, and no idea what to do."

"While I sympathize –"

"Yeah, like hell you do," she spits.

I roll my eyes and decide that I don't really need to be polite, or political with this woman any longer. Who in the hell is she? Or maybe more importantly, who in the hell does she think she is? She positions herself as the voice of the poor. A champion of the people. Yet, she's full of youthful idealism and arrogance – the same arrogance she keeps accusing me of. The irony of it all is baffling.

"Ok. I don't sympathize. Honestly, I don't care. I'm just a guy trying to do a job," I snap. "I've got enough shit of my own to deal with, and I don't have the time or inclination to worry about other people's problems."

She looks at me for a long moment. "Wow, what a true humanitarian you are."

"My job isn't to be a humanitarian," I growl. "My job is to build better communities."

She points to the construction site behind her. "And how is this building a better community?" she asks. "You displaced at least thirty people. Honest, hard-working people who'd lived here for years and years. It's the only place they can afford, and you still come in and pull it right out from under them. You sent them packing without a single care about what happens to them."

"Again, that's not my job or my responsibility," I say. "I'm running a business. Not a charity, and certainly not a homeless shelter."

"How can you possibly be this cold and unfeeling?" she asks, the contempt plain on her face.

I shrug. "I guess it's just part of my charm."

She snorts and shakes her head. "Unbelievable," she says. "Just another greedy corporate pig."

I chuckle. "If you say so."

"You really are a son of a bitch," she spits. "Gentrification of these working class neighborhoods –"

"You mean neighborhoods full of drugs, violence, and crime?"

She gives me a long, level look. "There are good people in these neighborhoods that you're so callously carving up," she fires back. "You're driving them out."

I sigh, my breath coming out in a plume of steam. I pull my coat tighter around me as a gust of cold wind buffets us. Bailey is only wearing a light sweater. Her cheeks are flushed, but other than that, she doesn't seem to be affected by the cold. It's probably her anger keeping her warm – righteous indignation can be a hell of a personal heater.

"I do admire your dedication to the cause," I say. "I don't know of many people who are capable of getting a group of folks to chain themselves to construction equipment on a cold November morning in Boston. That's impressive. My hat's off to you on that, Bailey."

"Some of us feel the need to take a stand against corporate pigs," she sneers. "People before profits."

"Your charisma is also undeniable," I say. "Now, imagine what you could do if you channeled that energy and charisma into something important or useful."

"Oh, so caring about people isn't important?" she asks, planting her hands on her hips, a serious look of disapproval on her face.

"I'll tell you what's not useful. And that's trying to block a deal that's already done," I say. "You're not going to stop us from developing this land. The contracts have been signed, the permits approved, and we're ready to break ground. All you're doing is putting yourself and your people in harm's way."

Her eyes narrow and her jaw clenches. "Are you threatening us?"

"I'm not doing anything of the sort. All I'm saying is that when you and your people do stupid shit like this, I'm forced to call the police to clear you out. And as I'm sure you know, when the police are involved, tensions sometimes escalate, and..."

I let my voice trail off, not needing to finish the statement. We've had clashes with Bailey's group before, and a couple of them have gone very sideways when the police show up. More than a few of her group – and a couple of my guys – have ended up in the hospital when tensions overflowed. Nothing serious. All of the injuries were minor, thank God. But, it's an unnecessary delay, and a headache more than anything.

"Some of us are more committed to the cause than others," she says.

"The cause," I say, a wry laugh escaping me. "And what exactly is the cause, Bailey?"

"Ensuring justice and equality for all people," she replies, like it's the most obvious answer in the world.

"You know what you could, and probably should, be doing?"

She rolls her eyes. "I'm sure you're going to tell me whether I want to hear it or not, so go ahead."

"You should be helping these people get jobs. Learn a skill. A trade," I say. "You should teach them how to be self-sufficient, useful members of society, rather than lazy assholes sucking off the government's teat."

Her eyes grow so wide, I'm half-afraid they're going to pop right out of her head. She looks at me like I've suddenly sprouted four arms or a second head or something. The look of shock though, quickly disappears – and is replaced by a dark shadow that flickers across her face before morphing into an expression of barely controlled rage.

"You are such an elitist asshole," she says, her voice low, and tight with anger. "You arrogant son of a bitch. How dare you generalize people like that. Do you even know that seventy-five percent of the people who live in this neighborhood are blue collar workers? Sixty-two percent have families they're working to support –"

"Oh, here we go," I cut her off. "It's the statistics portion of our program."

"Well, somebody clearly needs to educate you, Colin," she hisses. "Because, you have some really screwed-up perceptions of the working poor."

"Well, since we're going to educate one another," I say. "Let me lay a little knowledge on you. Last year, in this neighborhood, seventeen people were shot and killed. Two more were stabbed to death. There were three hundred and forty-three drug arrests on this street alone. So, tell me again, that this neighborhood isn't a cesspool, and that the people of Boston have no right to demand it be cleaned up."

I'd read that somewhere, and it stuck with me – but I honestly can't remember if they were talking about this exact neighborhood. I'm just hoping Miss Sparkly Rainbows and Sunshine over here, is too busy living in her self-righteous fantasy world to actually look up the crime statistics.

The bottom line is that I have a client who purchased this land and wants to construct luxury condominiums. He's wealthy and connected, and he has big plans to develop the entire surrounding area, making it not just safer, but more profitable as well. Which means that I need to have this project done on time, and under budget.

If I can do that, if I can impress the client, I'm in line to make an absolute killing. He has plans to take this area, and build it into a thriving center of nightlife and commerce in the city.

And I'm all on board with that.

"The point, Mr. Anderson –"

"Oh, we're back to Mr. Anderson? We were at Colin not that long ago. And here I thought we were making progress with our burgeoning friendship," I say, clearly amused – she's not.

"The point is," she says, her voice firm, "that you are putting profits over people. You are valuing your business more than human life. You're driving good, hard-working people out. You're treating them like the criminals and drug dealers you're complaining about. You're just lumping them all together and throwing them out in one swoop, just so you can make way for some rich hipster douchebags to come in and take over the neighborhood."

"Well, to be fair, with this development, we're targeting the upper-middle class family," I retort with a smug smirk. "The hipster douchebag demographic, we're trying to keep down the road about a mile or so."

Bailey looks like she wants to punch me. And if she'd been standing on a ladder, or something that would put her up closer to nose height, I think she actually might have taken a swing. She's feisty. Fiery.

As we stand there having a stare-down, the sound of sirens in the distance fill the morning air. She looks back at her people, then at me.

"Yeah," I say. "We had to call the cops again. But, you still have time to get your people unchained and out of here."

"What kind of monster are you?"

"The kind with a job to do," I say and gesture to the crowd behind her. "Unlike most of your friends, apparently."

"You know, with your money and influence, you could be doing so much good – actual good – for this community," she says. "Instead, you choose to tear it all down in the name of profit."

"One of these days, you're going to have to grow up and learn how the world really works, Bailey," I say. "I admire your passion. I really do. But, your anger is misplaced. I'm not the bad guy here. I'm just doing my job."

The sound of glass shattering and the shrieking of metal draws my attention. I turn around to see a couple of the protesters taking a hammer and a shovel to my car. I cast one contemptuous glare at Bailey, who seems positively stricken.

"Son of a bitch!" I curse.

Without giving her a chance to respond, I stride over to the men thrashing my car. The first one sees me coming, and comes straight at me, swinging the shovel viciously. I sidestep it easily enough and drive my fist into his face. He's out cold before he crumples to the ground with a meaty thud.

By then the second guy is on me, delivering a hard shot to my kidneys from behind. I grunt as the air is driven from my lungs, and when I turn around to square up, he catches me with a shot to the jaw. It's a glancing blow, but it stings like hell.

The rage within me is at critical mass, and I'm dimly aware of the screaming and shouting going on around me from both the protesters, and my crew. I catch a glance of Bailey, who's staring wide-eyed at me, her hands up on her head, clutching and pulling at her dark hair, a look of absolute shock and dismay on her face.

The man wades in again and throws another punch. I'm ready for him this time though, and deflect the punch, driving my knee upward into his gut. The man lets out an "oomph" sound as he doubles over. He gasps and wheezes as he collapses on all fours.

He's gasping for air. I manage to quell my rage and restrain myself from literally kicking him while he's down. As the cops start to hassle the crowd, there are shrieks and jeers from the protesters, and cheers from my crew.

I turn and stare at my car, shaking my head in disbelief. The body is dented to hell, tires slashed, and most of the windows shattered. One of those assholes keyed the word, "pig," on one side of the car in giant, crooked letters.

As the police move in and around, taking some of the protesters into custody, I stand there, staring at my car. It's an older model BMW –not a top of the line car in any way, shape or form. The vehicle itself can be easily replaced. That, I'm not at all worried about.

What isn't replaceable is the sentimental attachment I have to this car. I doubt many would understand it, given the fact that I grew up pretty privileged, but this car is all mine. It's the very first thing I purchased, totally on my own, without a dime of my family's money. The money for it was earned through hard work and determination.

And now it's ruined. Destroyed. Just like that.

On the one hand, it's just a car. I realize that. On the other, it's a symbol to me. It's a reminder of the taxing labor and sacrifices needed to achieve my goals. People might scoff at the notion, given my background, but that car keeps me grounded. Perhaps, even humble. I know people like Bailey would dispute the notion that I have *any* humility to me.

Whatever. They don't know me. *She* doesn't know me or what I've been through. Fuck that and their judgment.

"I am so sorry," she says softly from behind.

I turn and face Bailey, my face burning with anger. Tears well in her eyes, and she looks genuinely stunned. I can't blame her for the actions of those two assholes – but, it never would have happened, had she not brought them down here. Had she not worked up the crowd with her anti-corporation rhetoric.

"These are the good, decent people of the neighborhood, huh?" I spit.

"You can't blame everyone –"

"You're right," I say. "I can't blame everyone. So, I'm blaming you. I'm holding you personally responsible for this. For all of this shit."

A large, burly cop comes over and puts his hand on Bailey's arm. Fear flashes across her face as she looks at me. I just stare back at her, my expression hard, too consumed by anger to feel anything else. Maybe spending a day in jail will give her some time to reflect on the reality of this world. Maybe, it'll take her down a couple of notches and give her a much-needed lesson in humility.

I'm betting not though. I'm betting this will only stoke her fires even more. She'll most likely see it as a form of persecution. Just another way the rich and powerful are crushing the little guy. Stifling them.

"Come with me, ma'am," the cop says.

Bailey looks at me like she's hoping I'll interject on her behalf. Say something that will get her off the hook. That's a train that's never coming. My fury towards her and her group made sure of that. I simply stare at her, making sure to hold her gaze, as the cop hauls her away.

She organized this fiasco – it's only right she pay up when the tab comes due.

After she's loaded into the back of a squad car, I slip my phone out of my pocket and make some calls. I need to have my car taken somewhere until I decide what to do with it, and I'm going to need a replacement vehicle brought to me.

With those tasks done, I glance at my watch, and see that it's just past nine. Great. It's not even *close* to lunchtime, and my entire day has already gone to shit.

Chapter Two

Bailey

I pull into my spot in the parking lot and sit behind the wheel of my seven-year old Volkswagen Bug. I need to ground and center myself again. Yesterday, after a few hours in jail, most of us were released, thankfully, without any charges. Donnie and Eric are getting hit with vandalism and criminal mischief charges – and anything else the cops think will stick.

I don't condone what Donnie and Eric did. I'm opposed to any sort of violence or destruction in pursuit of any goal, really. It is utterly counterproductive to what we're trying to accomplish. It makes us look like a bunch of crazy anarchists, when all we're trying to do is fight for equality, and social justice.

In my view, forcing people out of their homes – in some cases, homes they've lived in for decades – just because these damn developers want to build luxury high-rises that cater exclusively to the wealthy, isn't only unjust, but downright evil. Unnecessarily cruel.

People are being turned away because they're poor. There's no other way to put it. It's classism and elitism at its finest. I see it every day, and it pisses me off that people like Colin Anderson walk around, willfully ignorant to it all. Or he does see it, and just doesn't care. I don't know which is worse.

Either way, it makes him a creep and a jerk.

If only he wasn't so damn attractive. He's tall – probably around six-foot, or so. He's got dark brown hair, and steely grey-blue eyes that are damn near hypnotizing – and they don't seem to miss a thing. When he turns his gaze on you, you can almost feel him breaking you down, taking you apart, and seeing what makes you tick. He seems capable of stripping you down to your barest parts with nothing more than a glance. It's somehow terrifying and exciting all at the same time.

He's got broad shoulders and a thick chest, but he's lean and strong rather than bulky. He's got a thick, neatly-trimmed beard, and is always fashionable, and well-dressed. His suits are all designer, and well-tailored to his trim, strong frame – I've never seen him in anything but a suit. I'm not sure he owns anything else.

I just need to keep reminding myself that, yeah, he's smoking hot, but he's also an arrogant ass. With his company doing so much development in the area, it's inevitable that I'll run into him again, and I need to remember that I can look, but I can't touch. He's the enemy – and you shouldn't sleep with your enemies.

Glancing at my phone, I see that it's time to go in and get some work done. I'm a paralegal at a small law firm that specializes in cases dealing with the poor and disadvantaged – especially as it relates to housing. My coworkers are just as passionate as I am about helping those without hope and giving a voice to the voiceless. It's one reason I love doing what I do. Well, that and I have a pretty flexible schedule.

Since I can do most of the research from home, they pretty much allow me to come and go as I please, so long as I get my work done on time – which I always do. I pride myself on my work ethic and my ability to do my job well. I'm a bit of a perfectionist, truth be told. I have a real knack for detail.

I think that's a trait that also helps me with my art –my real passion. It's my creative and emotional outlet. I'm mostly a photographer, although I also paint. My subjects are always the poor. The homeless. The destitute and desperate. My hope is that one day – sooner, rather than later – my art will shine a big, bright light on the plight of the poor here in Boston. My hope is that my creativity and passion will inspire people to help those less fortunate than themselves.

Of course, it would help if I could get myself seen. Getting your foot in the door of the galleries around here – the more prestigious ones anyway – is impossible without money or connections. Or, more accurately, both.

And, unfortunately for me, I have neither.

I'm a hit with small, indie galleries – the ones nobody but the hipsters like to go to. They all love my work. But, that's not doing a damn thing to get my foot in the door of the bigger, more well-known galleries. One that could really put me on the map as an artist and shine a light on the subjects of my work.

I grab my bag, get out of my car, and cross the lot. I know something's wrong about a microsecond after I walk through the doors. Tammy, the office receptionist, is looking at me with wide, nervous eyes, and an inscrutable expression on her face. Almost everybody else in the office seems to be making a very pointed effort to avoid looking at me.

Feeling incredibly self-conscious in the moment, I step over to Tammy's desk. Even though everybody's not looking at me, the fact that they seem to be going out of their way to do so, only makes me feel even more self-aware. It's as if their non-looks carry more of a pressing physical weight than if they were openly staring at me. As crazy as that sounds.

"What's going on?" I ask in a whispered hush.

Tammy looks around quickly, then cuts her eyes to me. "You might want to make yourself scarce for a bit," she says. "Maybe work from home if you can?"

"Why?" I ask. "What's going on? Are they laying people off?"

Tammy gives me a strange look and a slight shrug of the shoulders. "Not exactly," she says. "But Deacon found out about what happened down at the Chadwick Street protest."

I groan and run a hand through my hair. "Great."

"Oh, it gets better," she says softly. "The guy – that Connor Andrews guy – the guy whose car you trashed –"

"Colin Anderson?" I ask. "And I didn't trash his car. That wasn't me."

She waves me off. "Yeah, whatever. Him," she says. "He's in Deacon's office right now."

I feel like I've been dunked in a pool of ice water imported straight from the Arctic Circle. My stomach churns and feels like it's folding in on itself, my heart is beating so hard, I fear it's going to bruise the inside of my chest, my throat is as dry as the Sahara, and I feel like I'm on the verge of either hyperventilating or passing out.

Yeah, other than that, I feel just great.

"Do you know what they're talking about?" I ask.

Tammy shakes her head. "No, but I'm pretty sure they're not discussing a promotion for you right now."

"I didn't do anything," I protest.

"You don't need to convince me," Tammy says and chuckles. "I have a feeling you're gonna be pleading your case in front of Deacon in a minute if you don't get out of here, though. Take off and I'll tell Deacon that you're working from home –"

She never gets to finish that statement because Deacon's office door opens, and I see him escorting Colin to the front door. As they pass the reception area, Colin shoots me a wry smirk – one with all of the warmth of Wisconsin in the middle of winter. Deacon's face flushes the minute he sees me – and it's not because he thinks I'm cute.

"Thanks again for stopping by, Mr. Anderson," Deacon says.

"Colin," he replies. "And I appreciate your time, Deacon. Thanks for having me in."

"Of course, of course."

Colin disappears through the front doors, and Deacon rounds on me. The expression on his face has darkened considerably, his eyes have narrowed, and his nostrils are flaring. Definitely not good signs for me. As I stand there, waiting for him to say – something – I become aware of the furtive glances from the other office dwellers. They're trying so hard to avoid looking at us, but I know they're dying to watch the drama unfold – waiting for the inevitable bloodshed.

Bunch of ghouls.

"My office," Deacon growls, his voice low and menacing. "Now."

He doesn't wait for my reply, he simply turns and stalks back to his office, grumbling under his breath the whole way. I look up and catch all of the office dwellers staring at me. And when they see me looking, they quickly turn away, suddenly engrossed in whatever is on their desk in front of them.

With a yawning chasm opening in my stomach, I cut a glance at Tammy, who's staring back at me like I'm a dead woman walking.

"Good luck," she whispers.

I grumble under my breath, and I adjust my bag on my shoulder. Stiffening my spine as much as I can, I raise my chin, and march across the office floor, trying my best to look unaffected by it all. I kind of feel like a duck on a pond – smooth and graceful on top, but whose feet are churning like mad below the waterline.

I just hope I'm projecting the smooth and graceful bit as much as I think I am.

I step into Deacon's office. He looks up at me, already sitting behind his desk, and the perpetual frown on his face has grown even deeper than usual.

"Close the door and sit down," he barks.

I take a glance out at the office and see everybody looking at me again – and then quickly look away when I catch them at it. Jesus. Bunch of snoops and gossips. I close the door and sit on the edge of the seat across the desk from Deacon. He closes the folder in front of him and gives me a long, icy glare. Now, I suddenly know what it's like to be on the witness stand and have him staring at me. Even though I didn't do anything, I still feel like I'm guilty of something.

As gruff as he is, Deacon is a good man. He's also an incredible lawyer. He's in his late fifties, has iron gray hair, deep chocolate-colored eyes, a neatly-trimmed goatee, and is partial to flamboyantly-colored and patterned ties. He'd be a sweet, doting grandfather-type if he wasn't so grouchy all the damn time.

"You mind telling me what in the hell you were thinking?" he asks.

"It was a protest, Deacon," I say. "Like the dozens of other protests against corporate greed and gentrification I do every month. You know about my activism. I've told you about it before."

"Yeah, I know about 'em," he says. "And I've always told you to walk that line carefully. You may not like it, but you represent this law firm. That you let this spiral out of control and turn into a total shitshow the way you did – it's infuriating."

I sigh. "It wasn't supposed to happen like that," I say. "A couple of our –"

"Maybe it wasn't supposed to happen like that, but it did," he snaps. "When I found out what you and your group did, and that you were in jail –"

"I wasn't charged with anything, Deacon," I say. "I wasn't even booked. None of us were – except for Donnie and Eric."

"You're lucky you weren't charged as an accessory, Bailey," he growls.

Deacon sits back in his seat and lets out an angry puff of breath. He stares at me from beneath his thick, bushy eyebrows, obviously upset. Deacon's always admired my passion and advocacy efforts for the poor. Frankly, it's why he gave me this job in the first place – though, I like to think that I've shown my worth since then, and that I'm an asset to the firm. When I came in for my first interview, I had no experience, but he told me that I spoke so forcefully and passionately about the mission and goals of his firm, that he felt like he had to hire me.

"What was he doing here?" I ask.

"Colin Anderson?" he asks. "Your people destroy his car, get into a fistfight with him, and you still have the gall to ask what he was doing here?"

I don't have an answer to what is obviously a rhetorical question, so I don't say anything. I look down at my hands, and pick at my fingernail polish. I've never seen Deacon this upset before – at least, not this upset at me. I mean, I can't entirely blame him, but at the same time, I didn't do anything wrong.

"Colin Anderson is one of the richest, most influential people in this city," he says. "You really stepped in a steaming pile of shit this time."

I swallow hard and try to control the emotions whipping through me like a hurricane. I have no idea what Deacon is going to do. All I know is that I can't afford to be out of a job, and the thought that Deacon might actually fire me is turning my insides to terrified mush.

I honestly don't know what I'm going to do if he fires me. My art alone won't sustain me. At least, not yet – or ever, at the rate I'm going. I know I'll never find a job as good and flexible as the one I have right now – and I'm scared to death I'm about to lose it.

"Are you firing me, Deacon?"

He tugs at his goatee – one of the things he tends to do when he's seriously irritated. "Against my better judgment, no, Bailey, I'm not firing you," he says. "Don't think I didn't seriously consider it after this bullshit, though."

A profound sense of relief sweeps over me.

I don't dare let out a sigh of relief or self-congratulatory whoop, though – not with Deacon still looking like he'd feed me feet first into a wood chipper if he had the chance. As I cower beneath his withering glare, a thought suddenly stands out to me.

"I don't want to sound ungrateful, because I am – very grateful," I stammer, "but, why aren't you firing me?"

"Because Colin didn't want me to," he says flatly.

His statement leaves me stunned, and I lean back in the chair as I absorb his words. Of all the things I expected, that would have been last on my list. Dead last.

"He – didn't want you to?" I ask.

Deacon shakes his head. "For reasons I sure as hell don't understand, no," he says. "He specifically asked me not to."

I'm dumbfounded and I don't quite know how to respond to that. Colin Anderson and I are adversaries. We stand on two different sides of the philosophical divide. Plus, I'm a giant pain in his ass. I don't know why he'd go to bat for me.

"Why would he do that?"

"Hell if I know," Deacon grouses. "But I promised him I wouldn't terminate you the second I saw you, like I'd planned on doing."

My hands are trembling, but I'm trying my best to not let Deacon see that. I don't want him to know how close I am to actually losing it. I want to project an image of strength and dignity. For some reason, it's important to me. So, I sit up straighter, and lift my chin again.

"I appreciate that, Deacon –"

"Don't thank me, Bailey," he snaps. "I was about to send you packing, if not for your guardian angel. I didn't do it for you."

"Well, I appreciate it anyway."

He points a finger at me, his expression growing even more grim than usual. "But, you're on a short leash, kid," he says. "You're done with your activism. You either find somebody else to run your protest group, or you disband it. I personally, don't care which. If I hear about you out there causing problems on one of Anderson's construction sites again, I will run you out of here. Do you understand me?"

I nod, but inside, my heart is breaking a bit. Boston4All is a small group of like-minded people I met through social media. We came together to advocate for the poor, and to stop the gentrification of our neighborhoods. It's been my baby for a while now. I think we've become a powerful force for positive change in our community.

To be told that I have to abandon my baby, or risk losing my job, hurts. It's like an ice pick straight to the heart.

"Bailey, you know I have a ton of respect for you. For your passion and commitment," Deacon says. "But, I mean it. You're either done with that group, or you're done here. You can't have both. I won't stand for exposing my firm to liability because you can't control your group."

My eyes are stinging with the tears welling up in them, but I nod.

"I understand, Deacon," I say. "And I'm sorry. I never meant for any of this to happen."

He lets out a long breath and his face softens somewhat. "I know you didn't," he says. "And believe it or not, I know this isn't your fault. But, I've spent the last thirty years building this firm up and trying to effect some real change in our community. I can't risk that."

"I know," I say, nodding as a lone tear races down my cheek. "I know."

"Go," he says. "Work from home if you want. I need the research on the Peralta case by tomorrow. Just email it over to me."

"Thank you," I say.

"Like I said, don't thank me. I love you, kid, but my firm comes first," he replies. "If you want to thank somebody, thank your guardian angel."

Deacon opens the folder on his desk back up and starts shuffling through the papers inside. It's a clear signal that he's done, and the meeting is adjourned. I take a deep breath, and let it out slowly, dabbing at my eyes to avoid smearing my mascara too badly. I take another moment to compose myself before turning and heading out of his office again.

The moment I step out, all heads turn away from me, and a hush falls over the office floor. My stomach is still roiling, and I feel like I might be sick. Working from home is probably a good idea.

I walk through the office, avoiding eye contact with everybody, though I can feel their gazes pressing down on me like lead weights as I pass. I stop by Tammy's desk on my way out. She looks up at me, a sympathetic smile on her face, and likely words of condolence for getting canned on her lips.

"I'll see you soon," I say.

She looks stunned. "Y - you will?"

I nod. "I'm in trouble, but not fired," I say.

A look of relief crosses her features and she sits back in her chair, a smile gracing her face.

"I'm so happy to hear that," she says.

"That makes two of us."

"See you later then," she says.

"You betcha."

I step out of the office, and out into the cool morning air. I pull my coat around my body tighter, as a blast of cold wind envelops me. Winter is almost here.

As I walk back to my car, I'm filled with a deep sense of relief, but also with a tremendous amount of heartache. I hate having to leave my group. I'm beyond saddened that I can't be a part of it anymore. But, for now, my need to eat and keep the lights on at home, need to take priority. I can't afford to be jobless. That's not an option at this point.

Slipping in behind the wheel of my car, I'm filled with a sense of gratitude that Colin saved my job – along with a deep sense of contempt for everything the man stands for.

I just wish he wasn't so attractive – and thoughtful, apparently – it would make it much easier to flat-out hate him.

Chapter Three

Colin

"We were finally able to break ground on the Chadwick Street project two days ago," Mason says. "We're excavating the foundation now, and we've made plenty of progress."

"How much progress?" I ask.

I pace my office with Mason, my foreman on the project, on speakerphone. I stand at the window of my office, which affords me a terrific view of Boston Common. Personally, autumn is my favorite time of year – the leaves are turning, and the world is bedazzled in shades of reds and orange. It's simply gorgeous out there. I'm half-tempted to go take a walk through the Common, just to enjoy it.

Not that winter doesn't have its own appeal, but that is a cold, stark beauty – and one that is best viewed from indoors. In front of a fire. With a warm drink in your hand.

"We're almost back up to speed," he reports. "We've made up for most of the time we lost after the – vandalism."

The scene at the site was just that – a scene. It didn't turn into a full-blown riot, but it seemed precariously close for a while. Trying to get the people unshackled from the equipment they'd chained them-selves to was problematic. There were a few skirmishes between the cops and the protesters, some blood was shed, and quite a few arrests were made. And my car was absolutely trashed.

It forced us to shut down the site for a couple of days, until all the damage could be cleaned up, and replacement equipment brought in. Luckily, I tend to pad the timelines for construction a bit, just in case something unpredictable happens, but I never like to use up those extra days. I much prefer my crew to come in on time, and under budget. It's something my clients appreciate, and what keeps us landing such lucrative deals.

I'm glad we're almost back on schedule, but I'm still pissed off about the property damage and the lost time.

"That's good news, Mason," I say.

"I have the crews going hard," he replies. "I'm keeping them on task."

My crews always go hard, simply because they're sufficiently motivated to do so. But, if Mason wants to think he's the one driving that train, I won't deprive him of the notion. My crews have been with me long enough to know that if we come in ahead of schedule and under budget, I'm always happy to share some of the spoils of war. They get bonuses for completing a project early and cheaply. I think of it as profit sharing, and I know the crews are always appreciative of it.

It may not seem like much to me, but it's enough to keep them firing on all cylinders, and motivated to push the production envelope. That holds even more true at this time of year, with Christmas bearing down on us like a Boston winter.

God, Christmas. I don't even want to think about it. For the fourth year in a row, I'm hosting my brothers – and their families – for our annual holiday get together. It's become an Anderson tradition – whoever's territory was the least profitable the previous year is the one who gets stuck hosting the event.

It's not that I mind. I always love seeing my brothers – we don't get to spend nearly enough time together. In fact, we barely get to see each other anymore. Liam, Brayden, and Aidan all have wives and kids now, so that keeps them busy. The holidays are the only time we have to get together and just enjoy being around each other.

Truth be told, I miss my brothers. I miss hanging around with them like we did when we were younger. I know it's stupid. You have to grow up, and that entails taking on adult responsibilities. But, being with them for a week every year always takes me back to those carefree days. Everything was so much simpler back then.

Oh well. At least we have Christmas. That's something I always look forward to. Even if I'm the one who's hosting the damn thing every year.

All of us Anderson boys are competitive as hell, and this holiday deal is just an extension of that. I'm a bit handicapped in that, while I was in the Navy, they were all already setting up their territories. They were figuring out how the business ran and how to get things moving. I didn't have that advantage. In that regard, they got a running start over me.

It's a bit of a competitive advantage I'm having to overcome, but I'll get there. The last two years, I've managed to cut into the lead the others have over me. It won't be long before I'm passing them. I have the drive, and I'm accumulating the know-how on the fly. It's my personal formula for victory, and I'll surpass them soon enough.

"Good. I'm glad to hear it, Mason," I say. "We need to make up some more ground. This is a new client, so we want to be sure to impress. I'm counting on you."

"You have nothing to worry about, Colin."

"Good. Thank you, Mason. I'll touch base with you again soon."

I disconnect the call and grab the water bottle from my desk. I'm taking a long swallow of it when my phone buzzes again. The call is coming from my receptionist, Maureen. I set the bottle back down and punch the button.

"Yes, Maureen?"

"Sorry to bother you, Mr. Anderson," she says, her voice as crisp and efficient as she is. "There's a young lady in the lobby here to see you. Bailey Janson?"

I stare at the phone for a long moment. That's a name I didn't expect to hear today. I look out the window at the gorgeous fall day and decide it's too nice to be cooped up.

"Have her wait a moment, Maureen," I say. "I'll be right out."

"Very good, Mr. Anderson."

I disconnect the call and shake my head. No matter how many times I've tried to get her to just call me Colin, she refuses to do it. Says it blurs the line between employer and employee. Maureen is very much a by-the-book kind of woman. She takes no shortcuts and suffers no fools. And I love that about her.

Grabbing my coat from the rack near the door, I throw it on and head down the short hallway that leads to the lobby of my office. Maureen is seated behind her desk, her back ramrod straight, her hair in a severe bun at the back of her head. She's a middle-aged widow with soft, clear skin, blue eyes, and her hair has more gray than brown at this point. She refuses to color it and believes in allowing herself to age naturally and gracefully. She's a grandmother who does a spin class three times a week, hot yoga twice a week, and MMA classes twice a week.

As big as I am, I would not mess with Maureen because she might be capable of kicking my ass.

When I see Bailey though, standing over by the coffee machine Maureen dutifully stocks and runs every day, my breath catches in my throat. She's staring down at her phone and doesn't see me right away, so I have a chance to admire her for a moment.

She's wearing a red and white dress with black tights underneath, and a black cardigan that falls to the middle of her thighs. Her raven-black hair flows out from beneath her white knit cap, and her cheeks are ruddy from the chill outside. Bailey looks up at me, her dark eyes piercing me to my very core. Her full, red lips curl upward into a small smile as she slips her phone into her bag.

I look over at Maureen and find her staring at me with an inscrutable expression on her face. She's suppressing a grin, but there's a mischievous twinkle in her eye. I open my mouth to put a pin in what I know is going through her mind. Then, I remember that Bailey is standing right there, so I close my mouth again without saying a word. Maureen just quietly chuckles to herself and turns back to her computer.

I sometimes forget she's not always so uptight and straight-laced. The woman has a wicked sense of humor and an oftentimes subtle, but cutting, wit.

"Mr. Anderson," Bailey says.

I clear my throat and turn to the raven-haired beauty. "Ms. Janson," I greet her. "This is an unexpected surprise."

"I hope not a bad one," she says.

I can't be certain, but I almost thought I heard a flirty, almost seductive tone in her voice. Which would make no sense, given our combative history. Feeling the woman's eyes on me, I cut a quick glance at Maureen. She's still grinning to herself and starts to quietly hum – and if I'm not mistaken, she's humming the wedding march. She turns back to her computer again as I roll my eyes and reorient myself to face Bailey.

"No, not at all," I say.

"I hope I'm not catching you at a bad time," Bailey says, pointing to my coat.

"Not at all," I respond. "It's a gorgeous day out, so I thought I'd take advantage of it and go for a walk. Would you care to join me?"

"I'd like that," she replies. "As long as I'm not intruding on your time."

"No, please," I say.

I hold the door open for Bailey. When she passes by and has her back to me, I point my finger menacingly at Maureen, which only makes her laugh out loud.

I let the glass door close behind me as I put my hand on the small of Bailey's back, ushering her down the long corridor that will take us through the main lobby of the office to the elevators.

"Your receptionist –"

"Yeah, I'm firing her when I get back," I say.

The elevator doors open and Bailey steps into the car, a puzzled look on her face that makes her already large doe-eyes look even bigger.

She obviously doesn't know I'm being facetious.

"I'm not going to fire Maureen," I say. "Truth be told, I couldn't function without her."

She nods, but still looks hesitant and a bit uncertain. The ride down to the ground floor is quiet, and the atmosphere is tense and filled with a strange electricity – like the air after a storm has rolled in, right before it breaks.

The chime sounds and the doors slide open. I wait for Bailey to exit first, then follow her out. She turns to me, not sure where we're going.

"How about a cup of coffee to start?" I ask.

"Uhh... sure," she replies hesitantly. "That'd be great. Thanks."

I step away and walk into the small Starbucks that occupies a corner of the ground floor of the office building. I get a couple of drinks and head back out, handing one of the cups to Bailey.

"I hope a pumpkin spice latte is okay," I say.

She gives me a long look. "Are you calling me basic?"

I let out a small laugh when I realize she's joking. "No, personally, I'm addicted to the stuff," I say. "Don't tell anyone, but I'm always happy when they bring it back this time of year."

"Wow," she replies. "Big, strappin', Colin Anderson is a basic bitch. Who knew?"

"No one," I answer. "And if anybody does, I'll know who snitched on me and where to find you."

The comment, though a joke, seems to cast a bit of a pall over her. She looks down at her cup as a shadow crosses over her face, and I'm not sure why.

"You okay?" I ask.

She puts on a smile that I can clearly tell is forced. "Fine," she says. "Shall we walk?"

"Yeah," I say. "Sure."

We head out of the building and out into the cool, crisp air of the afternoon. Work crews are busy putting up holiday decorations – shiny tinsel and oversized ornaments on light poles, and sparkling, off-white Christmas lights on the trees, among other things. Now that Thanksgiving is over, the city has squarely turned its attention to the Christmas season.

The sidewalk is choked with people, but Bailey and I manage to make our way over to the crosswalk. When the light turns green, we head across the street, and head into the Common. With the leaves turning, as the calendar crawls closer to winter, the Common is a riot of festive colors. The world around us is dazzling in vibrant shades of red, orange, and gold, and I can't help but admire it all.

Growing up where I did – along California's central coast – autumn was never this dazzling. I never got to experience the leaves turning or feel this growing chill in the air. And I certainly never got to experience an all-out, city-crippling blizzard before.

Still, something about autumn and winter in Boston really appeals to me. After all these years, the first snowfall of the season still charms me. It still has a powerful magical atmosphere to me.

"How long have you lived in Boston?" she asks, finally breaking the silence between us.

"Eight or nine years now, I suppose?"

"And before that?"

I take a sip of my drink and smile as the flavor explodes on my tongue. I'd heard people raving about it for years before I tried the pumpkin spice myself two Christmases ago. Now I'm hooked.

If that makes me a basic bitch, I'm okay with it.

"Before that, I was in the Navy," I respond. "I lived all over. After I rotated out, I settled here. Went to Boston College, got my degree, and loved it so much, I decided to stay."

She chuckles softly. "So, where did you grow up?"

"California," I answer. "Central Coast. Small town near Big Sur. Have you been out that way?"

She shakes her head. "I've never been outside of Boston."

"Never?"

A look of irritation crosses her face. "Not all of us have the financial independence to go wherever we want at the drop of a hat."

I hear the hard edge and bitterness in her words. She obviously grew up without the privileges I did. I'd say, she probably grew up working class, if not poor, judging by her attitude – not to mention her strong advocacy for the downtrodden.

We stop in front of a place the locals call the Frog Pond. In the summer months, it's a spray pool, where you can come down on a hot day, and cool off. In the winter, it's frozen over and turned into an ice-skating rink. It's a popular place, and usually attracts hordes of locals and tourists alike. Which is why I try to avoid it.

"Have you ever been ice-skating here?" she asks.

I shake my head and take a sip of my drink. "Nope."

"Never once?"

"Never."

She looks at me like I'm a space alien who just descended from the mothership. I turn to her and grin.

"What?"

"You've been here almost a decade and you've never been ice-skating on the Frog Pond."

"Not really my thing. I just enjoy walking around the park and taking it all in. Especially, this time of year. It's so beautiful. Inspiring, really," I reply.

She gives me an odd look. "That's kind of surprising coming from you," she counters.

I arch an eyebrow at her. "Why is that?"

She shrugs. "You just don't strike me as the being awed by nature type, I guess."

"No? And what type do I strike you as then?"

She chuckles and takes a sip of her drink but doesn't answer. I'm curious – though, I'm sure I can guess. She and I are on the opposite end of the spectrum in – probably every conceivable way. Despite that, I find her opinion matters to me. I don't know why, but I don't want her to think badly of me.

Which is strange, because ordinarily, I couldn't give a damn what most people think of me.

But, there's something about Bailey that's just different. Different in ways I don't understand. I can't quite put my finger on. I can't make any sense of my feelings toward her.

Feelings and emotion often don't make sense to me. They're messy, complicated, and can lead to all sorts of crazy, impulsive, and stupid things. More than that though, they can also blind you to the truth. Keep you from seeing what's literally right in your face. It's why, at least for now, I tend to shun anything emotionally driven. I don't want or need it in my life. No, right now, I need to focus on building up my slice of the ADE empire.

Maybe, after I get this ship sailing in the waters that I want it to be sailing in, I can revisit the issue.

Until then, it's better for me to stay on the sidelines. Once bitten, twice shy, and all that.

Still, despite my best efforts to shut down the emotional side of myself – something I've been successful at for quite some time now – there's something about Bailey that's threatening to undo the knot I've tied around my heart. I can't say what it is. It makes no sense. But, despite our enormous differences, I find her incredibly attractive and appealing. She intrigues me. Compels me.

Which is why I need to get the hell away from her.

"Honestly," she finally answers, "I see you as more of the Captain of Industry type. Sitting up in your ivory tower, sipping brandy, smoking a big fat cigar, and doing everything in your power to avoid us – the unwashed masses. Those of us you consider less than yourself."

"Wow," I say. "I see you've given this some thought."

She shrugs again. "I just know your type."

"And what type is that?"

"The corporate, wealth-before-people type," she snaps. "The type who values money and things over the health, welfare, and dignity of people."

Ouch.

"That seems a touch harsh."

"The truth often hurts," she says, her dark eyes boring into mine.

"You don't even know me," I retort angrily.

"I don't know Charles Manson, but I feel *pretty* comfortable saying he's repulsive."

A wry laugh escapes me. "So, now I'm Charles Manson."

"That's not what I said," she responds, her tone growing more hostile by the second.

This conversation is starting to spin out of control, and I'm not sure how we got to this point, or how to stop it. I only wanted to enjoy a nice walk in the autumn air. I didn't want to have a sociological debate with her.

"Listen," I say. "I'm just a guy doing a job. My clients tell me where to build, what to build, and I do it. It's no different from you doing your job at work."

"Yeah, except my work doesn't displace people from their homes," she says. "In fact, we fight to help keep people in their homes."

"What do you want from me, Bailey?" I growl. "I'm not the bad guy here."

"You sure about that?" she hisses. "Because I'm not."

I'm really trying to keep my cool. Trying not to lose it. She's not making it easy. We're coming at this issue from two very different sides, so I don't blame her for how she feels – but, she's just so wrong about it.

"Look, I'm just a guy doing a job," I say coolly. "And if I don't, somebody else will. I guarantee you that."

"I know that. That's the problem," she snaps. "There's an endless stream of you vultures lined up, ready to pick at the carcasses of those less fortunate than you."

"What do you want me to say, Bailey?"

"That you care about people. That you're not just some evil, mindless, corporate – whore," she practically shouts. "I want to hear you say that displacing all these people, buying up their neighborhoods, and sending them to shelters or the streets, bothers you on some level."

I grit my teeth and take a long moment to collect my thoughts, trying to keep my temper in check. I keep reminding myself that Bailey is young. Idealistic. Naive. She doesn't understand how the world works – and she knows even less about how my business operates.

"Bailey, when a property is purchased for redevelopment, the people in those homes are given more than fair market value for their homes. I'm not just tossing people out on the street."

"No? What about people who rent? Do they get a cut of that? What about the apartment complex over on Walford you tore down about six months ago?"

"They were given at least ninety-days notice that the property was being redeveloped," I answer. "They were given first right of rental in the new property –"

"Yeah, like any of them could have afforded it," she snaps.

I shrug. "That's not my problem," I reply.

"Like I said, I'm running a business. Not a charity."

She opens her mouth to argue again, but I know that if I let her, and this debate continues, it's only going to become more intense and more heated – and there are already enough people subtly eyeballing us. Curious onlookers who want to see the drama unfold.

"Listen," I say coldly, cutting her off. "I'm not going to stand here and debate this with you. What was it you came to see me about today?"

She closes her mouth and suddenly looks deflated. And for a moment, she looks lost. But she quickly regains her footing and clears her throat.

"I wanted to come by to thank you for saving my job," she says, her voice stiffer and more frigid than the air around us. "And to apologize, again, for the damage that was done to your car."

"You're welcome," I respond formally. "And don't worry about the car. With the salary I earn as a corporate whore, I'm sure I can afford to get it fixed."

We stand there awkwardly, staring at each other for a minute, neither of us knowing what to say.

I can't tell you exactly what I expected or wanted from this walk with her, but I can tell you, this wasn't it.

I guess I was hoping for a good conversation, and to get to know the captivating woman in front of me. Obviously, I need to learn to manage my expectations better.

"Is that all?" I ask.

She hesitates, and I can see the uncertainty on her face. She looks like she has more to say, but the moment passes, and she looks away from me.

"Yeah, that's it," she says softly.

"Great," I reply. "Then I appreciate you stopping by. Have a nice day."

I turn and walk away, my mood deteriorating quickly. Part of me wants to go back to her and talk things out. To return to the free and fun conversation from before things went south. But, I don't turn back. I simply keep on walking and fasten another lock on the chain around my heart.

Chapter Four

Bailey

I unlock the door to my studio and step inside. I breathe in deeply, savoring the thick scent of paint hanging in the air. I know I shouldn't – that it's bad for me – but, the smell of paint has always been something I found enjoyable. To me, it smells like – art. Beauty. Passion.

My studio is small, but it's everything I need. I rent it out from a guy who built an artist's commune of sorts – a safe space for artists to work. It's located in one of the shadier parts of town. A neighborhood that I'm sure Colin and his ilk will eventually tear down in the name of wealth and progress.

Until then, I'm determined to keep creating art here. And I'm going to keep working my ass off to get my art noticed by the right people. Influential people. People who can help get my message out to the world, where it might do some good for the people who need it the most.

I flip on the lights and look at the row of canvases leaning against the wall. I think I'm a better photographer than a painter, but I don't think my painting is all that bad. I'd stack it up against some of the works I see in a few of the posh galleries downtown. It's my subject matter that's the problem. My art doesn't come close to resembling what passes for provocative and challenging these days – mostly abstract works.

My paintings trend more toward realism with elements of pop art blended in. It's a mixed media deal, where I use photographs, or magazine cutouts – anything that strikes me, really – in combination with the focus of the piece, which is always painted. My work depicts scenes from the world around me.

Perhaps there are a few abstract concepts thrown in, but only for effect. The main subject of my work is the people.

I walk over to the canvas on the easel right now. It's of a woman I know named Mona. She's in her early thirties and has been living on the streets since she was nineteen or twenty. She's had a hard life and it's taken a toll on her. You can see it in her eyes, and in every line on her face. The portrait I'm doing of her – based on a photo I took – shows her juxtaposed against obvious symbols of wealth and privilege.

Maybe my work isn't the most revolutionary, but I think it's striking and bold, all the same. I think it tells a story that needs to be told in a clear and concise way. I think that other people would see and understand that –if I somehow got my message out to a wider audience. They would connect with it, and my work would have a genuine impact on them.

Of course, I could be biased, but whatever.

I'm not here to paint tonight, though. No, tonight I'm here to develop some photos I took the other day. I personally don't feel photography is appreciated enough, and that it can be as beautiful and striking as any art form. Photography has an immediacy that other mediums don't. They can elicit a really visceral, emotional response. And it's because they're real. There's no fancy elements, no different brush techniques – a photograph is raw and in your face. To me, that makes it all the more powerful.

Locking the front door behind me, I cue up some music. As Janelle Monáe's voice echoes throughout my small studio, I step into my small darkroom and draw the curtain tight. I line up all of my chemicals, and check the last batch of photographs still hanging up. In my opinion, there are some good ones, and some that are simply garbage. They're dry, so I take them all down and slip them into a folder. I'll go through them later.

With that done, I flip on the red light and start to develop the latest batch of pictures. It's a tedious process but going through all the steps is something I always find soothing. Because I know the process like the back of my hand, I can do it without much thought or effort.

In this age of digital everything, developing your own film has become a lost art form, and I take pride in my work from start to finish.

The entire process takes a while – it's not nearly as fast as you see in the movies – but, because I can pretty much do it blindfolded, it gives me time to think. To clear my head. Doing this is like meditation, in a way, and it puts me in a calm state of mind.

As a picture I snapped of Colin at the protest the other day starts to resolve itself, I think back to our encounter earlier. I hadn't meant to go off on him like that. I didn't mean to debate or engage him. I know we're on opposite sides of the divide, and I don't know if such opposing views can be truly reconciled. Which is why I never intended to debate the issue with him.

No, all I wanted to do by going to his office was to thank him for saving my job, and to apologize for what happened to his car. I really can't afford to make restitution for the car, but I can at least apologize that everything got so out of hand.

It's the thought that counts, right?

I hang the picture of Colin up on the line to dry, studying his handsome face for a moment. His tall, lean, strong body is framed perfectly in the designer suit he's wearing. His face is chiseled and rugged, the thick beard only adding to his gruff allure. He really is a gorgeous man. If only he weren't so damn infuriating.

He's deeply entrenched in that elitist, corporate mindset. He's steeped in that, "screw the people in the name of profit," attitude. I find it incredibly appalling, and despicable.

Having grown up poor, I know what it's like to live like some of the people in those buildings.

When you're poor, you don't know where your next meal is coming from. You don't know if you'll be forced to choose between keeping a roof over your head or feeding your child.

And when some rich developer swoops in and pulls the rug out from under you, essentially kicking you to the curb, they're pulling out whatever small shred of security you have in your life. And to my way of thinking, there is nothing more cruel or callous than that.

Yet, Colin, and other developers and real estate agents like him, speak about it so cavalierly. But, they're not the ones who have to worry about where to lay their heads down at night. Nor do they have to worry about how they'll feed their family. They frankly don't have to worry about anything – ever – because their wealth makes them immune to such trifling, pedestrian problems.

Still, despite all of that, the fact that we are so incredibly different – and I loathe his mindset – I can't shake my attraction to him. I *should* find him utterly repulsive. And yet, I don't. I've tried. I've tried to hate him. Despise him. See him as a monster. The ugliest man on the planet.

Try as I might, I can't shake the feelings he inspires in me. Whenever I see him, hell, whenever I think of him, I feel a flutter in my breast, and a warmth spreads through my belly – and even further south.

I can't explain it, and I can't help it. I feel a raw, animal magnetism for the man, no matter how hard I try. I just can't deny it. It's strong and powerful. And it consumes me.

I lean back against my worktable and look at the picture of Colin again. I focus on the lines of his face, and the contours of his body and feel the familiar sensations flowing through my body. As I look at those perfectly kissable lips of his, I suddenly feel myself becoming aroused.

I bite my bottom lip as I imagine having his big, rough hands on me. The heat between my thighs flares as I imagine the way they'd feel sliding across my body. Heat spreads through my body like a raging wildfire.

Lifting my dress up around my waist, I slip my hand down into my leggings. I let out a gasp as I circle my clit and imagine Colin taking me into his arms and kissing me passionately. I close my eyes and try to feel his lips pressed to mine. I let my mind drift, imagining what it would feel like to have his tongue in my mouth, feeling our kiss growing in heat and intensity.

A shudder passes through me and I feel goosebumps raise along my skin. I picture Colin pressing himself against me, and feel his long, thick cock grinding against me.

Even though I'm still a virgin at twenty-three, I do my very best to imagine how it would feel to have Colin's hard cock slipping into me as I slide two fingers past my velvety lips. In my fantasy, Colin has me up on my worktable, my dress pushed up around my waist, my leggings in a crumpled heap on the floor. He's driving his cock into me with immense force.

I cry out, calling his name softly as I grind myself against my fingers, pretending that it's Colin instead. The waves of pleasure washing over me are intense and tendrils of flame engulf me as I picture him flipping me over and taking me from behind. He's rough and commanding. He grabs my hair and pulls it hard, wrenching my head back, and makes me call out his name.

I'm so firmly in control of every aspect of my life, and I refuse to cede that control for anything. In my fantasy though, Colin takes it from me. He strips me down totally and completely as he pounds himself into me, taking me, doing everything he wants to me – and I let him.

I completely give myself over to Dream Colin. Let him have me. Let him command me. I drive my fingers deeper, wishing it was Colin's long, thick cock filling me instead.

Fantasy Colin is gripping my hips tightly, and I can hear him grunting and groaning with pleasure. I look back over my shoulder at him, see the look of absolute rapture on his face, which only takes my own excitement higher.

I picture Colin fucking me. As hard and fast as I want him to fuck me.

"Mm... God, yes..." I murmur.

I feel stretched so wide – just how I imagine Colin would feel inside of me – and feel the pressure building up deep within.

In the theater of my mind, Colin is pressing me down hard against the table, keeping me pinned there so I can't move as he pounds his cock into me vigorously. I hear the deep baritone rumble of his voice as he talks to me, whispers dirty things that only draw me closer and closer to climax.

My body starts to spasm and shake. The explosion of pleasure deep within my body shakes me from head to toe. I'm moaning loud as I'm hit with wave after wave of sensation.

My knees grow weak, and I have to hold onto the table to keep myself upright as a powerful orgasm rocks my body.

Slowly, the trembling fades, and I'm able to stand on my own two feet again. The orgasm passes eventually, but I find myself wrapped in a warm afterglow, as images of Colin flood my brain.

It's a fantasy I know will never come to pass, but rather than sate my desire for the man, masturbating to him seems to have only increased my hunger. I want Colin Anderson. Want to feel him inside of me.

It's a desire I know I need to shut down – ruthlessly and immediately. It's a fantasy that will never play out in real life. I won't let it.

I want the man, but I will *never* give myself to him. Not in this lifetime.

Chapter Five

Colin

It takes the workmen a few minutes to get the fifteen-foot Blue Spruce centered and set in the corner of the living room. It's a massive, but regal-looking tree, and it has that wonderful, festive smell I always associate with the holidays. I'm not an overly senti- mental man, or one who gets too warm and fuzzy about anything, but I can't deny the rush of nostalgia I get around the holidays.

"So, what I was thinking was that we could do lamb shanks for your meal on Christmas Eve..."

Diane, who's been my party planner for years, is going on about decorations, meal planning, and a thousand other things I really couldn't care less about. I trust Diane to put together a good time and to make sure everything is taken care of. She's never failed me in the past, and I highly doubt she's going to fail me now.

Yet, despite my complete faith in her, she still feels the need to run every freaking thing by me for my approval.

It's boring and tedious, but she insists on going over every minute detail with me. I'm so busy staring at the tree and letting my mind wander that it takes a second to realize she's stopped speaking and is now looking at me expectantly.

Knowing I missed everything she just said, I clear my throat and give her a weak smile. "Everything sounds great, Diane," I say. "As usual."

She gives me a small frown of disapproval, obviously not missing the fact that I'd tuned her out a while back. She lets out a long breath and taps her finger against the clipboard in her hand.

"We can go over it again –"

"No, no. It's fine. Lamb is great," I say, seizing on the only thing I recall from her monologue. "Love lamb."

She looks at me a moment longer, and slowly shakes her head. After jotting down a couple of notes on her clipboard, she returns her gaze to me. Diane motions with her hand, asking me to walk with her, so I fall into step beside her.

"So, as far as decorations go..."

Here we go again. No matter how hard I try, my brain automatically goes elsewhere. The last thing I want to do is talk about decorations for forty minutes.

That's why I hire people to worry about it for me.

But, I walk along with her anyway.

I honestly don't know why I bought this house to begin with. Being a single man, I don't need ten bedrooms and the assorted other rooms in this place. Even though I can afford the extravagance, it was far from necessary. At the end of the day, it's just not practical. Not in any way, shape or form.

When I first started looking for a place, I wanted something larger than your standard apartment or a condo. I wanted something with space, and a big backyard – back when I had the idea of getting a couple of dogs. That's when I stumbled onto Sterling House. The architecture is classic Gothic revival, and simply stunning to look at. It's set on two acres of land, complete with heritage trees, and a large, well-stocked lake in the back.

As impractical as it is, I fell in love with the property the moment I saw it. Stepping through the front doors for the first time felt like I was coming home. The first time I entered the place, it gave off an energy that really resonated with me. Something about the house struck a chord deep within me, even after I'd finished touring the grounds.

It's impractical, and really, I have no use for most of the rooms in the house, but I had to have it anyway.

I'm not the impulsive type and usually think things through very carefully before doing anything big or important. I look at all of the pros and cons, practicalities, and impracticalities of every situation. I study it from every angle, and make sure I have a very thorough understanding of everything. That's just the way I am – the way I've always been.

Except when it came to Sterling House. I was so enamored with the house, it took me less than a day to put an offer in on the place. I wander around this monstrosity alone most nights, but it suits me just fine. Some people might think it's a lonely existence, but there's an energy about the place that makes it so I never feel alone. This place simply feels like home to me.

Jesus, with all of this talk about feelings and energy, I'm starting to sound like Bailey.

But, that's the truth. I fell in love with the place, had to have it, and bought it without thinking twice.

And hey, at least it's big enough to host my brothers and their families for the holidays.

Diane is still chattering away, talking about decorations, but my mind pivots, and is suddenly consumed with thoughts of Bailey. In my mind, I see her dark, raven-black hair set against her smooth, delicate skin. I'm imagining those dark, penetrating eyes of hers – the woman has a gaze that can break you down completely in a matter of moments. She doesn't just see you – she sees into, and through you.

There is something I find totally mesmerizing about Bailey, and even though I'm pissed that she chose to read me the riot act the other day, I'm not surprised. She's a woman ruled by her passion and ideals.

Unlike me, she is impulsive. Unpredictable. She doesn't always think things through, and as far as I can tell, she gives into her emotions quite easily.

That's not to say she isn't smart. In the few interactions I've had with her, I can tell she's intelligent.

Despite being so different from her, I have a lot of respect for Bailey. I may not agree with her on – well – almost anything, but I respect her passion and dedication to her beliefs.

Not to mention, that woman is sexy as hell. If there's one thing I wish I could do, it's to stop thinking about her in that context. It's not helping me out at all. And as strange as it sounds, her going off on me like she did the other day was kind of arousing. It was pretty hot to have her give it to me like she did.

It feels crazy that I was actually turned on by her righteous condemnation.

"Something funny?"

I give my head a quick shake and turn to Diane. "Pardon?"

"Oh, you just had a strange smile on your face," she says. "I thought you disagreed with some of the decorative decisions."

"Oh, no, not at all, Diane," I say quickly. "The decorations sound amazing. As usual. No, I guess a stray thought just popped into my head."

"Ah," she says, a critical frown on her face again.

My phone rings in my hand and I see that it's a Facetime call from my brother. Saved by the bell. I give her a small shrug.

"I need to take this," I say. "But seriously, everything sounds great so far. Just keep doing what you're doing. I have confidence that you'll put on a great show, just like you always do."

She gives me a small cluck of approval as I turn away and connect the call. Brayden's face fills my screen as I walk away from Diane, and head for my home office.

"Hang on one second," I say.

Brayden waits until I get into my office and shut the door behind me. I let out a long breath of relief and drop down into the chair behind my desk.

"Tough day at the office, little brother?"

I smirk at him. "Tough day being bored to death, is more like it."

"Let me guess, you're meeting with your party planner, and she wants to go over every excruciating detail with you?"

"How'd you know?"

"Because I got the same look when I've had to host," he says dryly. "Been there plenty of times, my friend. I'm just glad it's you and not me."

"Gee, thanks," I say. "Is that why you called? To gloat?"

"Among other things," he replies.

"Well, I guess listening to you rub it in my face is still better than discussing what color tinsel and garland I want around the house," I joke.

I lean back in my seat as my brother and I catch up. It's been over a week since we last spoke, and it's good to hear from him. Plus, it keeps me away from Diane and her checklist from hell.

"How are Holly and Jace?" I ask.

"Driving me crazy," he says. "But, I wouldn't have it any other way."

Holly is Brayden's wife, and Jace is their baby boy. My nephew. Of my brothers, I'm the only one without a wife and a child, actually.

"They're out on a playdate with one of Jace's friends right now, but they're looking forward to seeing you," he says.

"I'm looking forward to seeing them too."

"So, when can we expect a wifey and a wee baby Colin running around?" he chuckles.

"Well," I check my watch theatrically. "Does ten minutes past never sound good to you?"

He laughs. "Come on, Colin. You can't take yourself out of the game just yet."

"I never got into the game," I correct him. "I've been sitting comfortably on the bench for a while now."

"Ever think it might be time to suit up and get off the bench?"

"No, not really," I answer honestly. "Tried that once, remember? Didn't go all that well."

A few years back, I was engaged to my college sweetheart – Laurel Frederickson. She was gorgeous, smart as a whip, and had a hold over me like nobody before – or since. She was also manipulative as hell, selfish, and oh yeah, she was cheating on me with one of my closest friends. They'd apparently been screwing for a while, right under my nose. I never suspected a thing. At least, not until I came home from class early one day and found her bent over the dining room table in the place we shared – or rather, the place I let her stay – with Nick jackhammering her from behind.

Yeah, that wasn't my best day ever.

She tried to apologize and smooth things over between us. Tried to make it up to me. But really, how can you ever move past a betrayal like that? How can you ever repair a trust that's been shattered as badly as that?

The short answer is, you can't.

I kicked her out of my place and never looked back – though, that was more than a bit difficult. Although she was my college sweetheart, I'd known Laurel for a long time before that. Her parents were friends with my parents, so we grew up around one another. Cutting her out of my life wasn't a clean and easy thing, given that our families were so intertwined.

Something passes across Brayden's face, though he's careful to try and hide it. I'm pretty good at reading people, and know that there's something on his mind. Something he isn't telling me.

"What is it?" I ask.

He shrugs. "Well, it's funny you should mention that."

"Mention what?"

"Just – Laurel."

"And why is that funny?"

He grimaces, and I can tell he's having a hard time getting the words to form in his mouth. Which tells me I'm not going to like what comes out of it. Not at all. I steel myself, getting ready for whatever bombshell he's about to drop.

"Spill it, Brayden."

"Well, I ran into Laurel about a week ago," he says. "You know her parents passed away, right?"

"Yeah, I was at the funeral, remember?"

"Right," he says.

"She has nowhere to go for Christmas, man."

I stare at him, completely dumbfounded. I can't believe he'd even dream of asking me to allow my ex – the woman who cheated on me and broke my heart – into my home.

"Dude," I say. "You realize she was fucking my friend behind my back, right? I literally caught her in the act."

On the screen, he runs a hand through his hair, and looks uncomfortable. Good. He should. He should feel downright ashamed for even asking me to consider it.

"Yeah, I know," he says. "But, it was a while back, man."

"Doesn't change what she did."

"No, it doesn't," he says calmly. "But, her family has been friends with ours for how long?"

"A while," I respond, trying to remain calm. "So?"

"So, our families always looked out for another," he says. "When Mom and Dad died, who was there for us? The Fredericksons. They were always there for us."

"You're saying I should just forget what she did to me? That you want me to host Laurel in my own fucking home?"

He shakes his head. "Nobody's asking you to forget, little brother," he answers. "But, maybe just, put it aside for the holidays. She's got nobody, man. Nobody in the world."

"I can't believe you're asking me to do this," I say. "My own brother."

He sighs. "I'm not telling you to forgive her. Hell, I will never forgive her for what she did. All I'm asking is that you do what Dad would have done – put aside the differences for now, and invite somebody who has nobody, to the table. You remember how many strangers he brought home for a meal, right?"

"Sure. But those strangers didn't fuck our best friends," I snap.

"The point is, Dad invited those strangers, with nowhere to go, into our home," he says. "He was compassionate that way."

"You don't need to remind me who Dad was, Brayden," I snap. "I remember quite well, thanks."

"All I'm asking is that you show some compassion for an old family friend," he says. "This is her first Christmas without her folks –"

"Fine," I say. "Whatever. Just keep her the fuck away from me."

"I will," he replies.

"You better. You're bringing her, that means you're in charge of her," I growl. "I don't want her anywhere near me."

"Done," he says.

We sit in silence for a moment before he gives me a weak smile. "So, on an unrelated note, is anyone on your radar?" he asks. "Anybody going to be joining us for Christmas?"

I open my mouth to reply, and when I hear the words passing my lips, I want to punch myself in the throat.

"Yeah, actually," I say. "I've been seeing someone for a few months now. I wanted to keep it under wraps, but it's gotten serious."

Why in the hell did I just say that? I guess I'm finally fed up with coming dead last in everything in this family.

Brayden arches an eyebrow at me.

"Oh yeah? I'm glad to hear that," he says.

"What's her name?"

I grimace inwardly. I have no idea why I told the lie – maybe to get him off my back, maybe in the hopes he'd pass it along to Laurel, so she knows to stay the hell away from me, maybe – oh hell, I don't know why. All I know is that now that the lie is out there, I need to keep it going.

So, I reach for the first name that pops into my head.

"Bailey," I say. "Her name is Bailey."

That inward grimace transforms into an inward cringe. *Shit.* I'm just digging myself deeper and deeper. I already know what his next question is, and I really don't want to answer it.

"Great," he says. "I'm really happy for you, Colin. I mean it."

"Yeah," I say, suddenly eager to get him off the phone. "Anyway, I should –"

"Will your girlfriend be joining us for Christmas?" he asks. "We'd all love to meet her, Colin."

"Yeah, I don't know," I say. "She's got family, and –"

"Oh, come on," he presses. "Just have her over for Christmas Eve. Seriously, man, just for a while. It'll probably do you some good."

The hole is getting deeper by the second – it's practically a pit at this point – and I just keep shoveling out more. What in the hell am I doing? What am I thinking? I should probably just nip this in the bud now, and stop lying about it. Come clean and tell him I'm making it all up.

But, this should get them off my back about it for a while. So, as the old saying goes, in for a penny, in for a pound.

"Yeah, maybe," I say. "I can't guarantee anything. Like I said, she's got family of her own."

"Well, see if you can pry her loose for a bit," he responds with a chuckle. "She's gonna need to get the ol' Anderson brother consent. She's gotta pass our inspection."

"Yeah, because you guys have done such a bang-up job of it to this point."

"Well, do what you can to make it happen," he says.

"Will do," I say. "Anyway, I should run."

"Yeah, me too."

"Thanks for the call," I reply.

"Anytime, little brother," he says. "And don't worry, Laurel is going to be on her best behavior. I promise you that.

"She better be."

"Love you, Colin."

"Love you too."

I disconnect the call, lean back in my seat, and rub my hands over my face. *Great.* Now, I need to somehow drum up an imaginary *serious* girlfriend to fill the void of the one I just created.

Groaning, I get up and walk out of my office. Yeah, this is just fucking great.

Chapter Six

Bailey

"He's such an arrogant asshole," I groan.

"Who?"

I sip my mimosa and recline in my seat. I'm sitting on the patio of a local cafe having brunch with my best friend Cesar. We've been friends for years. He's a brilliant artist, unapologetically gay, and fantastic in every way. He and I have been through thick and thin together. He always has my back, and knows I'll always have his. Cesar is pretty much the only person in my life I ever truly and fully open up to. Safe to say, I trust him with my life.

"Colin Anderson," I say.

"Who's that?"

"One of the Captains of Industry who are carving up our city and making it a playground for the rich and powerful," I complain, rolling my eyes.

"Oh, is he the guy that had you arrested?"

"Basically," I say. "Technically, his guys at the site called the cops. Things got out of hand though and –"

"Yeah, I saw it all over Facebook and Twitter," Cesar says.

"You did?"

He nods. "Somebody was filming it and then posted it all over social media."

I groan and shake my head. "Ahh, that must have been how Deacon found out."

Cesar takes a bite of his omelet and chuckles. "How'd he take it?"

"Not well, I was really, really close to getting fired." I respond.

His eyes grow wide and he sets his fork back down on the plate. "Seriously?"

I nod. "Yeah, he called me into his office and totally chewed me out."

"Why didn't he end up firing you then?"

I roll my eyes and snort. "Yeah, the craziest part is he didn't fire me because Colin Anderson asked him not to."

"He did?" Cesar asks. "Even after you trashed his car?"

"I didn't trash his car," I scoff. "I didn't do anything. Why do people keep saying I did?"

He chuckles. "Because you're the ringleader," he says. "Heavy is the head that wears the crown, so they say."

"I guess," I mutter.

"So, it was this Colin Anderson guy – the guy you were protesting – that saved your job?"

"Weird, right?"

"That *is* pretty weird," Cesar retorts. "Unless... he has the hots for you?"

I roll my eyes again. "Yeah, I highly doubt that. He and I are about as polar opposite as two people can be."

He raises his mimosa glass in a toast. "You know what they say – opposites attract. They also make great bed mates."

It's my turn to chuckle. "Yeah, absolutely not. I know you made that last part up," I reply with a smirk. "He thinks I'm a pain in the ass. He even stormed away from me the other day. Plus, he's a corporate pig."

Cesar eyes me for a long moment, his gaze cutting straight through me. He knows me better than anybody else on this planet. He knows when I'm not telling the truth – or at the very least, when I'm omitting something. Oftentimes, I don't even realize it. And I can tell by the look in his eyes that he knows I'm not telling him everything.

He's right – but I'm not about to tell him I got myself off thinking about the man. As deep as our friendship goes, there are some boundaries I just won't cross. We don't need to hear the extremely intimate details of each other's sex lives. Or in my case, my lack of a sex life.

"What?" I ask, giving him a wry grin. "Why are you looking at me like that?"

"Because you kind of sound like a girl with a crush," he says and laughs.

My mouth falls open. "What? That's bull."

"Is it?"

"Of course it is!" I snap. "I despise the man and everything he stands for."

His smile softens. "I hear your words," he says. "But, I don't see the same conviction in your eyes."

I snort and shake my head. "Please," I say. "You're just seeing what you want to see."

"Am I?"

"Yes," I reply, sounding outraged. "You're probably the one that has the hots for the guy. Now you're trying to project it on me –"

"I don't even know the guy," he interjects with a laugh. "Until you mentioned it, I had never heard his name before."

Okay, he's got me there. It's not like real estate developers regularly make the front pages of the papers or tabloids or anything. Not unless they do something outrageous or illegal. And if there's one thing I've learned about Colin, he's not the type to do anything outrageous. And he certainly doesn't strike me as the type to willingly commit a crime. He seems about as straight-laced and buttoned-down as they come. A straight arrow if there ever was one.

"Fine, whatever," I say. "But, you're wrong."

Cesar has his phone in his hand and is staring intently at the screen. I crane my neck to see what he's doing, but then sit back, figuring it's one of his flavors of the month. Cesar isn't big on monogamy. I like to think he just hasn't found the right one yet, but he seems to be enjoying the single life. Maybe a bit *too* much, but there's nothing wrong with that. It's a bit enviable even. I do hope he meets someone special, though. If there's one person who deserves to be happy, it's Cesar.

"Okay, so maybe I am projecting," he says. "That man is drop dead gorgeous."

He holds the phone up so I can see one of Colin's publicity photos. As if I need to see it. The man's face is practically permanently seared into my mind. If I close my eyes, I can picture that strong, masculine face, and tightly corded body. Which, of course, leads me straight back to my fantasy, starring none other than Mr. Anderson himself.

"Yeah, I know what he looks like," I say, trying to sound as casual as possible.

"Why are you blushing?" Cesar asks, his tone distinctly amused.

"I'm not!"

I laugh, but I feel the heat burning in my cheeks, and know he's right. Damn it. I avert my gaze and fidget with the napkin on the table. I feel Cesar's eyes on me. The unwanted attention makes me squirm in my seat. I grab my fork and take a bite of my Eggs Benedict – mostly to avoid having to say anything for a minute or two.

"You know I can read you like a book, don't you?" Cesar asks, his voice filled with barely contained laughter.

"Yeah, don't remind me," I mutter.

"Babe, there is *nothing* wrong with being attracted to the man," he says. "Hell, I am. He's beautiful."

"Then maybe you two can hook up."

Cesar laughs. "If I thought he batted for my team, believe me, I'd take a shot at him," he says. "I'm pretty sure he's not, though. Pretty sure he's not even close to playing the same sport."

"You never know."

"I have a sense about these things," he says. "And how often am I wrong?"

I can't stop myself from laughing, the embarrassment making me feel flushed and awkward. "Shut up," I say. "You're not helping."

"Bailey, why not see if there's anything there?" he asks. "A man doesn't go out of his way to save your job – especially after what happened – if he doesn't have some feeling behind it."

"Yeah, but that feeling was probably pity," I admit. "He probably knows what happens if I get fired, and he doesn't want to feel bad for forcing me out on the streets this close to Christmas. I'm sure he only did it to ease his own conscience, not because he's actually a decent human being."

Ugh. Christmas.

My least favorite time of year. I grew up dirt poor. My parents would spend any money we had on drugs and alcohol. Needless to say, we barely had enough to eat most days, so frivolous things like Christmas were just that – frivolous. There was never money for gifts or anything like that.

When I was eleven or twelve, my parents decided they'd had enough – that they simply weren't cut out to be parents. They decided that they'd rather live their life unencumbered by a child, so they dropped me off at my grandmother's in the middle of the night and took off. I sat out on the porch all night, in nearly freezing weather, sobbing my eyes out, too ashamed and embarrassed to wake my grandmother up to let me in. She found me the next morning, nearly frozen to death.

Life with my grandmother was never easy. She was poor too and having an unexpected mouth to feed only made things tighter. But, we got by. I was never short on love, just the material things – which I learned weren't that important anyway. My grandmother, an artist herself – died while still very obscure. She fostered my own creative drive, and helped me explore the different mediums, testing things out until we found one that suited me.

We started off with sculptures – which is what she did. My grandmother collected old, discarded items and made the most beautiful works of art with them. I wasn't suited for it, nor did I have passion for it. So, we moved on to other art forms before finally settling on painting. The brush and colors resonated with me. I found that I could genuinely express myself through my work.

In those early days, most of my work tended toward the darker side of life and emotions. It wasn't exactly bright colors, flowers, and rainbows. It was brooding and moody. But that shouldn't be too surprising, given how I'd been discarded like a piece of trash.

It wasn't until I got to high school that I took a shine to photography. There was – and still is – something about being able to capture a unique experience, or somebody's essence, on film, that engages my mind. That speaks to my soul.

They say a picture is worth a thousand words, but I believe it's worth much more than that. You can tell a story – an epic tale – with a well-framed, well-crafted picture.

Of course, being poor, my grandmother didn't have the money to set me up with any proper equipment. One teacher, Mr. Crandall, knowing I couldn't afford it, set me up with a camera and all of the equipment I'd need. He gave it to me and let me work it off by doing chores around the photo lab – something I was more than happy to do.

When I told my grandmother, she was appalled. She was a proud, self-made woman who was never comfortable with gifts or charity. She viewed handouts as a personal affront and refused them on principle. She was always gracious about it, of course, but her belief was that if we couldn't afford it, we didn't need it.

I remember being absolutely devastated when she told me we had to take the camera set-up back. She said we'd figure out a way to get me what I needed – code for, I'd have to do without. It broke my heart when my grandmother took me to the photo lab at school to give it all back to Mr. Crandall.

My grandmother was as gracious and thankful as she always was but explained that although we appreciated what he was trying to do, we simply couldn't accept it. Mr. Crandall patiently explained to my grandmother that I have a real gift for the art form. That I see things in a way others don't. He told her that I was his most promising student and it would be a shame if I couldn't explore my creativity over something as silly as pride.

He told my grandmother that he believed I desperately needed the creative and emotional outlet my art provided me.

It was the first and only time I ever saw my grandmother back-track and accept a form of charity. It was also the first and only time I ever saw her tear up. I remember telling her that I'd work off the cost of the camera, and the rest of the equipment, by completing chores around the photo lab. She made sure to tell me that I needed to work extra hard, to never give Mr. Crandall grief about anything, and above all, to become proficient at my art.

Whether it was working for Mr. Crandall, or my photography, she said I needed to be the best I could be. And that I should use all the passion I can muster to get me there.

My grandmother was the toughest, most caring woman I've ever known. I shudder to think what my life would be like – what I would be like – if my folks hadn't dropped me off at her house that cold winter night all those years ago. Which is why I try to live my life in a way that would make her proud – and be the type of person that would make her smile.

"Why do you hate this guy so much?" Cesar asks.

"Because everything he stands for is anathema to what I stand for," I say. "If we were in a superhero movie, he'd be my archnemesis."

Cesar laughs. "Who even says words like archnemesis or anathema anymore?"

"Oh, so now you're going to mock my vocabulary?"

I laugh along with him and push the food around on my plate with my fork. "I'm not wrong, though, if this were superhero world, Colin Anderson would be a super villain. Consider him the Bane of my existence, my archnemesis. No question about that."

"Listen here, Batman," he says. "Don't you think you're judging Bane a tad too harshly?"

"How do you figure?"

"He's just a man doing what he's paid to do. At the end of the day, he's just doing his job."

"Jesus," I say and roll my eyes. "Now you're starting to sound just like him. 'I was following orders.' Gee, where have I heard that before?"

Cesar tosses a grape at me. It hits my shoulder and bounces away. "He's hardly a Nazi," he says. "He's a business owner, and has to do what his clients want him to do."

"I can't believe you're defending him!"

"I'm not defending anybody, Bailey –"

"You're supposed to be on my side, Cesar."

"Honey, you know I'm always on your side," he says, "But, you should also know by now that I'm never going to sugarcoat things. It's because I love you that I'm going to tell you when you're being an idiot. And in this case, you're being an idiot."

"He kicks poor people out of their homes," I argue. "He tears down their homes and puts them out on the street."

"Look, I don't know exactly how all of this development works," Cesar says. "But, from my limited, non-professional understanding, his client gives him a project to work on – and a location. Colin has to do what his client wants, or his business goes under."

"There are more humane ways to do what he does," I say. "There have to be."

"Such as?"

I sit back and take another swallow of my drink. I honestly don't have an answer to the question. I don't know how he could do his job in a more humane, kinder way. All I do know, is the mere thought of these rich assholes coming in without any regard for those less fortunate, discarding them like trash – elicits a visceral reaction in me.

I relate to the plight of the poor well. Perhaps too well. Has my own experience made me lose all objectivity? My passion for the cause, I always believed, was one of my greatest strengths. It drives me to make a difference. But, am I being unfair? Am I painting everybody with the same broad brush?

It's true that I don't know Colin. The only times I've interacted with him have been in adversarial settings that usually broke down into some sort of verbal spat. I truthfully don't know what kind of man he is. But I can't shake my attraction to him. Maybe there are some redeeming qualities in him. Maybe, a deep part of me senses something good in him. Just maybe, he's not the same sort of heartless, greedy cretin I'm used to butting heads with.

Or maybe, I'm just rationalizing it all in my own mind because I think he's gorgeous.

"I didn't think so," Cesar says, interrupting my train of thought.

"That doesn't make you right," I say and chuckle.

"Doesn't make me wrong, either."

Cesar drains the last of his drink and looks at me as he sets his glass back down. Obviously waiting for me to come around to his way of thinking. To admit that he's right, and that my assessment of Colin is overly harsh and unfair. He may be right, but I don't want to admit it.

"It's pointless anyway," I say. "Even though you're wrong, and I'm not crushing on him."

"Why is it pointless again?"

"Because he hates me," I say. "We had a nasty fight."

"Lover's spat already?" he asks with a chuckle. "That's a new personal record for you. Usually, you wait until at least an hour or two after you get together with somebody to argue."

"I was trying something different this time."

"So, tell me. What happened?"

I fill him in on going to Colin's office to apologize, and how it led to a knock-down, drag-out fight. Cesar listens to it all, a bemused smile on his face, and when I finish, he laughs and claps his hands.

"What's so funny?" I ask.

"Honey, that's not a fight," he says. "That's called foreplay."

"Oh, the hell it is," I reply, my cheeks burning bright again.

"I can feel the sexual tension all the way over here."

"Oh, shut up," I laugh. "Not even close."

"Uh-huh," he says. "Then go see him. Apologize for being a brat."

"I wasn't a brat."

He cocks his head and looks at me. "Yeah, you were kind of a brat."

I lean back in my chair, feeling somewhat deflated, and put on a faux-pout. "You're the worst."

"The most horrible," he says. "You should go apologize."

"I have nothing to apologize for."

"You afraid of the sexual chemistry? The animal magnetism?" he chuckles. "Afraid you won't be able to contain yourself and you'll rip his clothes off and –"

"Okay, you can stop right there," I laugh, throwing a crumpled napkin at him.

"If you're not afraid of your clothes falling off the second you see him, why won't you do it?"

"I'm not afraid of anything," I say. "I just don't have –"

"You kind of do."

"Well, so does he then."

"Fine, then give him a chance to apologize."

"Why are you so bound and determined to put us in a room together?"

He pushes his plate away from him. "Because I think seeing you with a crush is cute," he says. "I don't see it all that often."

I sigh. "Because most guys aren't worth expending the energy."

"I hear that," he says. "The fact that you're letting yourself crush on this guy tells me something, though."

"What does it tell you?"

"It tells me that somewhere in that messed-up wiring in your head, you think he might be worth it."

"I think you're making a huge leap here."

He shrugs. "Only one way to find out."

I finish the last of my mimosa and set the glass down. I know

Cesar well enough to know this is something he's not going to let go of very easily. He can be stubborn as hell when he wants to – I've seen it more times than I can count.

"You're not going to let this go, are you?" I ask.

"You know me."

"I do," I say. "Fine, I'll talk to him. I'll apologize, and I'll prove to you that there is nothing going on between us. Nothing at all."

"You do that," he says. "And I'll expect a full and detailed report. The juicier the better."

"In your dreams."

"After seeing a picture of that man? You know it."

I laugh and shake my head. I love Cesar. He's the best. We spend the rest of a leisurely afternoon together, shopping and hanging out. I don't spend nearly enough time with him. At least, not nearly as much as I'd like to. But, we both lead busy lives. It's the price we pay for being adults, having jobs, and trying to get ourselves noticed as artists.

As we wander around I can't keep my mind from drifting to Colin – more specifically, to the fantasy I had about him the other day. And as that memory surfaces in my mind, I feel myself longing for him again.

Yeah, I need to do something to purge this guy from my head once and for all. We're just too contradictory to each other to ever work out. It's never going to go anywhere. Better to get him out of my system now. I shouldn't even be thinking of him like this anyway. I seriously need to get my head straightened out when it comes to Colin Anderson.

He's not my friend. He's not my boyfriend. And he sure as hell isn't my lover.

And he can never be any of those things.

A few hours later, I'm standing in the Covington Gallery – one of the more prestigious galleries in the city. I wouldn't even be here if it wasn't for Cesar's cheerleading and the plentiful amount of liquid courage I imbibed during brunch with him earlier.

"Yes, can I help you?"

I turn to the sound of the man's voice. He's tall, wiry, with slate gray hair, pasty skin, and an impeccably-tailored suit. He just reeks of snootiness. I'm half surprised he didn't have me thrown out the instant I walked through the door. Judging by the look on his face, he's still considering it. The man looks down his nose at me, like I'm a living, breathing piece of garbage. Like I'm some detestable, pathetic creature, not worth his time of day.

I straighten my back and lift my chin, returning his gaze with what I hope is defiance in my eyes.

"Yes, I'd like to speak with the gallery manager, please," I say.

"David Winthorpe," he replies. "I'm the manger. How may I help you?"

Damn. I was hoping he was one of the peons and not the manager of the place. The scowl on his face is more than a bit intimidating – and a whole lot irritating.

"I saw the notice for the breakout artist showcase and –"

"I'm sorry, the slots are already filled."

"What?" I ask. "How can that be? The entry window opened like two hours ago."

"The slots filled up quickly this year."

I can tell by the way he's looking at me, that even if there were a hundred slots open, he wouldn't give me a single one of them. I feel the anger welling up inside me. To be dismissed like this, completely out of hand, is beyond infuriating.

"Can I speak with your supervisor, please?" I ask through gritted teeth.

He lets out a dramatic sigh and barely stops himself from rolling his eyes at me. "He'll tell you the exact same thing I am, miss," he says, his tone haughty. "There are no slots left available. You should have had your paperwork sent to us sooner."

"This isn't right –"

"I'm sorry, but those are the rules," he says, gesturing to the door. "Now, if there's nothing else…"

I bite back the scathing reply that's on the tip of my tongue. The last thing I can afford at this point in my wannabe career is burned bridges. Boston is a big town, but there are only so many galleries. If I get a reputation for acting like a pompous jerk in one, it will spread to the others like cancer, and it won't be long before I'm blacklisted from them all. As much as it pisses me off, I'm going to have to bite my tongue this time.

The most upsetting thing is, if I knew the right people, or had some connections, I could get my foot in the door. That would make it much easier to get my name, and work, talked about in the show-case circuit. Once my name is in the circuit, it's even easier to get my own solo showcase – my own spotlight.

Until then, I have to beg like a dog at the table, desperate for whatever scraps the gatekeepers will give me – which, to this point, hasn't been very much at all.

"Thank you for your time," I say.

Turning on my heel, I march out the door, with my portfolio tucked under my arm. Had I known things were going to end up this way, I would have spent the rest of the afternoon with Cesar, getting pleasantly drunk on mimosas.

Chapter Seven

Colin

"What in the hell are you doing up so early?" I ask.

Liam chuckles. "Paige was mumbling in her sleep and rolling around on the bed," he explains. "I couldn't fall back to sleep after she woke me up, so I just decided to get up."

"Early bird catches the worm," I say.

"Not even the birds are up this early," he laughs. "I figured you'd be up, though, so I decided to give you a shout."

"Glad you did," I say. "It's been a minute. It's good to hear from you, Liam."

"Good to talk to you too," my brother Liam – the eldest of my brothers – says. "Hey, so Brayden tells me you're seeing someone."

I roll my eyes, thankful we aren't Facetiming so he can't see me. It's still a bit early, and I'd just finished working out when he called. It's barely past six a.m. my time, which means it's three in his part of the country. None of us ever sleep that late – a habit instilled in us by our father – but even by our standards, getting up at three in the morning is considered excessive.

"Yeah, word spreads fast, I guess," I say.

He snickers. "I'm sure Laurel was sad to hear it."

"God, I hope not," I say. "She should be long over me by now."

"You really think so? Don't worry, Colin. We'll make sure Laurel is on her best behavior around your new girl. Promise."

I groan. *Time to play pretend again.*

"She better. I don't want Bailey to worry."

Not that I think she will. Mostly because our relationship is totally fictional, but I'm not going to tell him that *just* yet.

I was actually hoping Brayden would forget all about it and not say anything to Aidan or Liam. I should have known better. Ever since all of my brothers have gotten married and started families of their own, they've constantly been on my ass about doing the same and following the trend. They want all of their kids to be around the same age so they can grow up together. Form a sports team, or a gang, or whatever.

I've never marched to the same beat as my brothers, though. All of them went to college straight out of high school, and worked for ADE immediately after that. I took a different route. I wasn't sure if going into the family business was my calling. If it was my true passion.

So, after graduating from high school, I joined the Navy. I spent four years in the service, finished my tour, went to college, and realized along the way that I appreciated what ADE does as a company, and that I wanted a part of it after all. Once I was ready, I was given the Northeast territory, and I've been playing catch-up ever since.

"Anyway, how is Paige doing?" I ask, trying to change the subject.

"Pregnant. More than a bit moody, and she's been craving the strangest things lately," he says. "But, she's fantastic, as always."

I laugh. "What's the latest craving?"

"It'll make you sick."

"C'mon, you know I've got a strong stomach."

"Cheese sticks and peanut butter."

"Yeah, okay, that's gross."

He laughs. "I told you."

I laugh along with him for a moment. "So, how are things going up in Washington?" I ask.

"Good," he says. "I love living in this town. It feels like I've finally settled in and made a home here."

"It's a beautiful place, man."

"Yeah, I'm lucky."

There's a small lull in the conversation – my first mistake, because it gives him the perfect opportunity to go straight back to the conversation I've been trying to steer us away from.

"So, how's it going with your new girl?" he asks. "Will we be meeting her at Christmas?"

"Yeah, I don't know," I say. "She's got her own family stuff, and –"

"I know, but the rest of us have been talking, and we think it's time you met a nice girl and settle down," Liam chuckles. "Maybe have a few kids –"

"Thanks for planning my life out for me."

"Somebody has to."

He's mostly joking, but I also know there's a small undercurrent of truth to his words. My brothers are all settled into their family lives – something I personally never thought I'd see – but, they seem happy. And now, they want to spread some of that happiness to me.

Truth be told, I'm more focused on my career and getting my slice of ADE running smoothly, than anything else. Things are definitely headed in the right direction, but until I'm not stuck hosting the family holiday every year, I won't be satisfied.

Maybe, once I get to the top, I'll take some time and see if anyone out there piques my interest romantically. Or, maybe not. My experience with Laurel left me pretty jaded and cynical. And as far as kids go, I'm not sure if that's in the cards for me or not. I really don't know if I've got what it takes to be a father, to be honest.

But before I think about any of that, I need to get my share of the company to where I want it to be. That's my number one priority in life right now, and it's where all my focus and energy are being directed. It's all that matters to me right now.

That's a can of worms I don't exactly want to open up with my brother, though. That's only going to lead to a debate about work/life balance, and enjoying the time we have, because we only have one shot in this world, blah...blah...blah. As if any one of my other three brothers were any different than I am before they got married.

Working until you drop, and ignoring all other distractions, is an inherited Anderson trait. It's kind of our thing – what helps set ADE apart from other development empires. Blame our father's insane work ethic, his stern discipline, or whatever, but it's part of who we are.

Maybe, I'll meet somebody one day. Maybe, I won't. Right now, it doesn't matter to me in the least.

"Look, all I'm saying is that I know how – selective – you are," Liam says. "Which tells me this girl must be something special. And, personally, I would love to meet her. So would Paige."

"You've talked to Paige about this?"

"Of course," he says. "She loves you, Colin. She wants to see you happy too."

"Damn, you know, all of this talk about feelings and being happy – you're getting soft on me, big brother," I tease.

We both laugh, but I can tell Liam's is more forced. Slowly, it tapers off, then fades away altogether.

"I worry about you, little brother," he says. "Too much isolation and loneliness isn't good. Trust me, I've been exactly where you are right now. I've probably had the same exact thoughts that are going through your head. Believe me when I say I know how you're feeling, Colin."

And maybe, he does. Liam originally moved from Seattle to the sleepy little town of Port Safira – where he lives now with Paige – to get away from the memory of a woman whose infidelity was only the tip of the fucked-up iceberg. I know it cut him deeply, and for a long time, he preferred being alone.

Not that it changes my thinking, really, but it's nice knowing that he can relate.

"I just want to see you happy, Colin," he finally says. "You're really missing out on a lot."

Why are my brothers so determined to marry me off? I'm more than ready for Aidan, Brayden, and Liam to get off my back about this. I'm in this deep already – what harm will one more white lie do at this point?

"I know you do," I reply, swallowing hard. "I wanted to keep this a secret, but I asked Bailey to marry me the other day. She said yes."

Liam inhales sharply on the other end of the line and is silent for a long moment.

Oh, God. That was the fucking opposite of a white lie. Why can't I stop digging myself into this hole?

"That's great, little brother. I'm sad we couldn't be there to celebrate with you. Have you told anyone else?"

"No, I wanted to keep it a surprise until Christmas."

"So, I definitely expect to see your mystery fiancée at our Christmas Eve dinner – at the very least."

"I'll see if she can work it out," I say. "That's about the best I can do."

"Fair enough," he replies.

We talk for a few more minutes, get into discussing some of our business deals, and what's going on with the rest of ADE – nothing terribly pressing. I'm just glad to finally be off the topic of my love life.

"I should probably grab a shower and head into the office," I say.

"And I should probably start preparing Paige's cheese and peanut butter toast," he replies.

I shudder. "Bon Appetit, big brother."

He chuckles. "Love you, Colin. Talk soon."

"Love you too."

We disconnect the call and I drop my phone to my desk. God, why didn't I just come clean and tell him I made my fiancée up? Even if I do tell them that Bailey can't make it because she's with family, it won't be enough for my brothers. If she can't come to us, they'll insist we go to her. I know them.

I know they're coming from a good place. They're only this annoying because they love me and want to see me happy. And I appreciate it. I want the same for them. I just wish, this one time, they'd care a little bit less.

———

I step beneath the soft spray of the shower, wading through the billowing clouds of steam as the warm water soothes my aching muscles. I run my hands through my hair, gently working the shampoo into a lather before stepping beneath the spray again, washing it all away.

I honestly have no clue what I'm going to do about this mysterious, non-existent fiancée I've created for myself. I wish I'd never even mentioned it. Honestly, I was so rattled by the fact that Laurel was coming to our holiday celebration, I wasn't thinking clearly. I just threw out the first thing that popped into my head.

For a long time after I'd kicked her out and ended our engagement, Laurel tried her best to win me back. She apologized profusely, doing everything she could think of to repair the damage she'd inflicted on our relationship. I got daily emails, text messages, phone calls, and knocks on the door – I never responded to any of them. I didn't want anything to do with her. Ever again.

Some things, you just can't come back from. When you break a trust that thoroughly and completely, there is no amount of, "I'm sorry," that's going to fix it. You just can't. At least, I can't. Maybe, I'm too cold and unfeeling. I'm sure that other people can find a way to heal and move past it. There must be people out there that can bounce back from a gut-wrenching betrayal like that.

I'm not one of those people.

Laurel broke my trust. I'm not a man that opens up to just anyone, either. You have to earn it with me. Once you have it, I'm one of the most fiercely loyal people you'll ever meet. I'd brave a fire for someone I love and trust. If that trust is broken, however, that person may as well be dead to me.

Laurel now belongs to the small group of people who are effectively dead to me – and now, I'm going to have to put up with her staying in my home.

On some level, I understand what Brayden was saying. I know it's exactly the kind of thing our father would have done. And considering she's the daughter of one of his closest friends, he wouldn't have hesitated, not even for a second. Regardless of the history between the two of us, he would have extended her an invitation without a second thought. He would have told me to suck it up and put it aside for just one day.

My dad was tough. He could be a strict disciplinarian, and was absolutely no-nonsense in his approach to everything. He also had one of the kindest, gentlest hearts I've ever seen in another person. Dad would literally give a stranger the shirt off his back. I saw him do it once. It was cold out, so my father gave a homeless man his turtle-neck and jacket. He wore an old t-shirt from the back of his car until we could get to a store to buy some replacements.

He told me he'd sleep better at night knowing that man would be warm. That was simply the kind of person he was. He was a tough, but great man – and I miss him every day.

My mind turns back to my supposed secret fiancée, and the fact that I said her name was Bailey. Why did I choose that name? Why was *her* name so near at hand in my mind that it came out so easily? Perhaps, the better question, the one I should be asking myself, is – why is Bailey always on my mind lately?

She's a beautiful girl, no doubt about it. Stunning, really. But, it's more than that. It's more than her physical appearance alone that draws me to her. It's her substance – the things that drive Bailey and make her tick. Her fire, her passion, and to some extent, her wide-eyed optimism. She has a zest for life that frankly, I kind of envy. The few times I've been around her, I've felt that energy radiating from her, and found it intoxicating.

As I stand beneath the spray of water with thoughts and images of Bailey circling endlessly through my mind, I feel my cock growing stiff – I obviously can't deny my physical attraction to the woman, either. Leaning my head back into the water, I close my eyes, and try to banish all thoughts of her from my mind.

Not that it works. The harder I try to clear my mind, the more vivid the images of her become. Reaching down, I grab hold of my cock. I think the only way to get Bailey out of my head is to give myself some release.

Squeezing the base of my cock, I slowly begin to stroke it. I picture Bailey stepping into the shower with me. Feel her hands on my back as she runs her fingertips down the length of my spine. I groan softly as I imagine the feel of her full, round breasts pressed into my back while she reaches around to hold my cock in her small, delicate hand.

I stroke myself harder as I imagine Bailey touching me. I feel the warmth of her breath and the softness of her lips on my back as she plants a long line of kisses along my shoulders, never breaking the rhythm of her hand pumping my cock in a slow and steady motion.

I moan quietly, my voice echoing around the tile chamber as I begin to stroke my cock harder, gripping it tighter. In my fantasy, I turn Bailey around and pick her up, pressing her hard against the wall of the shower. Steam billows around us as I press my lips to hers, kissing her hard, letting her feel all the passion inside me. She wraps her legs around my waist as I hold her up. Leaning down, I take one of her plump, stiff nipples into my mouth, and suck on it. She lets out a soft yelp as I give it a gentle nip with my teeth.

She locks her hands around the back of my neck as she kisses me deeply, the heat in her lips setting me on fire as she does. I slip my cock into her, plunging myself as deep as I can go. Bailey gasps, then moans, as I start to move my hips, thrusting myself in and out of her.

Leaning forward, I plant my hand against the wall to brace myself as I continue stroking my cock, imagining how Bailey's tight, sexy body would feel intertwined with mine, holding on tight as I fuck her relentlessly against the shower wall.

The pressure is building up within me, and I know I'll come soon. I squeeze my eyes tight, holding on to the image of Bailey's beautiful, naked body under mine as I fall over the edge. Waves of pleasure ripple through me as I groan loudly and explode. I throw my head back and call out her name as I come. I squeeze my cock harder, losing myself in the tsunami of sensations sweeping my body.

Slowly, the afterglow from my orgasm fades, and I'm left leaning my forehead against the shower wall, my breathing ragged, and my heart thundering inside of my chest. My orgasm was strong. Powerful. And just the release I needed.

Except for the fact that it didn't drive out thoughts of Bailey from my mind. If anything, it only made them stronger. Now I want her even more.

"Great," I mutter to myself. "Just fucking great."

After rinsing myself off, I step out of the shower and grab a towel. As I'm drying myself, a sudden thought occurs to me. Maybe an answer to two problems at once.

It's outlandish, but it just might work.

Chapter Eight

Bailey

I finished my work for today at the law firm earlier than expected, so I decided to use some of my ensuing free time to put in some work at my studio. I may have not been able to get myself into the showcase at the Covington, but there are plenty of other showcases I can get into.

Hopefully.

If I'm being honest, the whole pimping myself out and begging for table scraps from prestigious galleries isn't only exhausting, it's downright degrading. Discouraging, even. It's also a thousand other negative things that are completely soul-crushing.

And yet, I persist.

I tell myself that, sooner or later, I'm going to knock on the right door. Eventually, somebody will take an honest look at my work and be impressed enough to give me a chance. But more and more often these days, I'm starting to worry that I'm doomed to spend my life like my grandmother – one of obscurity.

My grandmother was a talented artist. Her works were gorgeous. She even made a bit of money at it. Enough that she didn't have to decide between food and house bills most months, but she was hardly commercially successful. She didn't make very much profit from her art, even though I think it's among the most beautiful I've ever seen.

I know some might call me biased, and that's fine, but when it comes to art, I can be critical. I try to be as objective as possible. But, to this day, I believe that my grandmother never received proper recognition for her brilliant creative mind.

I'm sitting at the worktable in the front of my studio, soft classical music playing while I scan the community message boards. The art community in Boston isn't all that big. And for those of us on the fringe, we tend to look out for one another. We've got each other's backs. The message boards are always filled with words of encouragement, and inspirational messages that tell us that no matter what, we have to persevere. Put our heads down and just keep grinding.

And while I appreciate that, I mainly frequent the message boards for one purpose – to get the scoop on upcoming showcases or other chances to have my work displayed and seen. I'm jotting down notes on a couple of upcoming shows, when there's a knock on my studio door.

I look over at the sound curiously. I'm not expecting anybody, and honestly, I get very few visitors in my studio. It's not like this is a widely-known, well-traveled place. Getting up, I walk over to the door and open it – and am shocked to see the person standing behind it.

"Selling Girl Scout cookies?" I ask. "If you are, I'd like some of the peanut butter ones, please."

Colin grins, and my heart melts on the spot. "Sorry, fresh out."

As my heart stumbles all over itself, I give myself a swift mental kick, and hold the door open for him. He steps inside and looks around the place. Not expecting visitors, I haven't done much in the way of tidying up. There are boxes of supplies stacked everywhere, about a billion frames lined up against one wall, and the place smells heavily of paint and photo-developing chemicals – which reminds me to open the window. Drop cloths litter one side of the room – stacked and piled around the easel my current work in progress is resting on. It's only half-done and looks like shit in its current state. He stands there looking at it though, the expression on his face one of a man who is seeing the bigger picture. It's almost like he understands where I'm going, and what I'm trying to say on the canvas.

Or, maybe I'm just projecting, and he's actually wondering why I'm bothering wasting my time when I'm nothing but a hack.

I close the door behind him and grab the long, unwieldy pole from its hook before rushing over to open a couple of the windows set high in the wall to facilitate better airflow and help circulate the fumes out of the place.

"Sorry," I say. "I wasn't expecting company today. I don't get very many visitors out here."

"I was in the neighborhood."

"Yeah, right," I say and laugh.

We stand there in awkward silence for a long moment, just staring at each other. Those piercing gray-blue eyes bore into me, reaching down into my very soul. It feels like I'm being exposed.

"So, if it isn't Girl Scout cookies, what brings you all the way out here?" I ask. "Just felt the need to slum it with the working poor today?"

The smile on his face falters for a split-second before he regains his composure. I can tell he's doing his best to bite back a snarky reply – obviously trying to avoid provoking me into another fight. Which is curious. I've always gotten the impression he enjoys verbally sparring with me.

"Actually," he answers sheepishly. "I was kind of hoping you'd like to get lunch with me."

My stomach threatens to fold in on itself and take my heart with it as I stand there. Colin's asking me to lunch? He's asking me on a date? *Me?* It shouldn't – it really shouldn't – but him asking me out fills me with a sense of joy I can't understand, let alone explain. Not even to myself.

I should hate this man. He stands for everything I think is wrong with the world. And yet, here I am, giddy as a schoolgirl that he asked me out.

"There was something I hoped we could discuss," he says, and then adds quickly. "A business arrangement, of sorts."

And just like that, the warm, fuzzy feelings in me evaporate like a shallow puddle of water in the desert. A business arrangement – not a date. I'm not going to lie and say it's not a crushing shot, but at the same time, it's also saving me from a moral quagmire, I suppose. At least, I'm not going to have to choose between my convictions and being arm candy for a man like Colin Anderson.

Silver linings, right?

"What sort of business arrangement?"

He shifts uncertainly on his feet, looking a bit uncomfortable, which is odd, given that he doesn't strike me as a man who is ever uncomfortable or uncertain. About anything. At all. Ever. He comes across as a man who, when he finally comes to a decision, sticks with it, come hell or high water – and expects everybody else to do the same.

"I'd rather discuss it over lunch, if you don't mind," he says.

"You mean – now?" I ask.

He nods. "Yeah. Now."

I look at his designer suit – doing my best to not admire how it clings so well to his tight, toned body – and then down at myself. I'm wearing black leggings, tennis shoes that are spotted with paint, and a baggy, oversized sweatshirt. I have my hair in a ponytail and a blue bandana covers my head.

Yeah, I'm a walking fashion nightmare right now. Get me onto a Paris runway.

"I don't think I'm exactly dressed to go out in public," I say. "I was working, and –"

"I think you look fantastic," he says. "Beautiful."

An inscrutable expression crosses his face, and something like panic rises in his eyes. It's like he suddenly realized he said too much. Like he just gave up some important piece of leverage in one of his business negotiations or something. He clears his throat and looks away, trying to gather himself on the fly.

Like I'm going to let him off the hook that easily.

"I'm beautiful, huh?"

He runs a hand through his hair, still refusing to meet my eyes. "I think you're a very attractive woman in a traditional sense, yes."

"That's not what you said," I tease him. "You said I'm beautiful."

"Can I take you to lunch?"

"You think I'm beautiful," I say in a sing-song voice.

Colin shakes his head and looks down at the ground, but I can see the grin on his face. And if I didn't know better, I'd say that his cheeks are flushing behind that big, thick beard of his. It's actually kind of adorable.

"What do you want me to say?" he asks, no longer bothering to hide his smile. "You're a beautiful woman. An absolute pain in my ass, but beautiful. Happy?"

I cock my head and pretend to think it over for a moment. "Okay, I'll take that."

"So – lunch?"

"Sure," I say. "Why not? After all, us beautiful girls need to eat too."

He lets out a long, dramatic breath. "Such a pain in the ass."

"I think you kinda like it though."

I close down my computer and lock up my studio behind us. The whole time, I'm aware of Colin's eyes on me. The few times I've caught him looking at me, it's been with a look of near awe on his face – like he's admiring a beautiful work of art or something. Unlike that day in the office, when it was a smothering, suffocating pressure, something about having his eyes on me feels – sensual.

And even though I'm in leggings and a baggy sweatshirt, the way he's looking at me makes me feel sexier than I've felt in a really long time.

"So, tell me, why exactly are you so passionate about the poor and the homeless?"

It's a curious way to start off the conversation, but I actually kind of like it that he's taking an interest in me this way. I enjoy that he wants to know what makes me tick. And I figure the best way to get through to him is by being honest.

"I grew up dirt poor," I say. "Never knew where my next meal was coming from, wearing hand-me-down clothes – usually, not much better than rags, really."

He pauses with his water glass halfway to his mouth and looks at me with a stunned expression on his face. He quickly recovers and takes a drink, but the pause is telling to me. It shows me that poverty is an abstract concept to Colin. It's something he doesn't understand because he can't relate to it. Oh, he knows there is poverty in the world, and that there are poor people all around us, but he's never had a personal connection with someone in poverty before.

Which is why I'm here to educate him.

For someone like Colin – who I can only imagine grew up extremely privileged – being poor is something that happens to other people. Not to anybody he knows. And if I had to guess, I'd say that he thinks people are poor simply because of their own choices. That they're lazy or shiftless. That they would rather sell drugs than get a job.

He doesn't understand that people sometimes wind up impover-ished through no fault of their own. Yeah, some people make poor life choices, but sometimes, all it takes is a bad break to send them into the poverty spiral. And what Colin doesn't understand is that not everyone who's poor is a drunk. Or an addict. Or a criminal. Some of the poor – heck, many, if not most of the poor in this country – are stuck where they are because of a confluence of really bad luck and crappy circumstance.

"I didn't know that," he says.

I shrug. "How could you?" I ask. "You don't really know me. But, it's why I do what I do and the reason I'm so passionate about it. I believe in giving a voice to the voiceless and fighting for equality for all."

Having lectured him on the issue of poverty, he nods slowly, letting my words sink in. I can tell that Colin is a thoughtful man. He's not simply dismissing what I say out of hand. I can tell by the look on his face that he's actually processing it. That he's really thinking about it, rather than writing it off as some liberal hippie garbage.

I like that about him.

The waitress comes over and sets our plates down in front of us, departing with a smile. The restaurant is busy and she's running around like a chicken with her head cut off. I'd half-expected Colin to take me to some high-end, snobby restaurant. Surprisingly enough, he brought me to *Bobby Boy's* – one of the more popular burger joints on this side of town. As I look at him, I pick up a fry and pop it into my mouth – it's salty and crunchy on the outside but tender on the inside – absolute perfection.

"Why are you looking at me like that?" he asks, a wry grin on his face.

"I guess I'm shocked you even know this place exists," I say, pointedly looking at his suit. "Doesn't seem to be the kind of place you'd frequent."

He chuckles and shakes his head. "As a painter, I'm surprised you'd use such broad strokes, Bailey."

"Sometimes, broad strokes are what's called for."

"And sometimes, you need a smaller, more refined brush for the finer details."

"Touché," I reply. "I just figured you'd be more comfortable in a place with linen table cloths, that serves food with names I can't even pronounce."

He laughs. "The picture of me you have in your head must be hilarious," he says.

Colin probably doesn't want to know the kind of picture I have of

him in my head. And as I look at him, the fantasy I'd had about him –
the one I got myself off to – rises like a leviathan from the dark depths
of my mind. I feel my cheeks blush as the warmth spreads through
my body. I squirm in my seat, my body tingling as I start to grow wet.

Jesus, how can this man possibly have this effect on me?

"I found this place when I was going to BC," he says. "I've never
had a better burger. It's kept me coming back for years."

Yeah, maybe I'm painting him with too broad a brush. I guess. He
always comes off as elitist and snobby to me, like he takes being one of
the one-percenters very seriously, and seems to relish the fact that he
belongs to the highest social circle.

"Is it possible – and I'm just putting this out there," he says, "that
your experiences growing up, and this zeal you've formed for helping
the poor, having been poor yourself, has given you a negative percep-
tion of anyone who has money? I mean, don't get me wrong, there are
some real assholes with money out there. I'm not denying that. But,
not all of us are evil just because we happen to be wealthy. Is it
possible that your own experiences have made you so cynical that you
see anybody with any sort of economic advantage as bad, as the
enemy, when maybe, they actually aren't?"

I sit back in my seat and pop another fry into my mouth,
pondering what he said. Colin takes a big bite of his burger and
chews slowly, watching me the entire time. If I'm being honest with
myself, I can't necessarily dispute what he's saying. As I sit there
pondering, I think over everything Cesar said at brunch the other day
– which coincides with what Colin seems to be saying. Yeah, I tend
to think rich people are the devil incarnate, and I have a habit of
lumping them all together.

He's right. Maybe I'm not being fair.

"Growing up like I did, I learned what it was like to not have
anything," I say. "And I also learned that the world is divided up into
two different kinds of people – the rich, and everybody else."

"The world is a lot more varied than that," he retorts, wiping his
mouth with a napkin. "Not everything is so black and white."

"When you grow up like I did, it kind of is," I say. "Poor kids get made fun of by the richer kids. I remember being teased relentlessly about the holes in my clothing, or the fact that I was dirty. I remember them teasing me about not having a lunch, or – anything else they could find to torment me about. It was brutal, and it was very much a case of the haves and the have-nots. Black and white."

"I'm sorry you grew up that way," he says, and then slowly adds, "I can see why you have the worldview you do. It makes sense."

"You don't even know the half of it."

"So, tell me," he says, sincerity etched upon his face.

I take a bite of my burger and wash it down with some soda to fortify myself before launching into my tale of woe. I tell him everything, sparing no detail, and holding nothing back. Half of me expects him to get up and run out screaming. But, he doesn't. He sits there, chewing his food in silence, his eyes riveted to mine, absorbing every single word that comes out of my mouth. I can see that he's shocked, and maybe even somewhat saddened, for me.

I don't want his pity, though. I want his compassion when dealing with the issues we've fought over.

"Your grandmother sounds like an extraordinary woman," he says.

"She was," I say simply. "I wouldn't be who I am today without her. I don't even know *where* I'd be without her, to be honest."

He sits back in his seat and chews on a fry. I can see the wheels in his head turning, as he ponders everything I just shared with him. I wish I knew what was going on inside that beautiful, frustrating head of his.

"You're an extraordinary woman, Bailey," he finally says. "You have strength and resolve. You didn't let your background strip you of your passion. I admire that. Respect it."

"Thank you," I say and look away.

My cheeks flush – I've never really been good with praise. To be honest, it makes me uncomfortable. I never feel worthy of the compliments I receive. I know that's my own baggage, and my personal issues working against me, but I can't help it. It's just part of who I am.

The way he looks at me turns my insides to mush. Those eyes of his are practically peering into my soul. I can feel them analyzing me, and breaking me down. And, for some reason, I like it.

We finish our meal with some light conversation, and I'm surprised to find that we actually have a lot in common. Once you get past all of the political and socioeconomic differences between us, we have more shared interests than I would have thought possible, given the circumstances.

When we leave the restaurant, I see Colin in an entirely different way. Or at least, I'm starting to. There's still a ways to go before that gap is completely bridged, but I think we're starting to get there. All I know is that I enjoy spending the afternoon with him. Even more, I relished the way he looked at me the whole time – like I was the only woman in the world.

By the time I get into his car to have him taxi me back to my studio, I'm practically aching for him.

———

I expected him to drop me off and go, but Colin follows me back into my studio. When he shuts the door behind him, I remember that we haven't gotten to the reason for this impromptu lunch date just yet – this mysterious business arrangement.

I have to say though, I'm kind of disappointed it wasn't just a date, but a business proposal that prompted him to ask me out in the first place. More so now that he and I actually had a good time out together and found a lot of common ground between us.

But, it is what it is. Sadly.

I watch Colin as he walks around my studio, checking everything out. On one of the tables, he picks up a flier for a showcase in an indie art house I'm showing at. I don't know why, maybe he thinks he's being polite, but he slips it into the pocket of his slacks. He takes off his coat, draping it over his arm, and loosens his tie. It's starting to get warm in here, so I flip on the small, portable air conditioner I have. It's not much, but it's something.

I walk over and take his coat from him and hang it on the rack next to the door.

"Thank you," he says.

"You're welcome."

He starts poking through some of the framed portraits I have lined up on the wall – some of the oils, as well as some of the photographs. He stops and looks up at me, an expression of concern on his face.

"I'm sorry," he says. "Do you mind that –"

I shake my head and smile. "No, not at all," I say. "Art is meant to be looked at."

He gives me a nod and turns back to my work. With his coat off, and him kind of bent over the frames as he picks through them, I can see just how well those nicely-tailored slacks frame and showcase his tight, sculpted ass. Talk about a piece of art that's meant to be looked at.

I'm so busy staring at his ass and feeling myself grow wet because of it, that it takes me a minute to realize he's looking back at me and had been speaking. I see the devilish smirk on his face a millisecond before my cheeks start to burn, turning what's an unnatural shade of red, I'm sure.

Thankfully though, Colin has the good grace to not call me out for creeping on his ass. He's probably used to it. Probably gets off on it, come to think of it.

"Tell me more about these," he says.

I clear my throat and walk over. We spend some time talking about some of the subjects of my work. He seems thoroughly impressed by my ability to create art, and even more impressed that I can do it well in two different mediums.

"Bailey, your work – it's amazing," he says, sounding genuinely surprised. "Seriously. It's absolutely stunning."

"Thank you," I say, uncomfortable with the praise. "Oh, let me show you some of my new pieces."

I lead him into my darkroom, mostly as a distraction from him heaping praise on me. The thing that hits me is how sincere it is. I have some people tell me my work is great and all, but I can tell it's a rote response from them. They're saying it because they think they're expected to say it. With Colin though, I can hear the sincerity in his words. What's more, I think he understands my message – which is good, since he's a member of the demographic I target with my work. But, he genuinely seems to appreciate it – something that warms my heart and excites me.

He walks around a bit, scrutinizing some of the pictures I have hanging up on the line, and seems impressed. It's then I realize the picture I took of him at the protest is still up. I don't think he's seen it yet, so I move over and quickly pluck it from the line. He turns around and looks at me.

"What's that a picture of?" he asks.

"Nothing," I say. "Didn't really turn out."

He grins and tries to reach behind me. I spin to block him, which makes him laugh. I really don't want him to see the picture – I'm afraid he'll think I'm some weird stalker, or that he'll somehow know that I got myself off in this very room looking at that very picture. Like he'll be able to somehow just divine the information out of thin air or something.

Colin moves one way and I move to block him – only realizing too late that it was a fake move, and he was actually waiting for me to block him, so he could slip around the other side and pluck the picture from my hand,

I start to protest, but he holds the picture up. "Not a real great shot of me," he says.

"It's fi – I didn't realize I'd even snapped it, to be honest."

He gives me a smile as he hands it back to me. I clutch the picture, feeling utterly humiliated – like he'd caught me peeking at him in the shower or something. With my face already scorching hot, it's only then I realize just how close he's standing to me. My dark-room isn't all that big to start with but feeling his presence so close to me makes it seem even smaller than it really is.

And that's the best way I can describe Colin – he has this presence about him. He displaces the atmosphere in ways most people don't. Standing so close to him is like what I imagine standing at the edge of a black hole must be like – you're inexplicably drawn to it. Into him.

I turn my face up and see his crystalline eyes focused on me. Not even the red light of the darkroom is enough to strip away the sheer breathtaking quality of those eyes. They make my heart skip a beat – or twelve. In his face, I see such longing. A yearning.

He reaches out and strokes my cheek with his fingertips, sending a bolt of white-hot electricity from my head straight down to my lower belly. My whole body tingles with the sensation, and every nerve ending crackles with it.

When Colin leans down and presses his lips to mine, I swear, all of the air in the room is suddenly sucked out. I feel completely breathless, and my head is swimming. As his tongue slips into my mouth and twirls around mine, I swear fireballs are exploding in the darkness behind my closed eyes.

He grabs me by the waist and pulls me to him, pressing his body hard against mine. I run my hands up his chest, feeling the solid, corded muscle beneath the shirt.

Our kiss grows hotter and filled with more fire, and I quickly start to unbutton his shirt. I've never felt this much desire before – I need to feel his skin on mine. I slip my hands inside and move my hands down the hard angles and planes of his chest and abs. His skin is smooth and warm.

Colin pulls back and looks at me, and the craving I see in his eyes for me makes my legs go weak, and they almost give out beneath me. He steadies me on my feet, then grabs hold of my ponytail, pulling my head back roughly. A soft moan escapes my lips as he kisses my neck, nipping at the skin. His one hand still pulling my hair, I feel his other hand squeezing and cupping my breast. He pinches a hard nipple through the fabric, drawing a soft whimper from me.

I reach down and touch Colin through his slacks. I grip his cock, squeezing it through his pants. He's long, and thick – and incredibly hard for me already. I have no idea how he is supposed to fit inside of me. I stroke him through his pants, hearing him draw in a sharp breath as I do.

Colin pushes me back a couple of steps until the small of my back is pressed against my worktable. He pulls my sweatshirt off over my head and tosses it to the side, quickly disposing of my bra. The second his mouth hits my nipple, it feels like something explodes inside of me. He licks and sucks on it, pinching the other one with his hand. I run my fingers through his hair, losing myself in the sensations that are rocking my body.

Needing to feel him in my hand, I quickly unzip Colin's slacks, reaching inside his boxers, and pulling his cock out. He's so long and thick, part of me worries that I won't be able to fit him inside of me. I'm determined to try, though.

Colin grabs me roughly by the shoulders and kisses me hard. I love how it feels for him to grab me so forcefully. Taking what he wants from me. It's just like in my fantasy from the other day – I feel myself giving up all my control to him and the mere thought of it only makes me hotter. I want him to take control. To use me like he wants. I'm tired of always being strong, and keeping such a tight grip on everything. I want somebody else to take charge for a change.

And he does.

Putting his hands on my shoulders, Colin forces me down to my knees. I know what he wants, but I want to hear him say it. I look up at him, pinning him with my gaze.

"Tell me," I say. "Tell me what you want."

"I want your mouth on me," he growls.

His voice is gruff and commanding and sets me ablaze with desire. Colin reaches down and grips my ponytail, pulling my head back. The hunger in his eyes is intoxicating. I grip the base of his cock, squeezing it hard, and draw a gasp from him. He steps forward and runs the head of his cock around my lips.

A salacious grin touches his lips as I run the tip of my tongue all around the head of his cock, teasing the sensitive underside of it. Never breaking eye contact with him, I lean forward and slide his hard erection into my mouth, swirling my tongue around it as I take as much of him in as I can.

When I tighten my lips around him and start to move my mouth up and down on him, Colin draws in a sharp breath. There's a look of absolute rapture on his face as I start bobbing my head up and down. Instinctively, I wrap my fingers around the base of his shaft and stroke him in unison with my mouth.

"Fuck, Bailey," he moans. "I need you. I can't wait to be inside of you."

I stand up, taking his hand in mine and leading him over to the small, dingy couch I have set up in the corner of the room. Colin pushes down my leggings and sits me down on the edge of it, a mischievous sparkle in his eye as he kneels down before me. I'm staring up nervously at the exposed beams of the studio as he parts my thighs.

I can't believe this is happening. Goodbye, virginity.

His beard feels scratchy against my delicate skin, tickling me, but the moment his tongue hits my clit, I feel like a bomb has been detonated in my most intimate parts. A line of fire shoots from the warm, wet center of me and straight into my heart and brain, and back again.

My entire body feels electric as he runs his tongue along my wet, swollen lips. Colin takes my clit into his mouth, sucking gently on it at first. He gently nips it with his teeth, then rolls it around his tongue. I gasp, feeling like I can't catch my breath as my body trembles and shakes.

He buries his tongue deep inside me as he uses his fingers to massage my clit. The double dose of pleasure fills me up, and I feel myself hurtling toward an orgasm at a record pace. Colin licks me up and down, moaning as if I'm the best thing he's ever tasted. The rumble of his voice coupled with the warmth of his breath on my most sensitive parts, sends shockwaves of ecstasy coursing through me.

"Colin... Oh my god..." I gasp.

I cry out, gripping the cushion as I writhe beneath him. When he spreads me open and slides his tongue deep inside, I press my head back against the couch and whimper. I feel completely out of control, as I grip his hair, pulling it hard and pushing his head down further into me. He takes the hint and starts to lick me with even more zeal than before, touching off explosions of sensation inside of me.

My eyes grow wide and I open my mouth, a strangled scream bubbling up from my throat when he adds two fingers to his tongue, all of them working inside of me in unison. He drives his fingers in deep as he takes my clit into his mouth, gently nipping and sucking on it. He moves his fingers in and out of me, sucking harder on my clit, driving me ever closer to the edge.

My belly grows tight, and my entire body becomes taut as he works his fingers and mouth in a perfect erotic symphony, playing my most intimate parts like a maestro. I start to tremble as the pressure in me rises, my breath growing desperate and ragged. I can't wait to feel him inside me.

"Colin, yes," I cry.

I grip his hair even harder, grinding my pussy against him, taking his fingers ever deeper. He responds, using his hand and his mouth in ways I never knew were possible. He brings me to the pinnacle, and then with a flick of his tongue, sends me toppling over the edge.

My stomach lurches and I fall into a chasm of sheer ecstasy. I thrash on the couch, crying out, my body arching up, feeling like my skin is on fire. I call his name over and over, as my orgasm tears through me.

Slowly, the grip of my orgasm loosens, and I lay there quivering, whimpering, but feeling absolutely amazing. I sit up as Colin looks at me. His beard glistens with my juices, and he runs the tip of his tongue around his lips, as if savoring every last drop of me.

"I can't wait any more," he growls. "I need you."

He turns me around and bends me over the couch.

I'm starting to feel self-conscious as he gets behind me. Should I tell him this is my first time? I hear the rustle of plastic, and when I turn and look at him over my shoulder, I see him tearing a condom wrapper open. He gives me a roguish grin and pushes me back down, so my belly is flat on the couch.

A moment later, my eyes grow wide, and I open my mouth, but no sound comes out. Not even having three fingers inside of me could have prepared me for what his cock feels like as he slowly penetrates me. Colin grabs hold of my hair and pulls my head back as he drives his cock deep into my pussy. He fills me up completely as he stretches me open, a sharp pinch of pain melding perfectly with the pleasure that has my body humming with an electrical current.

Colin is gripping my hair and pulling my head back as he starts to slowly and rhythmically thrust himself into me. Every thrust hits a spot deep within me that sets off a tiny, but powerful explosion of pleasure inside of me. My body is quivering, and I'm gasping for breath, but the pleasure rocking me is unlike anything I've ever felt before. It's as intense as it is amazing.

He drives himself into me again and again, driving me to the absolute brink of sanity. The sensations gripping my body make me feel like I'm balancing right on the edge between hyperventilating and passing out. As he plunges his glorious cock deep inside of me, I cry out. I call his name, and I hear him grunting, feel his body stiffening behind me.

I push myself back against him, taking him as deep as possible, and the muscles inside of me tighten even further, making my pussy feel impossibly tight around his cock. Colin cries out and I feel him start to shake, and his cock pulsing in the condom inside of me.

Feeling him coming inside of me sets off another orgasm within me. My climax hits me out of the blue, and though it's not as intense as the last one, it's still enough to cause me to dig my nails into the couch as my body tightens and shudders.

I tremble beneath him as Colin keeps me pinned to the couch, his cock deep inside of me, the condom filled with his come.

Slowly, the ecstasy recedes, and Colin slips his now-soft cock out of me. He drops the condom in the trash can near my worktable as I stand up and pull my leggings up, and grab my sweatshirt, slipping it back on over my head. Although the initial bliss has worn off, I still feel warm and sexy, if a little bit sore. I walk over to him as he finishes buttoning his shirt and nuzzle up against him.

He kisses me on the forehead, but I feel the stiffness and tension in his body. He doesn't say a word as he tucks his shirt back into his slacks, and zips up. He won't even meet my eyes.

'You okay?" I ask.

He nods, but still looks away from me. "Yeah. Fine," he says. "I'm fine."

He's acting strangely all of the sudden, and I don't know why. What we did – what we just shared – was amazing. It felt incredible. I can't believe it happened, honestly. But now he's acting like we did something wrong. There's an awkward moment of silence as we stand there, staring at one another, the chasm standing between us wider than it's ever been.

"I – I should probably go," he says quickly.

"Oh, so that's how it is?" I ask, planting my hands on my hips.

"What do you mean?"

"You get your rocks off, and now you're just going to bail?" I almost shout. "You just use me, and now you're going to throw me away like a piece of trash?"

Most girls would probably be crying at this point. Not me. I'm just pissed. I gave myself to him willingly, and I don't regret it. But now, he's acting like I'm going to be some crazy, clingy girl with a crush or something.

"That's not how it is, Bailey," he says. "That's not it at all."

"Then what is it?" I ask. "Explain it to me, because that's what it feels like."

He runs a hand through his hair and looks at me awkwardly, as if trying to find the right excuse that will let him off the hook. Maybe this is all he wanted. He just wanted a quick screw – maybe with one of the poor so he knew what it felt like. Maybe, fucking me made him feel all-powerful or something. I don't know.

All I do know, is that the longer he stands there, saying nothing, obviously trying to find some spin or excuse to mollify me, the more pissed I'm getting.

"You know what?" I say. "Get the hell out."

"Bailey –"

"No, it was great. I had a good time. Thanks for making me come twice, I appreciate it," I say. "We both got something out of it, so let's just say we're good, and call it a day."

"It's not like –"

"I said get out of my studio," I say, my voice low and tight with anger.

"Bailey –"

"Get out!" I scream. "Get the fuck out of here!"

Colin looks at me for a moment longer, then slowly turns and leaves my studio. When I hear the door close behind him, I grab a small jar, and hurl it against the wall. The sound of shattering glass, and the feel of destroying something, is satisfying for a moment – only for a moment though.

But, just like the rest of my life, I'm stuck cleaning up that mess in the end.

Chapter Nine

Colin

I sign the contracts, tucking them back into the folder, and silently handing the folder over to Maureen.

"Are you okay, Mr. Anderson?" she asks.

I look up, and see the concern in her eyes. "Yeah, I'm fine," I say. "Just tired, I guess."

She nods, though I can tell by the expression on her face that she's not necessarily buying it. Instead of leaving, she surprises me by perching herself on the edge of the seat across the desk from me. It's unusual for her, though not completely unprecedented. In addition to her outstanding work in the office, Maureen has become my unofficial mother-figure, and never hesitates to dish out motherly advice.

"That girl who was here the other day –"

"Just a friend," I say, cutting her off. "Though, I don't know that I'd even call her that anymore."

Maureen looks at me evenly. She's sharp, and always seems to know when I'm not giving it to her straight. And I can tell she's onto me because she has a small frown and slightly disapproving expression on her face.

"I was only curious because the other day when she was in here, you looked at her like you were in love."

"What?" I laugh. "You've gone and lost it now, Maureen."

"Have I?" she asks, arching one of her eyebrows at me.

"Yes, you have."

She looks at me long and hard, her eyes boring into me. Maureen has an uncanny ability to read people, and I really should know better than to try and sneak one by her. Maureen knows and sees all. Maybe, one of these days, I'll learn that lesson.

"Because the way you looked at her tells me otherwise," she says.

"Okay," I reply with a laugh. "Whatever you say, Maureen."

"I've been around the block a few times, Mr. Anderson," she says. "And believe me when I say, when a man looks at a woman the way you did, he's interested in being more than friends."

I laugh heartily. "Okay, now you're just being crazy," I say. "I'm not in love with her. Not even close. I barely know the woman, Maureen."

She shrugs. "My point is that you have more than just, friendly feelings, for her," she says. "Believe me, I can tell."

"You're crazy."

"Maybe," she says and laughs. "Doesn't mean I'm wrong though."

"Even if I were interested in her –"

"Which you are," she cuts me off.

"I'm not saying one way or the other," I say and chuckle.

"You don't have to," she says. "But, okay. If you were – go on?"

"We come from two totally different worlds," I say. "It would never work."

"Why not?" she asks. "Plenty of people have opposing views, and still find a way to make it work. The key is finding enough middle ground that you don't drive each other crazy."

"Well, it's kind of a moot point, anyway," I say. "She doesn't like me very much right now."

Maureen chuckles. "Why would you say that?"

"Our last – meeting – didn't end well," I say.

Memories of having her in her studio flash through my mind, and I feel the stirring in my groin. Being with Bailey had been hot as hell. Intense. Exciting. At least, until the end. Then it got awkward, before it got ugly. And that was totally my fault. But, I can't explain it to her because I don't really understand it myself.

"Well, I'll tell you," Maureen says. "She looked at you the same way you did. You two may have had a spat, but there's something going on between you. I can feel it, and I'm only on the outside looking in."

"I'm not so sure that's true anymore, if it ever was," I admit. "She seemed pretty upset with me."

"Well, I don't need to know the details, but I will tell you that sometimes, you need to open yourself up more. You need to let people in. I think that might be one of your biggest problems," she says. "Bailey seems like a free spirit. To me, it seems like she really enjoys life."

I nod. "That she does."

"And then there's you, with your iron grip on your heart and emotions," she chides. "You have these high, thick walls around yourself, and you never let anybody in. You know, in all the years I've worked for you, I've never seen you go on a date. I've never seen you smile when you see a pretty girl. You're all business, all the time."

"I'm trying to build a successful company," I say.

She scoffs and waves me off. "I've been with the company long enough to know that ADE is always going to be successful," she says. "This company, whether it be your division, or one of your brothers, are the gold standard in this industry. Trust me, I worked for a competitor for a while before coming over, and their biggest concern was how to catch up to you."

"I just feel like my focus should be on making this division as profitable as the others," I say. "It's my responsibility. My legacy."

She raises her eyebrows at me. "And who exactly are you leaving your legacy to?" she asks. "If you're not interested in dating or settling down and having a family, who will you pass on the fruits of all your hard work to?"

Damn. She has me there. I really never gave it that much thought, but looking at it from that perspective, I see her point. I lean back in my seat and scratch at my beard, giving her a sheepish smile.

"If I may be so bold –"

"Aren't you always?" I ask and chuckle. "When did you start needing permission?"

She laughs. "Perhaps. Call it a perk of being my age," she says. "I think the bigger problem here is fear."

"Fear?"

She nods. "You're afraid to get involved with anyone," she explains. "You're afraid of your emotions, of getting attached to anybody."

"I don't know about that," I say. "But, if that's true, I think I have ample reason to be."

"Maybe," she says. "But, we all bear scars from our past. We all carry baggage. What we do with those things is what's important. We can either use them to teach us and help us grow, or, we can let them define us in a negative way."

I blow out a long breath, absorbing her words, and turning them over in my mind. A lot of what Maureen is saying rings true to me. As much as I hate to admit it, I know she's speaking the truth. The question is – what I'm going to do with that truth. And at the moment, I don't have the first clue.

"I want you to be happy," she continues. "I've never seen you really, truly happy in the whole time I've worked for you. You're a good man. You deserve it."

"I've been happy," I say. "I just don't show it, I guess."

She gives me an expression that says she knows I'm full of it, and that no words even need to be said. Yeah, message received.

"Talk to her, Mr. Anderson," she urges. "You'll see that if you're honest, and you communicate openly and honestly, there's not much the two of you can't overcome."

I laugh. "I wish I had your optimism."

"Talk to her, Mr. Anderson," she repeats. "You'll see that I'm right."

"Thanks, Maureen," I say.

She stands up and gives me a warm, motherly smile. "You're very welcome, sir."

"So, are you going to bill me for our counseling sessions?"

She laughs. "You know I will," she says. "And you'll get no discount from me."

"Nor would I expect one."

I watch her walk out of my office, and through the glass wall until she drops back down into her seat and returns to work. I realize I'm a very fortunate man to have the amazing people around me that I do. It sometimes makes me wonder what I did to ever deserve such good fortune.

As far as Bailey goes, I really don't know if I'm going to be able to salvage that now. I really screwed that up in a big way.

I can't really explain what happened. After we had sex, the initial rush felt amazing. It was total bliss. But, as that glow faded, my baggage started to pop back up. Worse than that, my emotions started to creep in. I remember feeling a swell in my heart when I looked at her and realized that I was losing my grip on the control I had over myself. The control I have on my emotions.

Right now is not the time to be dabbling with romance. That leads to complications, things getting messy, and people getting hurt. At the moment, I have bigger things on my plate I need to worry about and focus on.

Such as the coming invasion of my family. I look at the calendar and feel a surge of adrenaline. I don't have too much longer before they arrive. And although the house will be ready – and there's nothing left for me to worry about on that front – what I *do* need to worry about is finding an imaginary fiancée. One who will answer to the name of Bailey.

I thought getting her on board would be simple. Or at least, not overly difficult. But, I'd gone and screwed that up in a big way. Now, it might not be anything at all, since I doubt she'll take my call after the way things ended the other day. I'm pretty sure Bailey hates me right about now, and probably feels like I used her. I can't believe she'd agree to be my fake fiancée at this point.

But, I need to do something. Time's running short, and if I want to be prepared for this – for whoever ends up as my fake fiancée – I need to make some progress on that front sooner rather than later. The sooner the better, actually.

I rack my brain, trying to find the solution, and the only thing my brain keeps circling back to is Bailey herself.

Opening my desk drawer, I see the flier I'd taken from her studio. It's for a showcase she's being featured in at a place called the Commons Gallery. I check my watch and look at the time the show starts. I still have time.

This is so far outside my comfort zone it's not even funny. But, I'm in desperation mode at the moment, and need some help. I also need to set things right with Bailey. Somehow, some way, I need to accomplish both of those tasks.

Yeah, this is going to be a whole lot of fun.

———

There's a good crowd in the small, but chic gallery. It's definitely unlike any art gallery I've ever been in before, but I actually kind of like the electric, almost punk, atmosphere of the place. The gallery-goers are more urban than I'm used to. Instead of suits or tuxedos, and formal evening gowns, I see a lot of leather, lace, and tattoos.

And hipsters. There's a *lot* of hipsters here.

I feel really out of place in my black suit and tie – a feeling further reinforced by people with weird-colored hair, and piercings on their face, who are staring at me like I'm some kind of alien.

The gallery has an interesting vibe, though. It's not the uptight, almost sterile atmosphere that I'm used to. Here, there's rock music playing and people are laughing, speaking loudly, and enjoying the experience. There's a vibrancy to the place that's engaging and exciting.

As far as the art goes, there are some fantastic and interesting pieces. I'm not an expert and don't pretend to be one, but my personal take on art is that the good pieces are the ones that grab you. The ones that strike a chord deep inside of you. Pieces that, for one reason or another, really resonate with you.

I can honestly say that in most of the gallery showings I've been to over the years, nothing in those fancier, high-end galleries have ever connected with me. This place, on the other hand, full of dark, gritty art across a wide variety of mediums, is filled with work that's compelling. I see half a dozen pieces from where I'm standing that really resonate with me.

To me, the artists in a place like this are trying to say something with their art. They're trying to communicate with the world around them and everybody who views their piece, while some of the artists in the more traditional galleries are more austere and abstract. They think they're being intellectual and are making a statement. Though honestly, most times I can't understand what that statement might be. With the pieces on display here, though, what the artist is saying is as clear as day. It punches you right in the face with its bold message.

Which is the perfect way to make a statement.

I walk around the gallery, checking out some of the work when I spot Bailey standing in a corner by herself. I recognize some of the pieces on the wall behind her. She's sipping a bottle of beer and doesn't look very happy. In fact, she looks downright miserable.

I notice that almost no one is viewing her work, with most of the people crowding around a series of provocative sculptures. I'm assuming that Bailey's work is getting lost in the shuffle – especially, because she's tucked away in a back room.

I want to give her a boost, but I'm not sure how – and then it hits me.

I look around, and I have a hard time identifying the gallery employees from the guests. Eventually, I find an employee and pull her into a corner with me. Keeping an eye on Bailey, I tell the employee exactly what I want.

After that, I take a deep breath and head for the back room. Time to bite the bullet and see how this all pans out.

Bailey sees me when I step through the doorway and into her room. Her face transforms from despondent to livid in the blink of an eye.

"What are you doing here?" she snaps. "Slumming again? Liked it so much last time, you're looking for your next lower-class conquest?"

The venom in her voice takes me back for a moment, but I shrug it off and push through. I knew she was going to be pissed at me, so it doesn't come as any surprise.

"Actually," I say. "I'm viewing some amazing art."

She scoffs. "Right," she says. "What do you want?"

"I wanted to talk to you."

"You made your feelings perfectly clear, and I've got nothing left to say to you," she says. "Please leave me alone."

"I think you misunder –"

Her eyes grow wide, and her lips curl back into a snarl. It's in that moment, I realize that was the wrong thing to come out of my mouth.

"Oh, so it's my fault?" she hisses. "It couldn't be that you're an asshole who was just looking for a cheap thrill, right?"

"Is this guy bothering you, Bailey?"

I turn and see a guy in all black, walking toward us. He's all of five-five, and one hundred and thirty pounds, soaking wet. But, he looks like he wants to rip my head off. He steps up to me – and has to crane his neck upward to make eye contact. His face is red, and his nostrils are flaring. He reminds me of a kid on the verge of a tantrum.

"Really?" I ask, arching an eyebrow at him.

"We're fine, Billy," she says. "It's fine. Thank you."

Billy the bodyguard gives me a withering glare before he turns and slinks out of the room. When he's gone, I turn back to Bailey to find that she's got a small smile tugging at the corners of her mouth. What Billy the bodyguard lacks in size, he apparently makes up for in balls. I'll give him that.

I step closer to Bailey and force her to look up at me. She finally looks at me with those bottomless, soulful dark eyes of hers, and my heart stutters. She's so beautiful, and she doesn't even seem to realize it.

"No, that's not it, Bailey. Not at all," I say. "What I meant to say, was that I didn't communicate properly, so how could you have understood? I know you're not a mind reader, right? I handled what happened between us incredibly poorly. I freaked out and completely fucked up. That's on me. I'm here tonight to apologize for that."

She opens her mouth, presumably to rip me a new one, but then closes it in the face of my apology. What can she say, really? I fucked up. I'm taking ownership of it. Case closed.

Not that she's not still pissed, but I know she's reasonable, level-headed, and mature enough that she can accept an apology.

"Believe me when I say it wasn't some weird conquest or me looking for a cheap thrill," I continue.

"Then why did you get all weird afterward?"

I sigh and give her a tight smile. "Because I don't handle my emotions well," I answer. "I don't handle my emotions at all, actually."

"I noticed."

"And after we – afterward – I kind of freaked out," I say. "I felt this rush of emotion for you, and –"

"Wait, did you just say you had a rush of emotion?" she asks. "For me?"

"Yeah. For you."

I see her cheeks color, and she looks a bit embarrassed but happy at the same time. A heart-melting smile stretches across her face, and for a moment, she's rendered speechless. Only for a moment, though.

"So, I guess you kinda like me, huh?"

I chuckle nervously and run a hand through my hair. "Yeah, I guess that's kind of what I'm saying."

"You like me," she says in that sing-song voice. "You have a crush on me."

I roll my eyes theatrically. "Don't let it go to your head or anything."

She steps over and throws her arms around me, wrapping me in a big hug. I feel somewhat stiff and awkward at first – I've never been much of a hugger, really. But, I give into the moment, and embrace her back, relishing how her body feels pressed to mine. She steps back after a moment and looks up at me, that smile still on her face.

"You like me. You've got a crush on me," she sings.

I laugh and shake my head. "How is the show going?"

She frowns and shrugs. "Great. For other people," she says. "Kind of hard to display your work when you're relegated to the back rooms."

"Yeah, I noticed the lack of traffic back here," I say.

"It's fine," she says. "It'll be fine. If I don't get spotted at this show, it'll happen at another one. It's just hard to get into the bigger, more prestigious galleries without connections."

She sounds frustrated, and I can't blame her. I guess art, like everything else, is a matter of who you know. Knowing the right person can open doors for you that you never dreamed possible. I hate seeing her down, and although I can see that she's trying to keep a chipper, upbeat attitude, I can see that it's wearing on her. I can see the bitterness around the edges and can hear the frustration in her voice.

That spark in Bailey, that fire, and passion – is something I never want to see her lose. I never want to see that fire extinguished. As far as I'm concerned, it's one of her most attractive, endearing qualities.

Which gives me an idea. Before I can pitch it, though, the gallery employee comes into the room, and gives Bailey a big smile.

"Your pieces are a big hit," she says.

Bailey's face immediately brightens, and she clasps her hands in front of her chest, bouncing on the balls of her feet like an excited child on Christmas morning. It's absolutely adorable.

"Really?"

The employee nods. "Yup. Somebody bought your entire collection."

Bailey's eyes widen, and the look of excitement on her face quickly transforms to one of shock. She watches the employee putting the red tags that denote a sale on the placards with something like awe on her face. But then, I see the wheels start turning in her head as she puts all the pieces together. A dark shadow crosses her face, and the excited smile morphs into a small frown as she turns to me. Shit.

"Congratulations again," the employee says as she departs the room.

"Really, Colin?" she asks.

"What?"

"All seven of them?" she asks, her hands on her hips. "Kind of obvious, don't you think?"

She's right. In hindsight, it's totally obvious. I should have been smarter about it. I just couldn't bear to see her look so unhappy. It was actually causing me physical pain.

"Bailey, I –"

She shakes her head and holds up her hand to cut me off. "You might think that's sweet, and maybe, on some level, it is," she says. "But more than anything, it's patronizing. By you doing that, you're telling me I'm not good enough. That I'll never sell my work unless I have some rich guardian angel sweep in and snatch them all up. Do you even know how degrading that feels?"

"Are you done?"

"Maybe."

"You're done," I say.

"I reserve the right to rebut."

"This isn't a courtroom. You don't get to rebut," I say. "Believe it or not, I love your work, Bailey. This wasn't a patronizing gesture. It was genuine. Those pieces will be hanging in my house before the end of day tomorrow. I want all my guests to see them."

My words aren't mollifying her in the least. She's still standing there, hands on her hips, that frown still creasing her face. Those dark eyes of hers are penetrating, and I know she can see right through me.

"Fine," I say. "Part of it is that I wanted to give you a boost. You looked so down –"

"And you thought buying up all my work would make me feel better?"

I shrug. "It did. For a minute," I say. "I would pay ten times what I just did to see that smile on your face again."

Her face softens – slightly – as she looks at me.

"Look into my eyes, though," I say. "I want you to believe me when I tell you that I really do admire your work, and that I'll be proud to display these pieces at home."

She searches my eyes for a long moment before seeing the truth in my words. Her hands come off her hips, and that ecstatic smile returns to her face. She pulls me to her and makes me hug her again. Her hair smells of citrus, and her body is warm, and carries a subtle hint of perfume. I've never been a hugger, but honestly, I can get used to this.

"Thank you," she says, her voice muffled in my jacket.

"You're welcome," I reply.

I let out a silent sigh of relief, having successfully avoided a couple of major catastrophes. I'm feeling better about where we are now, though, I'm still uneasy about having confessed to my feelings for her. Mostly because I don't know what I feel. Do I like her? Yeah, absolutely. What's not to like? But, do I mean it in the way she thinks I do? That, I'm not totally sure of.

This is why I don't do emotions – they're messy, complicated, and can't be easily defined.

"So, how about we go get a drink?" I ask. "I have something I want to talk to you about."

She looks up, a curious expression on her face. "Sure," she says. "Let me just wrap up a few things here, and we can take off."

"Great," I say. "I'll just wander around a bit then."

She lets go of my coat lapels, and starts to turn away, but then reaches up quickly, planting a soft, chaste kiss on my lips. When she pulls away, there's a warm smile on her face.

"What was that for?" I ask.

"Because I felt like it," she says. "You need to loosen up a bit, Colin. You need to give in to your impulses now and again."

"Yeah, I'm not very good at that."

A mischievous twinkle sparkles in her eye. "Good thing you met me then," she teases.

"You might be the death of me," I say and laugh.

"At least you'll go with a smile on your face then."

She turns and walks away, putting some added swish in her hips as she goes. She looks back over her shoulder at me and winks, knowing I've been staring at that perfect ass of hers the whole time, and all I can do is laugh.

We end up not going out for drinks after all. Instead, we're sitting in a fifties-themed diner called *Dickie's,* eating the most enormous hot fudge sundaes I've ever seen. As a rule, I usually don't eat sweets. I try to avoid them, but I have to say, this is a damn good sundae.

"What do you think?" she asks.

"I think I probably should have tried this place sooner."

"That's what I'm saying, Colin," she says. "Live life a little. Enjoy it."

"I think you enjoy it enough for the both of us."

"That's probably true," she says. "But, enjoyment and happiness are not finite resources. There is more than enough for everybody."

She takes a big bite of her sundae, making noises of pleasure that are almost perverse. I'm glad the place is mostly empty, and we're sitting in the back of the place, not easily seen. She sees how uncomfortable I am and laughs.

"This is what I'm talking about," she says. "Just loosen up a bit. Have some fun."

I chuckle. "I think we might have two different ideas of fun."

She shrugs. "Maybe," she says. "But, there's nothing saying we can't find some mutual fun together, right?"

"Right."

"Good," she replies.

She comes around the table and scoots into the booth next to me. She pulls her sundae over and starts to eat again, pressing her body close to mine. I'm not sure what she's doing, but she's acting kind of hesitant. Cautious, almost. Her eyes roam around the place for a minute, before she turns them to me, a fiendish smile on her face.

"In fact," she says. "I think I know some mutual fun we can have right now."

"Yeah?"

She nods, and her right hand disappears beneath the table. I groan softly when she grabs my cock through my pants and starts to stroke it.

"What are you doing?" I ask, a small grin on my face.

"What do you think I'm doing?"

"Starting trouble."

She runs the tip of her tongue around her lips. "Then that's exactly what I'm doing."

Bailey moves closer to me, biting her bottom lip, her expression full of mischief. Under the table, she squeezes my cock through my pants. I have to fight to keep from moaning out loud.

"You're going to be the death of me," I moan quietly.

She squeezes my cock and pumps her hand up and down the shaft. "And here I am, just trying to have a good time."

"In a public place?" I ask.

She shrugs. "Sometimes you need to live a little."

She leans forward and plants a soft kiss on the end of my nose, giggling the whole time.

The sensations coursing through me are intense. Vibrant. Probably made more so by the fact that we could get caught at any time. There's a look of hunger in her eyes, that makes me wonder if she's enjoying this as much as I am. I somehow doubt it.

She adjusts her grip on me, giving herself some more leverage. I can feel my cock swelling and starting to thicken as the pressure inside of me builds up.

Shit.

"As much as I want you to keep going, Bailey, I'm about to lose it," I say, sighing with disappointment.

She laughs, and moves her hand away as we snuggle close. Being so close to her, feels good. It somehow feels natural and right. I can't explain it. It makes no sense to me. After actively shunning any sort of romantic entanglements for so long, here I am, plunging headfirst into one. What in the hell am I doing?

As I sit there, breathing in the fresh, citrusy scent of Bailey, I find that I don't really care. I'm going to focus on enjoying the moment. It feels good. I watch other people coming and going from the restaurant, observe the wait staff bustling back and forth, and can't help but laugh to myself. None of them know what we'd just gotten away with, and somehow, that secret knowledge, shared only by Bailey and me, makes me smile.

"So, what did you want to talk to me about?" she murmurs.

I suddenly feel very odd about asking her what I had planned. I don't know why, but it feels strange now. Somehow it feels – dirty. But, then I remember that time is running out, and that, coupled with the desire to keep my brothers off my back about it, tips the scale. I want whatever's happening between Bailey and I to grow organically, but I don't have that kind of time.

I let out a breath and sit up straight in the booth. Bailey turns and looks straight into my eyes. I explain everything to her – from my ex-fiancée, and how that all imploded, to my brothers, all the way to the fact that they would be in town soon, and I need somebody to act as my fiancée to keep them from pressuring me.

She listens to it all with a bemused smile on her face, and when I'm done, she giggles out loud.

"What's so funny?" I ask.

"I just think it's kind of interesting that you picked my name out of the, literally, millions you could have chosen," she says. "I guess you really do have a crush on me."

"Shut up," I reply and laugh. "So, what do you say? Will you help me?"

"Well, I don't know," she says, sending a bolt of fear through me. "I'm going to have to check my social calendar."

"I'll pay you, Bailey," I say quickly. "I'll definitely make it worth your time. Not only can I pay you, I'll reach out to people I know and see about getting you into one of the galleries you want to get into. I know a lot of people who can help."

When her back stiffens and her jaw clenches, I get the sense that I said the wrong thing. Her expression changes from bemused to hurt.

"What's wrong?" I ask.

"Is that what I am to you? A prostitute?" she asks. "You'll pay me to pretend to be your fiancée? What the hell, Colin?"

I have no idea how this went sideways so fast, and I'm left speech-less for a moment. She stares at me with a cold fury in her eyes, completely silent.

"That's not it at all," I say. "I just thought —"

"You thought what, you could charm me, then flash some money at me, dangle an opportunity to get a showcase, and I'd do whatever you wanted? Like I'm a whore?"

"No, Bailey, you have it all wrong."

"Do I?"

I slam my fist down on the table so hard, the silverware rattles and our glasses clink. I catch a few people looking our way, but when I glare at them, they quickly turn back to their own tables. Bailey looks more than a bit stunned by my outburst — a little scared, even —

and I instantly regret it. The last thing I ever want is for her to be scared of me.

I reach out to stroke her cheek, but she recoils from my touch as if I'd slapped her. Undaunted, I reach out again, and lay my hand against her smooth cheek. I stroke it with my thumb and hold her gaze. Her big doe-eyes are wide, and her lower lip is trembling with unspoken emotion.

"I'm sorry. I didn't mean to startle you," I say. "I just wanted a chance to explain."

"Then explain," she says, her voice slowly regaining some of its strength. "You have my full attention now."

I take a deep breath, and let it out slowly, trying to keep my temper in check. It's a struggle, just like it has been my whole life. I've always been the hothead in the family. The first one to go in swinging. That attitude has gotten me in more troublesome situations than I can count, but I've tried my best to keep it under control.

"I like you, Bailey," I say. "More than I even realized at first. But, there's a reason I don't get involved with people romantically."

She looks at me, her expression softening as the fear recedes. "And why is that?"

"Because I don't handle my emotions well," I say. "Never have. I don't understand emotions. They make me nervous."

"Everybody gets scared."

"Not like me."

"Everybody thinks that too."

A wry smile touches my lips. "Maybe," I say. "But, like I told you, I've had some bad experiences. Laurel really did a number on me, and I haven't been able to fully move past it."

"Do you still love her?" she asks, a faint glimmer of fear in her eyes.

I run a hand across my face. "No. Any positive feelings I had for her died the day I caught her fucking my best friend," I say.

"Then why are you so afraid of her coming for Christmas?"

"Because I hate her," I retort. "I'm afraid I'm going to lose my temper and ruin everybody's good time. But, I know my brother is right. It's the right thing to do. It's what our father would have done – what he would have wanted us to do. He would have wanted me to suck it up and deal with it for a day. Like an adult. But, it would be a big help to have somebody by my side that could act as a buffer between us."

"A buffer?"

I nod. "For a while, she really tried to get me to take her back," I admit. "I don't know where she's at in her life or what she's doing, but, given the fact that she has nowhere to go on Christmas, I think it's safe to say she doesn't have a family of her own."

"Sounds like a reasonable assumption."

"I just don't want her getting the wrong idea," I say. "I don't want her thinking that because I allowed her to come, that I'm interested in taking her back."

Bailey nods as if she understands. Hopefully, she does.

"Also, having somebody there with me, will keep my brothers off my back," I say. "I know they want me to be happy, but they can be kind of – overbearing – at times. To put it lightly."

"I'm sure it comes from a good place."

"Oh, it does," I say. "But, I don't want them planning out the rest of my life or trying to play matchmaker between Laurel and me. I only offered to pay you because I wanted it to make it worth your time. I don't know where this thing – whatever it is – between us is going yet. It's really early yet, but honestly, I love the way you make me feel."

A small grin tugs one corner of her mouth upward. "I'm sure you do."

"That too," I reply with a chuckle. "But, I mean, overall. You've come storming into my life and have turned my entire world upside down, Bailey. You're making me feel emotions I've had shut down and locked up tight for years. No matter how hard I try, I can't shut down my emotions when it comes to you. And trust me, I've tried."

There's a smile on her lips, and a look in her eyes I can't quite identify. She leans forward and gives me a slow, sweet kiss that seems to last forever, and yet, not anywhere near long enough. Ordinarily, I'm not a PDA sort of person, but with Bailey, it feels natural, and I don't mind it. Like I said, she's turning my entire world upside down. When she pulls back, the look on her face is soft. Sweet. It's an expression I could get used to seeing a lot more of.

"I thought by paying you for your time, I could help you out. I know you've told me that you sometimes have a hard time making ends meet," I say. "But, I didn't mean for it to sound like an offer to be a prostitute."

"That's kind of what it sounds like though," she says, but without any of the heat or anger from before.

"I know," I say. "I see that now. But honestly, I only want to help you. I mean, I want you to help me, of course, but I genuinely thought it would be a win-win for both of us."

She lets out a breath. "I like you too, but I don't like feeling like a hooker, Colin."

"I'm not asking you to be one. Look, I want to get to know you and see how this develops, Bailey. But, I'm also in kind of a bind at the same time," I say. "I just thought, we could get through the weekend with my family. And once they're gone, we can explore what we have together."

She looks at me, the skepticism in her face more than obvious. I know it's an odd request. In a certain light, it even sounds sketchy. But, I'm being honest about this. I like Bailey and really want to see where this goes, but I also need help with my brothers, and their families.

"Believe me when I say, I'm not asking you to sleep with me. I'm not paying you to sleep with me. Sex isn't part of this deal," I say. "I just want to get through the weekend with them, get them off my back, and go back to our normal lives. And for me, that includes exploring this thing between us."

She sits back in the booth and stares straight ahead. I can tell that the suggestion still bothers her. I know it struck her the wrong way, though, and I can feel the air between us cooling down and becoming more frigid. She hasn't quite thrown up a wall of ice, yet, but it's definitely coming. I can feel it. And I want to kick myself in the ass for it.

"I need some time to think it over," she says.

"Of course," I say. "But, if you can get back to me in a couple of days, I'd appreciate it. If you don't want to do it, I'll need to figure something else out."

She gives me a rueful grin. "You're going through an awful lot of trouble just to pull one over on your brothers," she says.

"You don't know my brothers," I say. "If they've determined it's time for me to settle down with somebody, they'll move heaven and earth to make it happen. I'd just like to avoid that if I can."

She laughs softly. "Sometimes, I'm glad I'm an only child."

"Sometimes, I wish I were."

Chapter Ten

Bailey

"I'm not a hooker!" I cry, slamming my bottle down on the table.

It's an empty bottle, now, and I'm ready for another one. Cesar's glass is still mostly full, and he looks at me curiously, since we've only been at the bar for fifteen minutes – and I've already downed an entire bottle of beer.

I'm sitting across from Cesar in a local bar we like to frequent and have drinks together. I've already filled him in on the more pertinent details of what's going on, so he understands why I'm fuming. At least, I think he does. The way he looks at me, like I'm amusing him, tells me he may not.

Colin and I left things between us amicably enough, but after I went home, I had some time alone. Time to think. Time to dwell. Time to stew. And honestly, the idea that Colin wants to pay me to be his fiancée – his escort – is sitting more and more wrong with me as the minutes and hours pass. It just feels so dirty.

I want to believe him when he says he likes me and wants to explore this thing that's growing between us. I really, really want to believe him. But, the whole idea of pay-to-play with him is bothering me on a deep, profound level. Why can't he just introduce me as somebody he's recently started to see? Why does he have to invent this whole long-term relationship that doesn't exist – and then pay me to continue the lie?

Granted, I don't know, and can't understand the family dynamics at work, but I don't like feeling like I'm some dirty secret, either. When I left Colin the other night, I thought I was okay with it. Or at least, okay with it enough to think about it. But, now that I've had some time and distance to reflect on it, I realize I'm not okay with it. Not anywhere near okay, honestly.

I'm still silently fuming when I catch Cesar looking at me. He shakes his head, a smile pulling at his lips as he peers at me from over his cocktail.

"What?" I ask. "What's that look for?"

"Nothing," he replies.

We both know that it's not "nothing," though. I can see it in his face. I tilt my head to the side and glare at him until he bursts into laughter.

"It's just, I don't see what the big deal is," he admits.

"You think I should sleep my way to the top, Cesar?" I ask. "Or at least, sleep my way to a paycheck?"

"No, I said nothing about sleeping with anybody," he says. "You did, you little virgin."

I open my mouth to argue, but he's right. Cesar doesn't know that I've already had sex with Colin. Normally, I tell my best friend everything, but that fact has stayed tucked away in my brain until now. It's been fueling my own fantasies, but I haven't felt the need to share just yet.

From the look he's giving me, though, I can tell he suspects something is up. He's just waiting for me to fess up.

"*Fine*, I slept with him," I say. "And I might have played with him under the table at Dickie's the other night. But it's not happening again."

"At *Dickie's?*" he asks and laughs. "How appropriate."

"Shut it, Cesar," I growl, without any actual heat behind my words.

"Let me just say, for the record – I knew it!" Cesar says, wiggling in his seat as if celebrating the fact that he was right. "So, *it* really happened, right? It finally happened!"

I nod sheepishly.

"I knew you had a crush on Colin. I told you so."

"I don't have a crush on –" I start to argue, but then stop myself as I realize how silly the argument sounds. "It was a mistake. I shouldn't have let my guard down like that with him. He's hot, but he's an asshole. It was a one time thing. A total fluke."

"Uh-huh," Cesar says, grinning like the Cheshire cat. "If you say so, Bailey. But, it sounds to me like you're trying to convince yourself."

"I do say so," I say, "Which is why I can't accept his offer. If I accept his offer, I'm admitting that I'm nothing but a glorified prostitute, and my grandmother raised me better than that."

"Do you like him?" he asks bluntly.

I hesitate a moment and then nod. "Yes," I say quietly.

"And, does he like you?"

"He says he does, but I don't know if I believe him," I say. "I mean, if he likes me, why can't he just introduce me as somebody he's seeing? Why the subterfuge?"

"Oh, subterfuge. Another good word," he says. "Do you just sit around reading the dictionary in your spare time?"

"Blow me," I say.

"I would, but you don't have the right equipment, sweetie," he says and chuckles.

"My point is, why do we have to fake this relationship thing?" I ask. "Why can't he just – I don't know – tell them we just started seeing each other?"

"From what you told me, he already lied to them. Told them he has a fiancée – ergo, an established relationship," he says. "If he backtracks on it and introduces you as somebody he's been seeing for five minutes, they'll descend on him like a pack of starving wolves. Sounds like he's just trying to cover his own ass, honestly."

I sigh as the waitress sets a fresh round down in front of us. Cesar looks from his still half-full glass over to the fresh one, and shrugs. What he's saying sounds plausible, I guess. I'm assuming he talked to them before we slept together, which would make sense, I guess. I mean, the day we had sex, he did say he wanted to talk to me about a business proposal. That jibes with what he asked me the other night.

"Yeah, maybe," I grudgingly admit. "I just don't like the idea of being paid to be his fiancée. It makes me feel dirty – like a prostitute."

"He didn't mention sleeping with him as part of this business deal, did he?" Cesar asks.

"No, he actually insisted there'd be no sex involved," I say. "But I don't believe him. I can tell by the way he looks at me, he wants to jump my bones every chance he gets."

"What I wouldn't give to have him look at me that way."

"Yeah, but you're a slut," I say.

He shrugs. "That's true," he laughs. "But, you should see your face when you talk about him – or when I know you're thinking about him. You get this starry-eyed glow about you. It's actually adorable. I'm pretty sure there's something inside you that wants to jump him every chance you get, too."

"Oh, shut up. I do not," I say, though I feel my cheeks flushing, because Cesar's probably right.

"Bailey, sweetie, I think you're overthinking all of this," Cesar says. "The man just wants you to pose as his fiancée. According to you, he was adamant sex wouldn't be part of the deal. Meaning, there's no pressure coming from him, so if sex were to occur – again – it would only be because *you* wanted it to."

My cheeks flush bright red and burn as hot as the sun as I look away, staring at my bottle and wonder how it got half-empty already. I shrug and tip the bottle back, draining the rest of it. When it's empty, I slam it down on the table, my mind and stomach churning like mad, pulling me in a thousand different directions. I want Colin to like me, not think of me as some freaking business commodity.

I need another drink. Turning my attention to the bar, I search for our waitress. When I don't see her anywhere, I decide to take matters into my own hands.

"I need another beer," I mumble, standing up.

Cesar grabs my hand and holds me fast. "Do you really need another beer?" he asks. "Or are you just trying to avoid this conversation?"

Damn. He knows me too well.

I sit back down.

"He's toxic, Cesar. He's everything I hate," I say, falling back on the same, tired argument, just to try and preserve my sanity – and my heart.

"But, you can't resist him, right?"

I nod, biting my lip. I've never felt so vulnerable in my entire life. The idea that this man – a man who is the complete and total opposite of me in so many ways – can come into my life and do this to me, to make me question and doubt myself like this is crazy. Beyond crazy. I'm a lot like Colin in that regard – I don't handle emotions very well – another reason I was a virgin until *very* recently.

I mean, I'm not the type of woman who falls head over heels in love with a man just because he's easy on the eyes. I need more than a good-looking man. I need a partner who shares my passions. My values and morals. A man who shares my vision for how the world should be.

And yet, here I am, undeniably attracted to Colin Anderson – who represents everything I hate in the world. A man who stands on the wrong side of the divide I've fought so hard and bitterly against for so long.

Another voice inside my head tells me I know better than that. I've seen into Colin's heart, and I know he's not like the others. Not really. There's a nagging feeling in the pit of my belly that forces me to constantly re-evaluate what I think about him. There is so much about him that remains shrouded in mystery to me. So much of him that remains an enigma.

Maybe I don't know the real Colin? Maybe, the gap between us isn't nearly as wide or deep as I think. Maybe, the differences between us are ones that we can overcome – together. And maybe, I can get him to reconsider his views on poverty, and the poor, in general. I mean, I've seen signs of his willingness to at least consider it in the conversations we've had. I know he's started to realize that his perceptions may be entirely wrong. That's a start, isn't it? That means he can change, right?

Yeah, that sounds like crap, even to me. The type of crap girls tell themselves when they fall for assholes. Oh, they can change. They can be what you want. *Yeah, right.*

Cesar sighs. "Girl, you need to pull your head out of your ass," he says. "You know, I'd kill to be in your shoes right now."

"I know, I know," I say. "I have the opportunity to get a fat paycheck, and a showcase in a large, prestigious gallery –"

Cesar stops me with a chuckle. "Well, yes, that too. But I was more or less talking about being wooed and seduced by that rich, successful, gorgeous, hunk of man who seems to like you."

I frown at him, and Cesar sticks his tongue out at me playfully. He's teasing me, and I know it. At least, I hope he is. I'm pretty sure neither one of us would sell out our morals or betray our beliefs for something as petty as a man – even one as charming as Colin.

Although he's teasing me, I also hear the truth in his words. For whatever reason, he's giving Colin the benefit of the doubt, and obviously thinks I should too.

And here I am, considering committing to a fake relationship just to get myself ahead. Just because I know what Colin's contacts would mean for my art. For exposure. It feels like cheating. It feels like something my grandmother would be ashamed of me for. But nevertheless, I'm considering it anyway.

I want to kick myself, but I'm actually considering it.

The waitress finally makes her way back to our table, taking up my empty, and setting down a fresh bottle, while I contemplate everything Cesar has just said.

"It still feels wrong," I say.

"Why does it feel wrong?" Cesar takes a sip from his neon blue cocktail.

"Because – well – I'm against corporatists like Colin. I'm against the elitists, and those who have no care or compassion for the poor," I say. "And to have him help me succeed – only because I agree to be his on-call fiancée – goes against everything I stand for."

"Is it so wrong to want your work to be seen by more eyes? Your art is amazing, Bailey. It's important, and it can do a lot of good. Especially if you can change the minds of people like Colin through it," he says. "But, the only way to share your message with more people is to actually be seen by more people. You have the opportunity to do just that. Sure, maybe it's not the way you imagined, and some might call it cheating – though I'd argue it really isn't – but at the end of the day, the good far outweighs the bad. He's not paying you to have sex with him, so your morals remain intact. There really is no downside, and the only hang up is the one between your ears."

I groan, rolling my eyes at him. Not because he's wrong, but because he has a valid point. All this time, I wanted to fight against everything Colin has to offer just because. It's a natural reflex. I haven't fully let my guard down yet, because of who he is and what he stands for. Though, even I have to grudgingly admit, that unlike other elitists assholes I've dealt with before, at least Colin seems open to learning and growing.

But, at the same time, I also want to find success, and not dwell in obscurity like my grandmother. I want to get my art out to a wider audience. Maybe Colin is the means to that end.

"I was really hoping you'd tell me what a bad idea this was," I say.

Cesar shrugs, giving me the smug, annoying smirk he's practically patented. "Sweetie, how many times have I told you, that you're only getting the truth from me? What kind of friend would I be if I didn't push you outside of your comfort zone from time to time?"

I'm far, far outside my comfort zone with this whole Colin situation. And although I'm ashamed to admit it, I'm intrigued, and maybe, even a bit excited, by what Colin's connections can mean for me and my art, but there's more to it than that.

At the end of the day, I just want him to like me. I just want him to see me as a girl he can fall head over heels in love with and call his own. That's what I really want, as painful as it is to admit – even to myself.

Which is why I'm ultimately screwed, no matter what I decide to do.

C olin is already seated in the corner booth when I arrive at the *Sunny Side Up Cafe*. He doesn't see me when I come in, since he's sitting with his back to the door. He's not wearing his suit jacket, which is draped casually over the side of the booth, and from where I stand, his shoulders look broad, strong, and sexy in a pale blue dress shirt that clings to him enticingly.

"Damn it, Bailey, don't ever use the word sexy to describe this man again," I curse myself under my breath.

I slowly walk over to the table, reminding myself to leave emotion at the door and treat this for what it is – a business transaction. Nothing more, nothing less. And emotion has no place in business. When I get to his table, I clear my throat to announce my arrival. Colin looks up at me and smiles – and being the perfect gentleman that he is, stands up and greets me.

"Bailey, thanks for meeting with me," he says, his voice softer than I expected.

For a second, it feels like he might hug me, which might be kind of awkward, given the fact that I'm still warring inside internally – the thought of selling out versus using this man as a means to an end has been a bitter, repetitive fight in my mind lately.

Thankfully, he bypasses the hug, and reaches out, taking my hand in his instead – just like a proper business meeting. Though, honestly, there is some small part of me that is disappointed he didn't, and I would have really liked to feel him wrap me up in those big strong arms. But, this is business. Nothing personal, just business. Right. Got it.

His hand envelops mine and there's a warmth and softness to his touch that for whatever reason, surprises me. It's warmer and more personal than a normal handshake. Maybe I should expect it, given the things we've already done together, but I'm left speechless for a moment as my body tingles, and small starbursts of pleasure go off inside of me

"Uh, thanks," I say quietly. "Thank you."

I pull my hand away and slide into the booth across from him. It sounds stupid, even to me, and I scold myself for apparently forgetting how to talk. Just because he's hotter than hell, doesn't mean I'm contractually bound to behave like a love-sick fool in his presence.

Colin sits across from me. He waves for the server to come over to our table, and we don't say much until she takes our drinks orders and leaves.

"So, I'm assuming since you called, that you've given my proposal some thought?" he asks.

Now, there's the Colin I'm familiar with – always one to get down to business, straight away. The cynical part of my mind adds, *thinking about himself, first and foremost.* I know that's probably not fair, I mean, he does need an answer. I can't blame him for that. But, part of me is disappointed. I realize I was hoping, on at least some small level, that he'd tell me he'd reconsidered his idea, and had found another way to appease his family that doesn't involve me acting like a paid escort.

Doesn't seem like that's going to be the case, though.

"I have, and I just have a few concerns I wanted to discuss first," I say.

He raises an eyebrow, but gestures for me to continue.

"I want to be one hundred percent sure that, as long as I'm technically your employee, there will be no sexual contact. Nothing, whatsoever," I say. "I am not to be treated like your personal call girl.

I will pretend to be your fiancée for the weekend in question, and that's it. If this is a straight business transaction, then let's keep it professional."

His lips pull back into a smile, and he's clearly amused by me. *Bastard.* Holding his hand over his heart like a good Boy Scout, he flashes me a smile and speaks.

"I solemnly swear that I won't seduce you, Bailey," he says. "Like I promised you before, that's not what this is about. You can trust me to behave like a gentleman."

"You make it sound like you have some magical power of seduction that makes you irresistible to me or something," I mumble.

"Don't I?" he teases.

I scowl, crossing my arms in front of my chest. "You're not making this any easier, Colin," I snap. "If you want this to happen, stop with the games. I'm serious here. I am not going to make myself feel like some cheap, knockoff prostitute. Got it?"

I can tell he's trying to keep things light and not too serious. Part of me wants to believe this is as awkward for him as it is for me because he has feelings for me too. Romantic feelings have no place in this kind of deal, though. He knows better than that. And although it's hard not to give in to the mixed bag of emotions I feel for him, I'm smart enough to know that too.

He looks at me with an abashed look on his face. It feels pretty good to watch the smug smile slip from his face as the mask of emotional control returns. At least now, I know he's serious. Colin is no longer teasing or taunting me, and he's back to his normal, serious self. Which means I'm safe. For now.

"Fine. I promise. You have my word. I just need this one favor. Pretend to be my fiancée, and I'll make sure you're well compensated, and ensure that you get a gallery exhibit of your very own," he says. "And there will be no more sex. You have my word."

No more sex. I love how he throws that in there for good measure. I resist the urge to roll my eyes as the waitress brings us our drinks. Though, a small part of me is sad about it. By walking through the door of this partnership, it feels like we're closing the door on any potential for a relationship between us.

Maybe, I'm just naïve. But, it almost feels like it has to be one or the other, and that once we walk down this path together, we can't turn around and go back down the other one. That if I accept his money and influence to play house with him, I can't turn around later, and be with him for real.

That thought – that feeling – leaves an empty, hollowed-out pit in my stomach, and sends a sharp lance of regret straight through my heart.

"Would you like something to eat?" he asks, opening a menu.

"No thanks."

"Not hungry?"

"No. And besides, this isn't a date, Colin," I say.

He puts the menu back and waves the waitress off. I focus my attention on my iced tea, adding in some sugar and swirling it around a bit while I think over the next thing on my mind. I turn it over and over again, not quite sure how to phrase it that doesn't make me sound like some backwoods hick. All the while, Colin's watching my struggle with translating my jumbled thoughts into actual words.

I let out a frustrated breath and finally just spit it out.

"Listen, before we go any farther with this, there's one thing you should really give some consideration to," I say. "Something that may be a deal breaker, that might make you want to go in another direction."

And hopefully, if he does decide to go in another direction, we can actually explore whatever this thing is between us. Part of me hopes, really, really hopes, he'll choose door number two.

"What's that?" he asks.

"To be perfectly honest, I'm not sure I'll fit in with your family, you know? I'm not really the high-class, upper-echelon type," I say. "I don't have the fancy clothes or know which fork should be used with which course – honestly, I may just end up embarrassing you more than anything."

"I'm not worried about that."

"You're not?" I ask, feeling my heart deflate that much more.

"No. I already figured we'd need to work on a few things," he says. "Why don't I stop by your place tomorrow morning, and we can go out for a bit?"

"For what?" I ask.

He waves off my question. "Just logistics," he says. "Nothing major."

"Not a date?" I ask.

"No, of course not," he says, chuckling to himself. "Just ironing out some kinks and helping prepare you for meeting my family. That's all. It's all business, Bailey, I swear. I'm going to be above board with all of this."

"Of course," I say. "Sounds good."

Even though I agree it's for the best, there's a small part of me that's bitterly disappointed. That's absolutely crushed and heartsick. I shouldn't want to date this man. I know that we are on opposite ends of the spectrum – yet, despite that, I still feel like a silly girl with a crush.

"I'll pick you up around ten tomorrow morning," he says, slipping out of the booth. "See you then, Bailey."

He casually throws down enough cash to pay for our drinks before leaving. He doesn't wait for my response or for me to tell him ten works for me. I guess now that I'm his employee, I'm officially at his beck and call.

Bastard.

Chapter Eleven

Colin

I don't want to worry about driving, so I have a car come pick me up in the morning. We stop by a Starbucks so I can get my PSL fix – and I grab one for Bailey as well – and we head over to her place. On the ride over, I lean back in the seat, and let my mind wander, turning everything over in my head.

At the diner yesterday, she seemed so cold and distant. I'm not sure why. I mean, I would have thought she'd be excited. Not only is she going to get some financial stability, but more importantly, I'm going to make sure she gets her own show at one of the large, prestigious galleries in town. She's going to get her art seen by many, many people, and that kind of exposure could catapult her to heights she never dreamed of.

I'm excited for her, because I think her work is important. I think it should be seen by as wide of an audience as it can. While I haven't come around entirely to her way of thinking, I will admit, that she's given me a lot of food for thought lately. Surprisingly enough, I'm starting to see things a bit differently.

At the end of the day, though, I have a job to do, and I would be letting all of my employees down if I didn't take my responsibilities seriously, or put my best foot forward on any given project. My clients come first, and I have to do my job.

But, Bailey has opened my eyes to the realization that there are people being impacted by each and every job I'm trying to do, as well as the possibility, that in some cases, there may be a better, more humane way to do the job.

I don't think that's what was on her mind yesterday, though. She seemed bothered by something else. I mean, I know she feels weird about this whole arrangement. And if I had any other options, I would take them. I know it's not ideal, and the last thing I want to do is make Bailey feel like I've bought her. Like she's some call girl. I know she's got morals and values she cherishes. And I'll never put her in a position where she'd have to violate them.

Bailey is special. Unique. One of a kind. I've never met anyone even remotely like her. I wasn't kidding when I told her that she came into my life and turned my world upside down. She has. The girl is a force of nature, and she's pushed me well outside my comfort zone. She's challenged me in a thousand different ways and has opened my eyes to a new way of seeing and doing things.

She's opened my eyes to a new way of being.

I don't know that I'll ever be the free, unfettered spirit she is – in fact, I can almost guarantee I won't be – but, she's made me loosen my need for control and relax in so many different ways. And if I'm being honest, I like it. I can't recall the last time I've felt this free and loose. The last time I felt this genuinely happy.

I'm well aware that people around the office call me "Stone Face," behind my back. It's childish, and not very creative – I'd like to think I hire people who can do better than that, honestly. But, the point is very much taken, all the same. I'm about as emotional and expressive as a rock. I get it. Message received.

But Bailey has made me smile, and actually feel something for the first time in a very, very long time. And it feels really good.

I'm hoping that once we get past Christmas with my family that Bailey and I can pick up where we left off and explore the growing thing between us. I want more of her. I want to get to know her better. I want to know everything about her, actually. And I'm looking forward to doing just that.

Once Christmas is done and over with.

The car pulls to a stop in front of an apartment building that looks like it's been around a while. It's worn, but it's clean, at least. Bailey is standing at the curb, and when the driver runs around and opens the door for her, she slides into the backseat beside me. She gives me a smile as I hand her the cup of coffee.

"Pumpkin spice?" she asks.

"What else?"

"You're such a basic bitch," she says and flashes me a small grin.

The car drives away from the curb, merges out into traffic, and we're on our way.

"Where are we going?" she asks.

"You'll see when we get there."

She smiles, but I can see that it doesn't quite reach her eyes. I so badly want to reach out and touch her. Pull her to me and hold her. But, I get the sense that it wouldn't be welcome right now. There's definitely a barrier up between us after meeting at the diner. A wall of ice. I can tell Bailey is treating this as business, and I know that's how I need to think of it too.

If I let my emotions get involved, things will get messy and complicated. And God forbid, I act on the carnal impulses that are firing through my mind and body from just sitting next to her. Talk about making her feel like a prostitute.

No, the best course of action I can take right now, is to regard this as a business relationship. Once Christmas is over, we can go back to trying to figure out our decidedly non-business relationship. We can go back to exploring each other and the chemistry building between us.

Yeah. We can. And I'm very excited for that. Excited to explore everything with her.

She may not be what I expected, or even wanted – hell, I know she's not what I wanted, because I wasn't even looking – but maybe, just maybe, she's just what I need.

"You realize, if this was some stupid rom-com movie, and not real life, this would be the part where they have a music montage," she says.

"Yeah, that sounds about right," I reply with a laugh.

Bailey is holding a nice, vintage-style dress up to herself, and spins around in the mirror, giggling the whole time. She stops and looks at it critically for a moment before disappearing into a dressing room.

When she found out I was taking her shopping, she was hesitant at first. She obviously inherited her grandmother's sense about charity and taking handouts. At first, she refused to come into the shops with me, and I had to tell her that I'm considering it a business expense – that this is part of the gig she signed on for. I told her that it was now her job to come in and pick out some clothes for the weekend that will make her presentable.

It took a lot of badgering and cajoling – and I received more than a few empty threats from her that she'd rather quit this job than take a handout – but I was finally able to persuade her, and she relented.

I'm seated in a chair in the dressing room area, waiting for Bailey to come out and show me what she's picked out for herself. Truthfully, it doesn't matter to me. She can wear a burlap sack for all I care. I think she's perfect the way she is. But, I know wearing nicer clothes will make her feel better and less out of place, so it seems like the least I can do.

"What song?" I call through the dressing room door.

"What's that?" she yells back.

"What song would be playing in your music montage?"

She's silent for a moment, and I can just picture her as she concentrates. She usually cocks her head to the side, and kind of screws up her face as she thinks. I think it's adorable.

"*Girls Just Wanna Have Fun*, I think," she answers with a giggle.

"Cyndi Lauper?" I ask. "Really?"

"Yeah, I think it's kind of fitting."

I can't help but laugh to myself. Bailey is always surprising me.

"What do you think it would be?" she asks.

"Oh, I don't know," I say. "I was never big on movie montages."

"But you know music," she says. "Everybody knows music."

"Maybe something by Vivaldi?" I call. "Chopin?"

"Classical? Really, Colin?" she asks, her voice deadpan. "Come on. You can do better than that."

I laugh. "How about something by Taylor Swift?"

"Wow, you really suck at this game."

She pulls the curtain back and as she steps out into the viewing area, I feel my breath catch in my throat as I look at her. She's in a deep, rich blue vintage-style dress that seems to perfectly accent her cool, pale skin, and darker than night hair. It falls to just above the knee and has a sweetheart neckline. And she looks absolutely stunning in it. Beyond stunning. She looks almost ethereal.

"Well? What do you think?" she asks, as she turns in a circle to show me.

I can't really say what I think, because it would be highly inappropriate on several levels. When I open my mouth to say something, however, I find that my throat is dry, and I can't seem to form the right words. I just nod and give her a smile.

She laughs. "Okay, what's that supposed to mean?"

I quickly work up enough saliva that allows me to function like a normal human being and open my mouth again.

"Stunning," I say. "You look absolutely stunning, Bailey."

She flushes and waves me off, but I can tell she appreciates the compliment. She might even like it deep down somewhere.

"I don't know about that," she says.

"I do," I say.

Her smile is small, and she looks away to keep me from seeing the embarrassed look on her face. I've noticed that she's not great with compliments. She always finds a way to discount, if not outright reject, them. She can't seem to just accept a compliment at face value.

"So, this one's a yes?" she asks.

"I'd say so," I reply. "You look breathtaking in it."

"Thank you," she murmurs softly before turning around and scampering back into the dressing room.

She comes out a few minutes later, back in her regular clothes – a green floral dress with white leggings on underneath, and a baggy cardigan. She's holding the dress up, admiring it, and it makes me smile.

"It really is a beautiful dress," she says.

"And it looks great on you," I say. "Let's get it."

She fumbles around with it for a minute, and finally sees the price tag. Her eyes widen in disbelief, and she shakes her head.

"I can't –"

"You're not," I say.

I stand and walk over, plucking the dress from her hands. One of the shop attendants stops by to check on us, and I hand it to her.

"We'll take this one," I say, and look around the shop. "And do you have anything else with a similar style?"

The attendant smiles. "We do," she says. "We have a lot of great pieces similar to this."

"Great," I say. "Have them brought over so Bailey can try them on."

Bailey looks at me and shakes her head. "Colin, I –"

I turn to the attendant. "Any color you think would look good on her."

She looks between Bailey and me, and then gives me a nod and a smile. "Right away."

As the attendant steps away, Bailey turns to me, her face a mask of concern. "I can't ask you to pay for this, Colin," she says. "Business expense or not, it's too much. Did you see how much that dress cost?"

"Doesn't matter," I say. "I don't care. I thought it looked great on you, so we're getting it."

She looks at me for a long moment, and I can see the conflict in her eyes. I see her grandmother's influence – so strong and proud – starting to slip through the cracks, and know I need to snuff that out before it takes over.

"This is how it's going to be, Bailey," I say. "It's not up for debate."

She bites her bottom lip with a sheepish, goofy smile on her face. "It is a very pretty dress, I guess."

"It's gorgeous," I say. "And it looks even better on you."

The attendant returns with a pile of dresses, all in a vintage-style that seems to flatter Bailey's figure, in a wide variety of colors. She gasps in wonder at all of the dresses, and we spend the next couple of hours in the shop as she tries them all on, squealing with delight every time she puts a new one on.

There wasn't a single one that looked bad on her, and by the time we left the shop, we ended up purchasing a dozen different dresses. We find a valet stand just outside the shop and load the bags onto one of the carts. I contact my driver and tell him to expect some packages to be delivered, and to pull the car around. The valet runs the cart out while we continue to shop.

By the time we're finished, we've gone through at least ten different shops, and it feels like we've picked up enough clothes that she can wear something different every day for a year. At least. Though Bailey was mortified the entire time, and worried about how much money we were spending, I brushed off her concerns. I told her over and over again that it simply wasn't up for discussion.

Yeah, we might have overdid it for the one weekend my family is going to be here. We probably could have stopped a long time before we did. Truth be told, it warmed my heart to see Bailey getting so excited about the clothes. She was literally like a kid in a candy store, and I wanted nothing more than to encourage that. I love seeing her smile and hearing her laugh.

More than anything, I love being around her.

With all of our packages being hustled out to the car, Bailey and I sit at a small cafe in the mall and snack on some coffee and a pastry. I think we earned the treat after a long day. Usually, I hate shopping, and avoid it like the plague. I've got a personal shopper who normally handles all of this for me. But, I wanted to be here with, and for, Bailey.

Mostly, I just wanted to be with her. There's something about being with Bailey that makes me feel good. Makes me happy to be alive. She gives off an energy that's intoxicating and infectious. She just makes me – happy.

I guess I never really give a lot of thought to whether I'm happy or not. I've always assumed that I'm as happy as the next guy. It wasn't until Maureen mentioned it to me, and I really took stock of how I feel when I'm with Bailey, that I realized there's a void in my heart and my life without her. A void I never even realized existed. And now that I know it's there, it becomes even more obvious when she's not around.

"Thank you, Colin," she says.

"No need to thank me."

She shakes her head. "No, there is," she says. "I never dreamed I'd have a closet full of clothing this nice before. Growing up, I was grateful to find a nice pair of jeans on sale down at the thrift store without too many stains or holes in them. Honestly, I still shop at the same thrift store. One thing my life has taught me is how to be frugal."

"But, aren't you the one who's always telling me to enjoy life? And to enjoy everything about it?"

She nods. "Easier to say when you're sitting on more money than Scrooge McDuck," she laughs.

I shrug. "Maybe," I say. "But, what's giving me a lot of enjoyment in life right now, is seeing you smile. Seeing you happy."

Her expression softens, and I can see her eyes shimmering with tears. I can't honestly say I know or understand what she's feeling in the moment. I never grew up wanting for anything. Yeah, my father wasn't the kind of man who indulged our lavish, impractical desires.

But, I never went without. And I never had to wear hand-me-down rags.

I know Bailey had it a lot rougher, and that she often had to go without. Often had to make do with what was on hand. And it breaks my heart. So, no, I can't understand or relate to what she's feeling right now. Not really. All I know is that shopping today made her feel good for a little while. It made her happy. And that's worth every last dime I spent. I know I'm not going to be able to take it with me, so why not spend some of it now, to do some good, and spread some happiness to somebody I like?

Damn – Bailey is having more of an impact on me than I originally thought.

Her phone rings, so she slips it out of her bag and connects the call. She presses the phone to her ear and gives me a little smile.

"Hello?"

All at once, her face falls, and I can see grief become etched upon her features as she listens to whoever's on the other end of the line.

"Oh my God," she says softly. "Yeah, I'll be right there. Okay. Thanks."

She looks up at me, and I can see the pain radiating in her eyes. "I need to go," she says.

"I'll take you wherever you need to be."

Her lips compress into a tight line as we get to our feet and head to the car. I don't know what's going on, but I can see that it's breaking her heart – which, in turn, breaks mine. Yeah, Bailey has gotten under my skin. I can't deny it anymore.

Not even to myself.

———

"How is he?" she asks.

"He's okay," replies an older Hispanic woman. "The EMT's are back there with him now. They're taking him to the hospital soon."

We're standing in the industrial-sized prep area behind the cafeteria of the soup kitchen at St. Bartholomew's. Bailey spends a lot of time volunteering here, and we got here right before the evening dinner rush, apparently. The place is crowded, but there's a subdued buzz of conversation, and all of the people stopping by for a hot meal are speaking in hushed, reverent tones. No doubt, they saw the ambulance out front, which is making them all curious.

"What happened?" Bailey asks.

The older woman, her face etched with as much sadness as Bailey's, shrugs. "We were just starting to set up for the night shift, when he just collapsed," she says. "Heart attack, I think."

I look around the cafeteria, and see the crowd milling about. Everybody is craning their neck, trying to get a look at what's going on. As we headed over here, Bailey explained to me that Father Gus is the parish priest, and the one who does most of the cooking for the soup kitchen. Not only that, he's the closest thing to a father figure to her. I gather that they're incredibly close – which is why they called Bailey to let her know.

"Is he going to be okay?" Bailey asks.

The older woman, whose nametag reads Olivia, shakes her head. "I don't know anything much right now, hon," she says. "They've been back there with him a long time, though."

Tears roll down Bailey's cheeks, and she angrily scrubs them away. A moment later, the doors to the rear offices crash open, and two EMT's push a gurney out. On top of the gurney is an older black man with a thick head of white hair. An oxygen mask covers most of his face, and he's unconscious. Bailey runs over and falls into step beside the gurney. She takes the old man's hand in hers and murmurs a few words I can't make out over the rest of the background noise.

"Ma'am, we're going to need you to clear the way," one of the EMT's tells her gruffly.

The other one, seeing her tears, gives her a compassionate smile. "He survived the initial heart attack. Now, we just need to get him into the hospital for some more tests and treatment," she says. "We're taking him to Three Angels. Do you know where that is?"

Bailey nods, and steps away from the gurney. She stands there, silently watching them take the old man out the front doors to the waiting ambulance. The crowd falls silent as the gurney passes, each of the people seeming to bow their heads respectfully, and some say a little prayer for the man. It's a heartbreaking yet touching scene.

I step up next to Bailey and put a hand on her shoulder, giving it a gentle squeeze. "You okay?"

She shakes her head. "Not really," she says. "Gus is basically the father I never had. He's been so good to me."

"Three Angels is a good hospital. They've got one of the best cardiac care units in the country," I say, hoping it's reassuring. "He's going to receive top of the line care."

"I don't think he has insurance," she says.

"Don't worry about it," I reply. "I'll handle it."

"I can't ask –"

"You're not asking me," I say. "I'm telling you."

She takes my hand in hers and gives it a squeeze. Olivia steps up next to her and takes her other hand. Together, they watch the doors. The sound of the siren fades in the distance as they take the priest to the hospital. Olivia turns to Bailey.

"We still have a shift to do," she says gently. "People are hungry, and Father Gus wouldn't want us to let them go without, no matter what."

"No, he wouldn't," Bailey says, her voice sounding completely disconnected from the reality of the situation.

She scans the crowd and seems to be trying to gather herself. She's collecting her wits, and mentally and emotionally readying herself to do what needs to be done. What Father Gus would want her to do.

She turns to me and gives me a small smile that doesn't even come close to reaching her eyes. "I can't ask you to stay," she says. "I'll be fine here, if you want to go ahead and take off. Olivia can give me a ride home later."

I shake my head. "I've got nowhere better to be," I say. "And I'd like to help you in any way I can."

Her smile becomes softer, more genuine, and grateful. "Thank you, Colin."

"Anytime," I reply.

We walk back to the kitchen to get ready. I take off my coat and hang it up while Bailey hands me a full-length apron. A couple of men are standing at the stoves, cooking away, trying to make up for lost time.

"What do you need me to do?" I ask.

"Nothing just yet," she says. "We can't get started until the food's finished cooking. After that, I'll have you on the line, dishing out some of the food, if you don't mind."

"Nothing would make me happier," I say.

"Thank you, Colin," she says. "I appreciate this more than you know."

"No need to thank me," I reply. "I'm just glad I can be here for you."

Two hours later, after dishing out the last of the rice pilaf I was in charge of, I take the pot back to the kitchen, and set it down in the sink to let the washers have at it. Bailey is still busy, running around like a chicken with her head cut off, trying to do everything I assume Father Gus usually tends to.

I watch her with the people and see the way they react to her and can't help but smile. It's easy to see that she cares for them all – and they care for her as well. As she tends to their needs, you can see the warm, genuine gratitude and appreciation for her in their faces. Seeing the way they interact tells me a lot about the woman – though, nothing I didn't know already. But, it only reinforces the fact that she's a genuinely good person with a large, generous heart.

Not knowing what else to do with myself, I wander around the cafeteria, picking up plates, throwing them away, and wiping down the tables with a wet rag.

"Haven't seen you around here before."

I turn to find a middle-aged man looking at me. He's white with dark hair, shot through with gray, green eyes, and a neatly-trimmed goatee. Dressed in black jeans, and a blue button-down shirt, he's a bit cleaner than some of the other folks who've come through here tonight. He's got a plate of food in front of him but he just seems to be picking at it.

"I'm here to help Bailey out tonight," I say.

He nods. "She's a good girl," he says. "One of the kindest, most compassionate people I've ever met. She really cares."

"I'm getting a sense of that," I say.

I sit down at the table with the man and can see the pain in his eyes – pain he's trying to hide, but failing at. There's an air of sadness about him that's as deep as it is dark.

"Are you okay?" I ask.

"Yeah, I just hate this time of year," he says. "But, I'll be fine. I'm always fine."

I've heard about the Christmas Blues, and that it's the toughest time of year for a lot of people. I've never met one of them, though. Not until now, at any rate. I can see the shadow cross his face and know that he's not actually fine. Nor is he ever, more than likely. He just puts on a good show.

"Can I ask you a question?"

He nods. "Sure."

"I don't want to sound rude –"

"Which is how people preface a comment that's going to be rude," he chuckles.

"I don't intend to be rude, but I'm curious. How'd you end up here?" I ask. "I mean, you seem –"

He cuts me off with a derisive snort. "Smart? Articulate?"

"Well, not to put too fine a point on it, but – yeah," I say. "I guess."

"Well, let's see," he says. "It all started with some really shitty luck, actually. First, my wife of twenty years was diagnosed with Stage IV, terminal cancer. It was aggressive as hell, and her treatments sucked our savings dry. When she passed, we were broke. But, I would pay twice that to have more time with her."

His cheeks flush, and his eyes well with unshed tears. I feel like I should do something to comfort the man, but I have no idea what to do. Instead, I sit there in silence, feeling like a heartless idiot.

"Anyway," he says, sniffing back tears. "Shortly after she passed, I lost my job. Downsizing. They were offshoring my department, apparently. With no job – and likely, because of my age, I got no bites when my resume made the rounds – no income, and no money left in savings, I ended up losing my home. And here I am."

I sit back on the stool, feeling completely stunned. His story has left me speechless. I don't know what to say or what to do. It's obvious the man is in emotional distress, and has been for a long time, I'd guess. But, he seems like the type to just bury it, put his head down, and keep trudging forward.

"Is that common?" I ask. "That you end up on the streets because of something like that?"

He shrugs. "It's a lot more common than you'd think," he says, pointing to a man in a blue baseball cap. "Rick over there was an airline mechanic for twenty-two years. They cut him loose to bring in some younger, cheaper mechanics."

I look over at the older Hispanic man sitting at the table next to us, eating his meal in silence.

"That's Darryl," he says, pointing to a man in a red coat. "He was a contractor. Fell off a roof one day, ended up in the hospital for a long while. Can't do the same work anymore, and ended up out of a job," he says. "He lost everything after that. Wife, kids, his dog – everything. So yeah, it's probably a lot more common than you think. It's why we're all grateful to have a place where we can come and get a warm, hot meal."

I look around the cafeteria, looking at the sea of faces out there and wonder what everyone's story is. Wonder how many of them are there because of circumstances beyond their control. Wonder how many ended up on the street through a series of unfortunate events, or a turn of bad luck. I turn back to the man, my mind swirling with a thousand different unasked questions.

"What did you do?" I ask for lack of anything intelligent or actually compassionate to say.

"I was an accountant," he says. "Headed the company's accounting department until they figured they could find cheaper labor overseas."

Sitting here with this man is something of a humbling experience for me. He's not a drunk. Not an addict. Not a criminal. He's none of the preconceived notions of the homeless I've held all my life. I don't like to admit it, but yeah, I guess the fact that I looked down on the poor and the homeless as lazy, or as somehow being in their situation because of something they did wrong, is a form of bigotry I never thought much about.

I feel like the air is being sucked right out of my lungs as I hear that phrase ringing through my mind on an endless loop – I'm a bigot. I've never been so ashamed in my life. And I know, if I gave voice to this epiphany, my father would be ashamed of me too.

Where did I develop this prejudiced, cavalier attitude toward others? Do my brothers have the same thoughts and beliefs? I think back and try to piece it all together, try to figure out where my prejudice against the poor first started, where it came from – and I really don't know. I have no idea whatsoever.

It's a revelation about myself that leaves me sickened. Stunned. I never actively treated the poor like they were trash – at least, I don't think I did – but, I realize now that I regarded them with a certain degree of callousness and coldness. To me, they just didn't exist.

"What's your name?" I ask.

"Matthew," he says and extends his hand. "Matthew Rehnquist."

I shake his hand and nod. "How long were you an accountant?"

He snorts. "Probably longer than you've been alive," he chuckles.

I fish a card out of my coat pocket and hand it to him. "My name is Colin Anderson," I say. "We're about to shut down for the holidays, but once they're over, I want you to call me at my office. I'm going to bring you in and we'll get you a job in our accounting department."

He takes the card and looks at it, then looks up at me. I can see the skepticism in his eyes.

"Aren't you a little young –"

"Family company," I say, cutting him off.

He looks at me a moment longer. "What's the catch?"

I shake my head. "No catch."

He chuckles. "I've been around long enough to know there's always a catch," he says. "Like they say, there's no such thing as a free lunch."

"Well, the catch then, is that you show up on time, and do a good job for me," I say.

Matthew looks at me for a long moment. The skepticism is still in his eyes, but now, I see the faint flickering of some other emotion – hope, maybe.

"Is this for real?" he asks.

I nod. "One hundred percent."

A wide smile crosses his face, and I watch as his nose and cheeks grow red. His eyes are wet with tears I can see he's doing his best to keep from falling. He rubs his hand across his face, doing his best to keep his composure in front of me.

"And what are you boys talking about over here?" Bailey asks as she steps over to the table.

She's looking at me with a look of pure adoration in her eyes, and it melts my heart. It's a face I could stare at every day and never grow tired of. Bailey turns and looks at Matthew, and when she sees he's struggling to contain his emotion, her face falls, and she rushes to his side. She casts a wary, slightly accusatory look at me – like she thinks I did something to upset the man.

"Matthew, are you okay?" she asks. "What's wrong?"

He shakes his head, but he can't hold the tears back any longer.

He covers his face with his hand as the tears start to roll down his cheeks. Bailey looks over at me with narrowed eyes and a clenched jaw.

"What did you do?" she hisses.

Matthew puts his hand on Bailey's shoulder and looks up at her. He shakes his head and gives her a trembling smile.

"I never believed in Christmas miracles, Bailey. Always thought they were Hollywood movie garbage," he says and looks over at me. "Until right now."

Confusion sweeps across her face as her gaze shifts between Matthew and me. She wants to be mad, assuming I did something horrible, but something in Matthew's face seems to be keeping her anger in check.

"How many years have I been trying to get a job?" he asks Bailey.

"A lot of years, I know," she says.

"I guess I have one now," he says. "After all this time, I finally found a job, Bailey."

She looks at me, her confusion only deepening. I just shrug and give her a small, enigmatic smile. She immediately thought the worst, so I'm enjoying seeing her squirm a bit.

"What are you talking about, Matthew?" she finally asks.

He looks over at me and brandishes my card. "Mr. Anderson here," he says. "He's giving me an accounting job at his company."

Her eyes widen, and I can tell she's not sure what to think. I nod, confirming what he's saying – though, it does nothing to lessen her expression of confusion. She stands up and motions me to join her.

"We'll be right back," she says to Matthew, giving him a gentle squeeze on the shoulder.

He nods, then looks up at me, his face filled with nothing but gratitude. "Thank you, Mr. Anderson. Thank you for this opportunity," he says. "I won't let you down. I swear."

"I know you won't, Matthew," I say.

Bailey drags me out of the dining room and into the now-deserted kitchen. She rounds on me with anger and distrust in her eyes. She steps forward and thrusts a finger into my face. To anybody seeing this from the outside, it has to look funny, I'm sure – this delicate, diminutive woman, standing with her finger in the face of a man two, maybe three times larger than her. But, seeing the fury in her eyes, I wisely bite back the laughter and any snarky reply.

"You had better not be screwing with him," she says. "That man has been looking for work for a long time. He's absolutely demoralized about having to come here to begin with. The last thing he needs is for you to come in here and mess with him."

She's red in the face, huffing and puffing, and I find it utterly adorable. Not that I'm going to say that to her. Not if I plan on getting out of this kitchen alive, that is.

"Are you done?"

"For now."

"Good. I'm not messing with him," I say. "I spent some time talking to him, and his story genuinely moved me. I think I'm a pretty good judge of character, and I can see that he's a good, decent, hardworking man. He needs to catch a break for a change, and I want to help him. Really."

She eyes me for a long moment, trying to decide whether or not I'm being sincere. "So, this isn't just some random, Christmas-fueled offer that you're going to change your mind about when the tinsel comes down?" she asks.

"No, it's not. It's a genuine offer. If he doesn't work out in accounting, I'm sure I can find him another position somewhere else," I say. "But hey, thanks for thinking the worst of me. I appreciate that."

Her face softens, and she looks down at the ground. Bailey shuffles her feet and pushes some loose tendrils of hair behind her ears. When she looks up at me again, she looks chastised and abashed. I'm not going to lie, the fact that her first instinct is to think the worst of me hurts a bit. But, given her past experiences with me, plus my previous attitudes regarding the poor, I can't blame her too much.

Still, I thought she knew me better than that by now. I mean, I know we still have a lot to learn about each other – and that we've only scratched the surface – but knowing that's her default reaction still stings.

"I'm sorry," she says softly. "I'm just so protective of the people here, and –"

"I understand," I say. "I get it."

She steps forward and wraps her arms around me, pulling me into a tight embrace. It's the first real physical contact we've had since she gave me the hand job at the diner, and it feels nice. There's something comforting about having her warm body against mine. Something that soothes and eases my mind, body, and soul. It's a completely unexpected feeling and reaction, but it's nice all the same.

She turns her face up to mine, and I lean down, pressing my lips to hers. Our kiss is slow, and sweet, our tongues dancing around each other in her mouth, and yet it's filled with unspoken emotion. It's filled with passion, desire – and something more. Something I can't put my finger on. But, it brings me no small amount of comfort and joy, all the same.

When I pull back, there's a small smile on her lips that I'm sure matches the one on mine. We stand there in each other's arms, staring into each other's eyes, and I have the absurd notion that I never want the moment to end.

The moment ends right when Olivia bursts through the doors, her phone in hand, and a wide smile on her face. Bailey and I step back from each other, both of us clearing our throats at the same time, pretending nothing was going on between us. Which is stupid – two grown adults acting like a couple of teenagers who just got caught making out in the basement.

Olivia, obviously realizing she walked in on something, looks away, an embarrassed expression on her face.

"I'm sorry, I didn't mean to –"

"No, it's fine," Bailey says. "We were just – talking."

Talking. Like anybody with half a brain would believe that. I almost want to laugh at how ridiculous the lie is, but I manage to hold myself in check.

"What's up?" Bailey asks.

"We just got a call about Father Gus," she says. "He's going to be okay."

The relief washing through Bailey is palpable, even from where I'm standing. It's like all of the tension in her body suddenly rushed out at once, leaving her limp and boneless. I'm half-afraid her legs are going to give out and she's going to fall right on her butt. She manages to hold it together though and remains upright. Soft tears roll down her cheeks, and the smile on her face makes my heart melt.

"That's good news," she says. "Really, really good news."

Olivia nods. "It's a blessing," she says. "I just thought you'd want to know."

"Yes, absolutely," Bailey says. "Thank you, Olivia."

"Of course," she says. "I'll leave you two to finish your – conversation."

I can hear her laughing through the door as she leaves, and all I can do is shake my head. Bailey turns to me with a look of pure, unadulterated joy on her face. It's a look that makes me smile. And I realize, I always want her to be this happy.

Always.

Chapter Twelve

Bailey

It's been a long, long day filled with the highest of highs, and the lowest of lows – and everything in between. We're sitting in the back of Colin's car, and I stretch out my legs. My feet are killing me. Colin looks at me, and even though his face is cloaked in shadow, I can still see the enigmatic smile he's wearing.

"What is it?" I ask.

He shrugs. "Nothing."

He grabs hold of my legs and puts them in his lap. I watch as he slips off my shoes and starts to rub my feet for me. My eyes practically roll into the back of my head as he rubs my stiff, sore feet. I melt into the seat and feel like I could drift off to sleep right here and now.

"You know," I say. "If the whole exploiting the world thing doesn't work out for you, I think you could have a real career in foot massage ahead of you."

"Foot masseuse doesn't quite have the same appeal as exploiting the world around me," he says. "There's no power trip to be had when you're rubbing people's feet."

"No, probably not."

"Definitely not," he says.

Between the gentle sway of the car and Colin's foot massage, I'm being lulled into a near catatonic state. And all the while, Colin is looking straight at me, his eyes glittering like chips of ice in the darkness.

I still can't get over the shock of him offering Matthew a job. It's one of the most generous things I've ever seen a person do for a total stranger. Not only is Colin giving Matthew a job, and a chance to build his dignity back up, he's giving him a sense of hope. A sense of purpose. And that's something you can't put a price tag on.

Seeing the unfettered joy in Matthew's face is something that will stick with me forever. It's a memory I'll cherish and treasure for the rest of my life. In a lot of ways, I feel like the people who come into the shelter are my children. I doubt I'm ever going to have any of my own, so I've taken on an almost motherly role with the people I care for. I love them. I want to see all of them succeed.

And, I'm fiercely protective of them. Which is why I went off on Colin like I did – something I feel terrible about, after finding out his offer was genuine and sincere.

"You know I don't actually think the worst of you, don't you?" I ask.

He shrugs again. "Kind of seems like that sometimes."

"I'm sorry, Colin," I say. "I'm just very protective of them."

"And I get that," he replies. "That's one of the reasons I'm not upset. Actually, I think it's sweet. Endearing."

A faint smile touches my lips, and I let out a soft moan of pleasure as he works one of the sorest spots on my feet.

"I was watching you with them tonight," he says. "The people in the shelter. You're really good with them. They all seem to love you. I can tell you've made a real difference in their lives."

"They deserve to know somebody cares about them," I say. "They deserve somebody who will fight for them."

"And that you do," he says with a soft chuckle. "In spades. It's one of the many things I respect and admire about you, Bailey. You fight for what you think is right."

I reach down and take his hand in mine, giving it a squeeze. "Thank you," I say. "That means a lot."

We ride in silence a few minutes, and I continue to watch him from the shadowy back seat. He seems content, just absent-mindedly rubbing my feet. Seems content – maybe even happy – to just be with me. And as I turn it all over in my mind, I know that I feel the same way about him.

"You're a good man, Colin Anderson," I say.

"And here I thought I was a greedy corporate pig," he replies with a grin.

"Those things are not mutually exclusive, you know."

He laughs as the car pulls to a stop in front of my building. I see flashing yellow lights strobing throughout the interior of the car and sit up quickly. I see work crews surrounding my building and notice that the doorway has been taped off. As I stare at the scene outside, I feel nausea and anxiety rising in my stomach.

"God, what now?" I groan.

"Let's find out," Colin says.

The driver opens the door, and we slide out – stepping into at least an inch of water. Actually, it's more like a raging river that flows past our feet, down the steps of my building, and out into the street. I look over at a man in a hard hat standing there, looking up at the building.

"What is going on here?" I ask.

"You live here?" he turns to me and asks.

"Yeah, I do," I reply.

"Bad news," he says. "Water pipes on the top floor burst. Everything's wasted."

"What?"

My heart falls into my stomach, and I feel like I'm going to be sick. I live one floor from the top, meaning that if the pipes on the floor above me burst, my place is completely flooded. Actually, judging by the amount of water flowing out of the building, I'd say it's a safe bet the whole building is flooded out.

"I need to get into my place," I say. "I need to see if anything can be salvaged."

The man shakes his head. "Can't let you in, lady," he says. "It's too dangerous. What floor do you live on?"

"The seventh."

His face is pinched, and gets the expression of a man who really doesn't want to deliver bad news. He looks over at Colin, and then back to me.

"If you're on the seventh floor, it's safe to say you're not gonna be able to salvage anything," he says. "The whole place is wasted, lady. Sorry."

It's a good thing Colin is standing beside me, otherwise I might have thrown myself into the river at my feet and let myself be swept away. He holds me as I burst into tears. It's as if all the emotion of the day is suddenly hitting me all at once. My body heaves as I'm racked with sobs, and salty, thick tears roll down my face.

"It's my home," I say. "All of my things."

Colin pulls me to him and wraps his strong arms around me. He holds me tight and strokes my hair, doing his best to soothe me.

"It's okay," he whispers softly into my ear.

"No, it's not," I wail. "It's really not."

I let him lead me back to the car and slide me inside. He closes the door himself, and then gets in on the other side. He scoots close to me, and puts his arm around my shoulders, pulling me tight against him. I bury my face in his chest and keep sobbing.

We spend the entire ride to his place like that, and it's only when he's helping me out of the car that my tears seem to dry up. I barely even look at his house as he leads me inside. I feel completely numb right now.

"What are we doing here?" I ask.

"You're going to stay here," he says. "You need a place to rest."

"I can go to a hotel, Colin."

"No," he says. "I have more than enough room. You'll stay here, and we can figure out what to do in the morning."

I nod, only because I don't have the strength or energy to argue. Everything I own – which admittedly, isn't much – was in my place.

And now, it's totally gone. All of it. I know it's just stuff. But, it's mine. I bought it myself. And when you grow up without anything to call your own, you cherish your belongings more than the average person.

Colin leads me into the kitchen and sits me on a stool at the large granite island. I glance around, noticing that there's a lot of brick in the place, and of course, all of the modern, state of the art gadgets a person could want.

He reaches into a cupboard, grabs a couple of glasses, and a bottle of something alcoholic. I don't really care enough to look at the label right now. All I know is that it's an amber-colored liquid that will help keep me numb – which, for now, is all I want. To shut down my emotions and feel absolutely nothing.

He pours a couple of fingers into each glass and slides one over to me. I reach out, grab the glass, and down it in one fell swoop. I grimace as the liquid fire slides down my throat. It hits my belly like an atomic bomb and starts spreading warmth throughout my body. Without a word, Colin pours me another, and I repeat the process. Only this time, it goes down with much, much less pain.

It feels like my body is glowing from the inside now, and although I'm numb, I'm starting to feel somewhat more human again. Colin sips on his drink in silence, just staring at me over the rim of his glass. There is an overwhelming amount of compassion and concern in his eyes, and it sends a warmth shooting through me that has nothing to do with alcohol.

"I'll be okay," I say. "I just need to get over the initial shock of it all. It's been a long, emotional day."

He nods. "I'm sure you must be exhausted."

I give him a weak, fragile smile. "I really am."

"There's a spare bedroom you can have," he says. "It's quiet, near the back of the house, and has its own bathroom. You'll have total privacy."

"Thank you, Colin," I say. "For everything. I don't even know –"

"You don't need to thank me for anything, Bailey," he says and then grins. "Besides, it might be nice to have some company in this big ol' place for a change. Come on, I'll show you the way."

I follow him through the house, really seeing it for the first time. The place is enormous – practically a palace. The floors are done in a dark-colored hardwood, and the interior design is soft, earthy, and muted. The architecture is unlike anything I've ever seen. I don't even know what to call it. Honestly, it reminds me of a castle.

We pass all the packages we picked up today. The driver has them all stacked up in the foyer, lined up and waiting for me. I don't even want to think about it right now. All I want is a hot shower and some quality time in a comfy bed.

Colin leads me up a spiral staircase, and down a long hallway decorated in the same earth tones and dark paneling. The further we go into the house, the more it reminds me of a castle. The art on the walls is classic – all of the old masters are well-represented, of course. And for good reason – they're not called the masters for nothing. I see many prints, obviously, but there are a few that could be original works, something which is mind-boggling to me. The price of an original is more than I make in a year. Hell, it's probably more than I'll make in my freaking lifetime.

The hallway ends at a rounded doorway which Colin holds open for me. I step through and into a room larger than my entire apartment. The room is dominated by a large, four-poster canopy bed. The bedding is a rich shade of crimson and looks heavenly soft from where I'm standing. There's a large armoire against one wall, a highboy dresser against another, and a luxurious walk-in closet that also might be larger than my apartment. A pristine daybed sits beneath a large, oversized window that overlooks what has to be at least an acre of land behind the house.

Wow. Must be nice to be rich as sin.

Colin disappears and lets me walk around the place, getting a feel for it. He comes back a few minutes later with a t-shirt, a pair of sweatpants, and some basketball shorts.

"I wasn't sure what you'd be comfortable in," he says. "I guess we should have gotten you some casual wear today too, huh?"

A regretful chuckle passes my lips. "If only we knew, huh?"

He takes my hands in his and gives them a reassuring squeeze. "It's going to be okay, Bailey," he says. "I promise you it will. You can stay here as long as you need to. I'm down the hall, but you'll pretty much have this side of the house to yourself. So, however long it takes to get your apartment squared away, is fine with me. You'll always have a roof over your head here."

As I look at him, I honestly don't know how I got so lucky, or what I did to deserve such good fortune. My eyes sting with tears I'm trying my best to bite back but failing at miserably. Colin's generosity humbles me, and I am profoundly grateful to him. It's a debt I don't think I'll ever be able to repay.

I lean against him and revel in feeling his powerful arms wrapped around me. Delight in the warmth and closeness of his embrace. Having him pressed against me makes me feel safe in ways I've never experienced before. I turn my face up to him and find a gentle smile on his lips as he looks down at me.

I put my hand behind his neck and pull him down to me, hungrily pressing my mouth to his. I part my lips, and let his tongue fill my mouth. Our kiss is sensual. Passionate. And exactly what I need right now. I feel so unhinged and untethered at the moment, that I need this human contact. Need this affirmation of life.

Colin leans into me, letting his hands roam my body as our kiss intensifies. He cups my breasts, rubbing my hard nipples through the fabric with his thumbs, drawing a soft moan from me. He slips the cardigan off my shoulders, and lets it fall to the ground at my feet. He presses his soft lips to my neck, planting a line of tender kisses down to my collarbone.

I reach around to my back and slide the zipper of my dress down. I let the straps slip off my shoulders, and it joins my cardigan in a pool of fabric at my feet. I stand naked before him and watch his eyes explore my body for the first time. He draws in a breath as he drinks me in from head to toe, his expression rapt, desire burning bright behind his eyes.

The way he looks at me makes me feel like the sexiest woman on the planet. Colin looks at me like I'm a goddess, and as those intense gray-blue eyes soak in every inch of me, I feel myself becoming more and more turned on.

"Are you sure you want to do this right now?" he asks.

I nod. "Very sure."

I need to feel something. I need to feel him. I'm teetering right on the edge of a nervous breakdown, and I feel like he's the only one who can pull me back and return me to reality. I step forward and reach for his belt. He stops me though, taking my hands in his. I cock my head and look at him, and he flashes me that enigmatic, roguish smile of his.

He leads me over to the bed, sitting me on the edge of it. Suddenly, Colin darts out of the room, and I hear his feet padding down the hall. I lay back on the bed and close my eyes, letting the sensations wash over me. My body is glowing with an inner light, and I feel a warmth burning bright between my thighs. I reach down and idly stroke my clit, teasing myself until he gets back.

I circle it with my fingers, making my body hum with a carnal electricity. I'm smoldering with desire, anxiously anticipating the feel of Colin's thick, hard cock deep inside of me for the second time. I bite my bottom lip and stifle a cry as I slip two fingers into me, pressing down on my clit with my thumb.

As I pleasure myself, I suddenly realize I'm not alone. My eyes pop open and I sit up to find Colin standing there, his cock already encased in the condom, his eyes lit with pure lust and desire.

"Sorry," I say. "I was getting tired of waiting."

"Don't let me stop you," he says.

"But I want the real thing."

"Your wish is my command."

I scoot up on the bed and he falls down on top of me, holding himself up on his arms. He looks down at me, presses his lips to mine, and gives me a kiss that's surprisingly affectionate. Sweet, even. I spread my legs for him, giving him access to me.

Colin positions the head of his cock, pressing it against my opening, and as he passionately kisses me again, he parts my lips with his cock. He slips between the velvety folds of my pussy with a surprising gentleness and ease. He slides himself all the way in until he's fully sheathed inside of me and holds himself there.

I press my head back against the bed and bite my bottom lip as he stretches me open, the slight stab of pain blending with the wave of pleasure sweeping through me. Colin starts to gently move his hips, his eyes locked onto mine as he slides himself in and out of me with a sense of tenderness. He kisses me, and our tongues meld together as he moves inside of me.

I grip his forearms, my nails digging into his flesh. We're moving slowly, making sure to take our time, and I'm savoring every single moment I have him inside of me. He never breaks eye contact with me, and somehow, it makes everything even more intense than the other day.

The way he fucked me in my studio was hot. Beyond hot. It was amazing. I was so turned on – so ready for him – it barely registered that I was finally losing my virginity. And I orgasmed harder than ever before. But I'm sure the way he's making love to me right now, sweetly, and without any sense of urgency, will make me come just as hard.

I gasp as I feel every inch of him slide deep into me as Colin slowly drives himself into my most sensitive spots. I shudder and gasp, digging my nails even harder into his flesh as I'm buffeted by waves of utter bliss.

His breathing is growing ragged, and his voice is hoarse as he moans, softly calling out my name. I arch my back, taking him even deeper inside of me, and his body grows even tighter. I know he's racing to the edge of bliss himself, and given the powerful currents of ecstasy raging through my body, I'm going to get there with him – if not before.

The intensity is driving me wild. The way he looks at me, and how he holds me with his gaze, like he thinks I'm the most beautiful creature in the world, only adds more kindling to the fires of desire spiraling wildly out of control.

He stutters and gasps, losing his rhythm for a moment. I see his jaw clench, and know he's holding back. Trying to draw this out and make it last.

"Come for me, Colin," I call softly. "Come inside of me. I want to feel you."

He squeezes his eyes shut as he thrusts himself into me deep, holding himself there. He hits that spot and sends me tumbling over the edge. I tremble and cry out as a powerful orgasm crashes over me. A moment later, Colin lets out a garbled breath. He shudders, and that's it. I feel his cock throbbing and pulsing within the condom inside of me.

He lowers his head and grits his teeth as he explodes. I cling to him as I tremble while he shudders on top of me. Together, we ride the twin currents of pleasure that have us soaring higher and higher.

Colin collapses on the bed next to me, his body covered in a thin sheen of sweat. His eyes are wide and he stares up at the canopy, doing his best to try and catch his breath. I lay my head on his chest, snuggling up next to him and relishing how his strong body feels next to mine. I've never felt safer in my life. And honestly, I've never felt more loved.

It's ridiculous, really. We don't know each other well enough yet to even be thinking, let alone saying the "L" word out loud. That doesn't mean, that I can't feel it, though. This man has demolished all of the walls and defenses I've built over the years. He's destroyed everything I used to keep myself out of harm's way – emotionally speaking, of course.

I wasn't necessarily looking for a partner when Colin came crashing into my life, but, here we are. Curled up next to him, feeling his body pressed to mine, listening to his slow, steady breathing, and strong heartbeat, just feels natural. It feels right.

And that scares me to death.

I don't know how Colin feels. I mean, I get the idea that he likes me. But, not knowing if his feelings are as intense as mine, or if he actually feels the same, scares me to death. I feel like I'm way out on a ledge without a safety harness here. And nobody's there to catch me if I fall.

It's a terrifying feeling – but it's exhilarating at the same time. In a weird, kind of perverse way. I haven't closed myself off to love as much as Colin has, I just haven't been looking. I've been focused on my art and activism, and haven't had much time or room in my life for anything else. It's not that I wanted to be alone, I just figured that when the time was right, the perfect man would reveal himself to me.

I never expected that man would be someone with totally opposite views from my own.

But, are we really that different? After seeing what he did tonight – all day today, actually – from buying me a closet full of clothing, to offering to pay for Father Gus' medical care, to giving Matthew a job – it makes me think the man might have a heart of gold. Sure, it's buried under layers upon layers of baggage and other dark stuff, but at the end of the day, Colin is a man with compassion and integrity. With love in his heart.

And that's the kind of person I want to be with.

The real question is whether or not I'm the kind of woman Colin wants to be with. I sometimes see glimpses of him that make me think so. Other times, I doubt myself. Doubt that what I'm seeing, and experiencing, is real.

His breathing is steady and regular. He's passed out, asleep. I curl myself around him tighter and try to shut out all of the negative thoughts in my head. Try to drown out the nagging voices of doubt. I just want to live in this moment and enjoy it to the fullest.

A small, satisfied smile upon my lips, I let the darkness of sleep wrap its tendrils around me and pull me under.

Chapter Thirteen

Colin

The sunlight streams in through the curtains, and for a confusing minute or two, I can't remember where I am. I lay there, having been woken from a dream that seemed particularly vivid, but the second I opened my eyes, it fluttered away like a dandelion on the breeze.

In that moment, nothing looks familiar to me, and my heart is beating wildly inside my chest as panic creeps in. I stare at the walls around me, trying to piece together my dream and my thoughts – trying in vain to understand where I am. At least, until my bedmate rustles the blankets beside me. When I turn my head and see Bailey, it all comes rushing back in sharp detail.

I'm at home. In one of the guest bedrooms. And with those realizations, I suddenly recall the night before, remembering how we'd made love. As snippets and flashes of making love to her scroll through my mind, my breath catches in my throat.

Bailey's eyes open, and when she smiles, I can't help but think to myself that she might be the most beautiful thing I've ever seen in my life. My heart swells to the point I'm afraid it might burst.

"Good morning," she says, her voice groggy.

Bailey stifles a yawn as she scoots next to me, nuzzling her body closer to mine. She moves as if she wants me to put my arm around her, but suddenly stops. Maybe she notices the look on my face, which I'm sure matches the sense of disconnect I'm experiencing in my head.

"Everything okay?" she asks.

"Yeah, I'm just a little disoriented," I say. "It's been a long time since I've had anyone stay over. I literally haven't woken up next to someone else in years."

There's a moment of tense silence between us as she looks at me and searches my eyes for something, though I'm not sure what. It's awkward for me, knowing what happened between us the night before. There's no denying it, I feel something for her, and judging by the way she looks at me, I can see she feels it too. It's more than just a simple crush. It's already deeper and more profound than some mild case of infatuation or simple puppy love.

Whatever "it" happens to be, neither one of us is quite sure what to make of it yet. At least, I know I'm not.

I pull her to me, letting her curl up closer to my body – savoring the warmth. Her naked flesh is soft and comforting against mine, and I can lay there and revel in it for hours, never getting tired of it. As we lay there in silence, our bodies intertwined, my eyes begin to flutter shut again. I can totally go back to sleep right now, nestled against Bailey's perky, supple body. But I can tell that even though she's not saying anything and is laying there in perfect silence, she's very much awake right now. I'd feel like a bit of an ass if I fell asleep while she was still laying there, wide awake.

"You okay?" I ask.

She nods. "I'm good," she replies softly. "You?"

"I'm good," I say.

We speak in hushed whispers, as if speaking in our normal tone of voice would somehow shatter whatever fragile, delicate thing is hovering between us.

"What are your plans for the day?" she finally asks.

"You know, destroy a few lives, tear people from their homes, the usual," I answer. "Maybe, I'll even start a genocide somewhere, just for kicks."

I pull away, propping myself up on my elbow to stare at her. She's smiling, but I can tell that she isn't finding my jokes very funny at the moment. Not in the least, actually. So, when I see the serious look on her face, I just sigh.

"Sorry, I was just messing with you," I say, tucking a wisp of loose hair behind her ear.

"Well, I'm not amused."

"I can tell," I say. "Though, I tend to find it adorable when you're mad. Just so you know."

"Then you must find me adorable a lot," she says, "since you seem to have a unique gift to provoke my anger."

Even though her words are harsh, there's much less heat and anger behind them than there would have been weeks ago. It probably has to do with the fact that we've slept together a couple of times now, if I'm being honest. Kinda hard to hold a grudge against someone you've just slept with the night before.

That's progress, though, right?

We had such a beautiful time the night before, that I really don't know what has her so rattled this morning. I don't know why Bailey seems so on edge. Did she have a bad dream? All I know is that last night, things seemed fine. We actually seemed to be drawing even closer to each other than before. And, of course, that culminated in our making love. In making each other feel good.

"Talk to me," I say. "You don't seem like yourself. What's changed since last night?"

She hesitates a moment, opening her mouth to say something, only to close it again without speaking. I reach out and stroke her cheek, looking deeply into her eyes, as I try to figure out what's going on with her.

"You can tell me anything, Bailey," I say. "It's okay. We can talk through anything together."

"I just – I like how things are going between us," she says. "And I guess I'm kind of waiting for the other shoe to drop?"

I cock my head and look at her. "What do you mean?"

She shrugs. "I don't know," she says. "I mean, I know you're not big on relationships. And I keep thinking back to the first time we had sex in my studio, and how awkward it was afterward, and how you couldn't get out of there fast enough. I guess I'm kind of expecting you to run at any moment."

I chuckle softly. "For one thing, this is my house, so it's not like I can go very far."

She remains stone-faced, not laughing at all. She doesn't even have the grace to give me a courtesy laugh. Which means this is more serious than I thought.

"I had a dream that you left me," she says. "Only, it felt like more than a dream. It felt more like a – premonition, I guess."

"Do you see me trying to go anywhere, Bailey?"

She shakes her head, but it seems to do little to mollify her.

"I'll admit, I'm more than a little nervous," I say. "But, something's changed between us. Or rather, you've changed something within me. And I like it, Bailey. I don't know what it is, and I obviously can't promise you anything right now, but I like what this is, and even more, I like where it's going."

"Really?" she asks me, her face so wide-eyed and innocent that it melts my heart.

"Really," I say.

She presses her body to mine with more force than before, wrapping her arms around me, and burying her face in my chest. She plants kisses all over my pecs and abs, seeming to take an enormous amount of comfort from having me right next to her, holding her. Touching her. It's almost as if she's drawing strength from our physical contact, and needs more, just to reassure herself.

I reach out and stroke her cheek, looking deeply into her eyes. The mood in the bedroom seems to be lighter now as the tension that marked our first moments awake slowly, but surely evaporates. I run my thumb across her soft, full lips, recalling how amazing they felt pressed to mine.

"You're lucky I don't bite your finger off," she teases.

"That might be okay," I say. "After all, I've always been fond of a woman who bites."

"Careful what you ask for."

"I usually am."

She nips at my hand unexpectedly and catches my thumb between her teeth. A playful light gleams in her eyes as she makes a vicious growling sound, and I yelp, pretending that she's hurting me. I know it might seem silly, goofy, and childish. But, I can't help it. I enjoy having fun and acting like a kid when I'm around her.

She releases my thumb before grabbing hold of it and placing a gentle kiss on it. Then, just for good measure, Bailey leans forward and plants a soft kiss on my lips. I chuckle to myself and can't help but look back in wonder at how we got here. It's crazy to think that one woman who had the power to get under my skin as deeply as she did, is now even deeper beneath my skin, for an entirely different reason. Whereas once, she made me feel little more than anger and annoyance, now, she makes my heart race, and makes me tremble with absolute passion and desire.

Now, I can't imagine my days without her. I can't imagine going an hour, let alone a day, without seeing that sparkle in her eye, hearing her laughter, or feeling her body against mine. I can't imagine not talking to her, debating with her, arguing with her, loving on her, sharing our hopes, dreams, desires, and passions. Bailey has brought something to my life I never expected, and now, it seems that I can't live without it.

What's more – and what's even scarier – is that not only can I not imagine it, I find that I don't want to.

"Penny for your thoughts?" she asks.

"I was just thinking about what a huge pain in the ass you used to be," I say.

"I hope I still am," she says. "I don't plan on changing anything about myself."

I laugh softly. "Nor would I ask you to," I say. "You know I admire you for your passion and the courage of your convictions, believe it or not."

"My convictions? As in criminal? I've been charged many times but have never been convicted. Not even once, believe it or not," she says, playfully poking me in the chest.

I roll my eyes but am still smiling. "I'm actually kind of surprised," I say. "I mean, it's not like you're a criminal mastermind, exactly."

She slaps me in the chest, laughing. "You just called me stupid."

"No, that's just what you heard," I say. "Think of it kind of like a Rorschach test. I have to say, your answer is very telling."

She laughs, lightly slapping me in the chest again, and my heart swells with an unfettered feeling of happiness. One that makes my soul feel like it's glowing. This is the kind of effect Bailey has on me – I think this might be the first time I've even considered the idea of having a soul, let alone one that glows with giddiness.

But with her, I feel like all things are possible. It's crazy, but it's true. That's what I'd like to refer to as the "Bailey effect."

As she continues to giggle, I roll over onto my back, and the blanket gets pulled down off my chest. Bailey rolls with me, and she lays her head on my chest, idly stroking the bare skin on my torso. The feel of her nails on my flesh sends a pleasant chill through me. I reach out and gently run my fingers through her hair, which she seems to like. We lay like that for a while, the silence between us no longer strained, but comfortable. Companionable. Filled with something a lot closer to love, than not.

"I admire you for standing up for what you believe in," I say. "Even if what you believe in goes against everything I stand for, I still respect the hell out of it. I admire your courage and your fearlessness. It's something uncommon in people today."

She raises her head and stares at me with her mouth hanging open, seemingly unable to say anything at all. The look on her face says she can't believe what she's just heard. Which is odd because it's not the first time I've expressed similar sentiments. Maybe not as forcefully, or convincingly as right now, perhaps.

Slowly, that look of awe and stunned disbelief melts away, and is replaced by that mischievous grin she sometimes gets. There's a devilish sparkle in her eyes as she looks at me and starts to sing.

"Colin likes me," she croons in that high-pitched, sing-song voice of hers. "He's got a crush on me. A big old crush. Oh yeah, Colin Anderson has a crush on me –"

Her impromptu concert is cut off when I smack her in the head with a pillow. She laughs and hits me back with her pillow. And together, like children, we're laughing and shrieking as we roll around, wrestling, and roughhousing in bed.

Once our wrestling match ends, we lay there, our bodies intertwined, for what feels like hours. We talk, sharing stories about ourselves and our lives. We get to know each other on a deeper level than before. We're open, honest, and share everything with one another – and the wonderful feeling of lightness, of being free, consumes me. It's foreign and strange, but all consuming.

And everything in the world, in that moment, feels so fucking right.

Chapter Fourteen

Bailey

"You ready for this?" he asks.

I swallow hard but give him a thumbs up. "Good to go, boss."

"Don't call me that," he says and laughs.

It's D-Day, and I can't recall a time when I've been more nervous. Not even before my very first gallery show. My body is trembling, and it's not because it's freezing cold outside, either. There was a light dusting of snow overnight, and although the sun is out and quickly slipping toward the horizon as the day gives way to night – it was never warm enough today to melt it all, so the world around us looks like it's been nestled into a smooth, white blanket. It's one of the things I love about living here – the natural beauty of the seasons.

"If everyone's scattered all over the country, how did they all get on the same flight out here?" I ask as the thought suddenly occurs to me.

Colin gives me a smirk. "One of the perks of being a family of corporate pigs is that we have a fleet of company jets," he says. "We each have one, and they coordinated their flight itineraries to touch down at Logan at the same time, more or less."

"Wow, you're never going to let me live the corporate pig comment down, are you?"

"Let me think about that for a minute – yeah, probably not."

"Jerk," I say and laugh.

"Just another facet of my charm."

"So, you've got private jet money," I mutter, cringing inside. "That's nice."

"It's practical."

The last few days have been wonderful. More than wonderful, really. Luckily, the firm has limited holiday hours in December, and I've been working remote a few hours each morning. The workload is light this time of year, so I've been able to fully enjoy my time with Colin. I've really started to fall for him. He's more different than I ever could have imagined, and he captures my mind and heart in ways I never thought possible.

I feel us growing closer, and even though neither one of us really acknowledges our feelings, we both know they're out there, hanging awkwardly in the air between us. It's almost as if we're afraid that if we give voice to them, they'll somehow disappear in a puff of smoke or something.

We're standing on the porch of his house, watching two dark SUVs rumbling noisily in our direction. Feeling uneasy, I look down at the giant, glittering diamond ring Colin gave me earlier today to reassure myself. Now that his family is almost here, however, I feel intensely guilty about deceiving them like this. *Oh well. What can I do now?* I check my dress one more time, making sure I look presentable. I've never been in the presence of so many wealthy people, and I'm afraid I'm going to stick out like a sore thumb.

But, I have to say, the dark blue dress really flatters me. It accentuates my small waist while highlighting the generous curves of my hips and breasts. Not to toot my own horn too loudly, but I look pretty smoking hot in this outfit. I look up and catch Colin staring at me with the purest look of love in his eyes – even though we have yet to even acknowledge that emotion exists in our little slice of the world.

"You look amazing, Bailey," he says. "Absolutely gorgeous."

"Thank you," I reply, feeling myself blush.

The SUVs pull to a stop, and I feel the tension in my body ratchet up about fifteen notches. There's a hard flutter in my belly that's quickly surpassed by the one in my heart. I don't know why I'm so scared to meet them. I've always been good with people. The only probable reason I can think of is the fact that this is Colin's family, and I want to make a good impression on them. I want to impress them. I want them to like me.

Yeah, this whole thing may have started as a business proposal. And who knows, maybe he still thinks of it that way. But, a lot has happened since we agreed to this mutually beneficial partnership, and I feel like the nature of our relationship has evolved since then. I feel like it's grown and changed in only good ways. It feels more genuine. Heartfelt.

It actually feels like we're a real couple, rather than two people pretending to be together to execute some shady business deal. At least, that's how it feels from my end; I can't really speak to Colin's state of mind right now.

Given how the last few days have gone, though, I tend to think that this has become something deeper than a business arrangement for him too. I want to believe it when I see the way he looks at me. In the way he treats me. Truth be told, I've never been treated better by a man in my whole life. He dotes on me. Caters to my every whim and desire. Colin spoils me.

It's an amazing feeling, but also a scary one – for the both of us.

The doors to the SUVs open and three men, four women, and two small children all come piling out – and I can't help but find myself wondering which one is Laurel. Colin rushes down the steps to greet them, and the brothers all cluster together, exchanging hugs, high fives, and bawdy humor – guys being guys, and all that. It's actually pretty damn adorable.

It's not often – or at all, really – that I see Colin this animated or excited. I can already see the love and connection between the Andersons, and instantly understand just how deep and strong their bond is. As I see the knot of people down there interacting, I feel a small pang of jealousy. Though, most of the time I'm okay with being an only child, every once in a while, like right now, I find myself wondering what it would have been like to have siblings.

A moment later, Colin rushes back up the steps, takes my hand, and gently leads me down to where everybody is standing. My throat is parched, and my stomach is flipping so violently, I'm afraid I'm going to throw up all over everybody's thousand-dollar shoes. I take several deep breaths in through my nose, and slowly let them out through my mouth, trying to steel my nerves.

"Guys, I want you to meet Bailey Janson, my fiancée," Colin says. "Bailey, these are my brothers, Aidan, Liam, and Brayden, and their wives Paige, Holly, and Katie. And Laurel is over there too. I'll leave you all to make the individual introductions."

He picks up a small boy and squeezes him tight. Colin plants a kiss on the boy's cheek, making him giggle. It's the cutest sight ever.

"Bailey, this is my nephew Jace," he says, and then blows a kiss to a small girl hiding behind her mom's legs. "And that is my niece Charlie – Charlotte, to be precise."

I raise my hand and give everybody an uncertain wave I'm sure looks awkward as hell – while inside, I'm kicking myself for being such a self-conscious goofball.

"Hi, everybody," I say. "It's nice to finally meet you all. I've heard a lot about you."

"And we've heard next to nothing about you, so let's go hook you up to the polygraph, and play twenty questions," says a man with a lean, trim build a lot like Colin's.

"That's Brayden," Colin says. "And he's kidding. I think."

Brayden laughs and steps forward, pulling me into a tight embrace. I return it, but feel more than a bit awkward, given that I just met the man. He steps back after a moment, and smiles at me.

"Congratulations, you two! It's very nice to meet you, Bailey," he says.

"It's nice to meet you too."

"Come on, kids," Colin says. "It's cold out here. Let's continue the getting-to-know-you part inside."

We all turn and follow Colin up the steps. A woman in a long black peacoat, maybe a couple of years older than me, falls into step beside me, and I do a double take. On the surface, the two of us could be sisters. We've got the same midnight-black hair and eyes. Our body types and height are even similar.

"Uncanny, isn't it?" she asks and laughs. "We could be sisters."

"I was just thinking the same thing," I respond, laughing nervously.

This has to be Laurel. I know guys have types and given that this woman and I are virtual clones of one another, I'm guessing I know what Colin's type is. At least, I know now, anyway. So far, she seems nice enough, though. Given what Colin's told me about Laurel, I expected hostility, or at the very least, a cold shoulder. But she actually seems nice. Warm. Friendly.

"I'm Paige," she says. "Liam's wife. It's really nice to meet you, Bailey."

Okay, not Laurel. One down, three to go. Apparently, Liam and Colin have very, very similar taste in women. I don't know how I should feel about that.

"It's nice to meet you too," I say.

"I know I just met you like a millisecond ago," Paige says, "but, I can already tell that you've been really good for Colin."

I let out another bark of nervous laughter. "Think so?"

"Know so," she says. "Colin is usually very somber and reserved. In the thirty seconds we've been here, I've seen him more animated than in the rest of the time I've known him. Combined. It's like you've brought him out of his shell or something."

I give her a warm, sincere smile. "We work well together," I say. "We complement each other in a lot of different ways."

"I'm glad," she says. "I've always wanted to see Colin happy. He's a good man and deserves to have an equally good woman by his side.

One who challenges him to step out of his comfort zone. I can already see you're having a positive effect on him."

"I'm glad," I say. "He's a very good man."

We step into the house and Colin's house manager, Rhonda, shuts the door behind us. She ushers us into the den, where everybody is standing around talking. There's a roaring fire in the oversized fireplace, and the decorations make it look like Santa's workshop exploded in here. Larger than life ornaments and gift boxes, are scattered around, while an ornately decorated Christmas tree – bigger than anything I've seen outside of a mall or Rockefeller Center – dominates the room from the corner.

The two small children, closely watched by their parents, play with the large Christmas train on one side of the room. I've never experienced anything like this, and it feels totally surreal to me. Talk about feeling like a fish out of water.

Paige links her arm through mine and gives me a reassuring smile. Now without her peacoat, I can clearly see her tiny baby bump. With how nervous I was, I almost forgot Paige was pregnant. "Trust me, I know what you're feeling," she says. "It's more than a little overwhelming, right?"

"Yeah, just a bit."

She laughs. "Just trust me when I say that you're not alone," she says. "The Anderson brothers apparently have a thing for picking up strays like us and keeping them."

She makes me laugh and I feel a bit better about the whole situation. "I just so feel out of place."

"It gets easier," she says. "I mean, the boys are all as down to earth as they can be."

"I don't know about that, I'm having to break Colin of some bad habits."

She grins. "About time somebody did," she says. "Honestly though, the whole family is very level-headed. Just give it a chance because I have a feeling that you're going to fit right in with us."

"And don't mind Laurel," whispers a voice to my right. "She's not one of us."

I turn and look at a redhead who's a few inches taller and maybe a year or two older than me. She's got milky-white skin, a figure to die for, and is model gorgeous. All of the Anderson wives are, actually. And then one thing stands out to me – all of the wives are right around my age, give or take a few years.

"The boys all like to marry young, don't they?" I ask.

Paige and the newcomer – not Laurel, obviously – giggle and nod.

"Yeah, it seems to be a trend with them," Paige says with a laugh.

"I'm Holly," says the redhead. "Brayden's wife, though I like to think of myself as far more than just that."

"Don't we all," Paige says.

We stand in a small cluster, and I look over at the woman watching both kids. I assume that has to be Katie – Aidan's wife, if I'm keeping score right. Which means, the tall, leggy blonde leaning against the fireplace with a drink in her hand, glaring daggers at me, must be Laurel.

"Not the friendly sort, is she?" I ask quietly.

Paige and Holly apparently don't even need to ask who I'm referring to, as both shake their heads in unison.

"I've felt more warmth from an ice cube," Paige says.

"I accidentally bumped into her and got frostbite," Holly adds.

All three of us burst into laughter together, and I can't help but feel like I've known these two women my entire life. They make me feel so welcome and accepted, which is crazy, since they don't know me at all. All I know is that we might only be ten minutes into this crazy adventure, but I already like these two – a lot.

"And what are we laughing about here, ladies?"

Colin slips his arm around my waist and places a soft kiss on the top of my head. It's an unexpected gesture, but one that sends a warm tingle through me. I lean against him, basking in the comfort I feel from being beside the man. Sneaking a quick glance over at Laurel, I watch her mutter something angrily to herself as she powers down the last of her drink. Casting an ugly glance at me, she stalks away.

Yeah, this is going to be a lot of fun.

"We were just grilling Bailey about you two," Holly teases.

"What's there to know?" he asks. "We've been dating for – about how long now?"

I rack my brain quickly, trying to remember the story I'm supposed to remember. But, Laurel has me more than a bit rattled at the moment. So, all I do is nod.

"Honestly, I don't recall," I say brightly.

"I think it's been about eight months or so," Colin lies, quickly covering my flub.

It's probably closer to something like eight days, but close enough. Honestly, it doesn't even matter to me anymore. I feel like Colin and I are on the right path. I want to believe that our feelings are real, and that we're actually building something together. But, I know he wants to avoid drama with his brothers – and after seeing Laurel's reaction to me, I can understand why he feels the need to invent this fiction – so I'm just going to play along.

But, he obviously doesn't know that the wives all hate Laurel. Or, at least, that's the vibe I'm picking up, anyway. And I have to say, judging by my first impression of the woman, I can understand why. She doesn't seem to be a terribly pleasant person.

"It's great to see you both," Colin says, giving both women a hug.

"It's wonderful to see you too, Colin," Paige says. "I was just telling Bailey here that it seems like she's inspiring some positive changes in you. You seem –"

"Different," Holly chimes in as Paige nods. "You seem lighter and freer than I've ever seen you. You actually seem – happy."

He laughs. "You make me sound like I was a dour old codger before Bailey came into my life," he says, then turns to me. "I really wasn't."

"Yeah, you really kind of were," Paige says.

"Grumpy as all get out," Holly adds.

Colin's laughter rumbles from deep inside of him. It's a warm and genuine sound – and honestly, really nice to hear. He gives both of the girls the finger, which only makes them laugh harder.

"I don't have to take this kind of abuse," he says.

"Sure you do," Holly teases. "We're going to be here for a few days, after all."

"About that... I'm thinking of going to stay in a hotel," he says.

"Like we wouldn't track you down," Paige says.

Colin turns to me. "Don't let these harpies get into your head and turn you against me," he says. "They're evil, the lot of 'em. Keep a sharp eye out."

Brayden grabs him and pulls him away, the four brothers standing together, taking selfies, and laughing raucously. I watch them all together and can't help but smile.

"He really does seem different," Holly says.

Paige nods. "Our girl here has had a very positive effect on him, I think."

I grin but shake my head. "No, that's all him."

"Bullshit," Holly says. "It might have been inside him all along, but it took the right person to bring it out of him. Obviously, that was you."

I feel my cheeks flush as a rush of gratitude fills me. Being around these two is helping me feel like I fit into this crowd. They're not the high-society, snooty as hell types – which is what I was expecting. They're incredibly down to earth, hilarious, and come across as genuinely good people.

"I'm gonna sit with the kids for a while so you can meet Katie," Holly says. "But, we've got some talking to do later, Bailey."

I give her a smile as she turns away and heads over to the kids. The other woman stands and crosses the room. I hold my hand out to her, but she pushes it aside, and wraps me in a tight, warm embrace, and I can't help but laugh.

"Hi, I'm Katie," she says. "I'm the treasurer of the We Hate Laurel Club, and you just became my new favorite member."

Paige and I laugh. Katie is a dirty blonde, with brown eyes, a shapely figure, and a Southern accent dripping like honey from her lips. Aside from all of us being around the same age, another thing I've noticed about the type of women the Anderson boys seem to be attracted to is that all four of us come across as feisty, independent women who like to speak our minds.

All three of the wives seem to have strong opinions, aren't afraid to share them, and have fierce, unique personalities of their own. Like Holly said, they might be Anderson wives, but they're so much more than that.

"Seriously, Bailey," Katie leans in, pitching her voice low, "don't let her rattle you. She thinks she's all that, but trust me, she ain't."

I watch as Rhonda enters the room and goes to Colin. He leans down as she whispers something in his ear. He smiles and nods, before turning to the room.

"Okay, folks," he says. "I hope you're hungry, because I've been informed that it's time for dinner."

"Who should we stick next to Laurel?" Paige whispers.

"Can we put her plate out on the back porch?" Katie whispers back.

All three cackle with laughter as we head toward the formal dining room.

Chapter Fifteen

Colin

I know I was dreading this day, but having everybody at the table, with the conversations loud and animated, feels good. I'm definitely happier than in year's past, and I know it has everything to do with Bailey.

I watch her, sitting between Paige and Holly, watching how quickly they've bonded, and smile. They're laughing and talking like they've been friends for a thousand years. It's really good to see. I was worried about how easily Bailey would integrate into the family, but it looks like my fears were totally unfounded.

"It's good to see you, Colin."

I look over at Laurel, who managed to worm her way into the seat to my right – a seat that should have been reserved for one of my brothers. I'm sitting at the head of the table, and Liam is to my left, engaged in a conversation with Brayden. To Laurel's right is Aidan, who's chatting up the girls, leaving me stuck with my ex.

"It's nice to see you too, Laurel," I say – not that I really mean it. "You look well."

"I am well," she says.

"I'm glad to hear it," I say. "What are you doing these days?"

She shrugs. "A little bit of this, a little bit of that," she says. "Always looking for the next challenge."

The way she delivers that line, her eyes fixed to mine, make it clear to me that she sees me as the next challenge.

Yeah, not going to happen.

"Yeah? That's good. I'm glad to hear it," I say and raise my wine glass to her. "I wish you many new adventures, and exciting challenges then."

She runs the tip of her finger around the rim of her wine glass, leaning her chin in her hand, her arm propped on the table, on her elbow.

"Why didn't you ever return any of my calls?" she whispers.

"I'm not getting into this with you, Laurel," I say. "Not now, not ever again."

She shrugs. "I think I deserve an answer."

I pitch my voice low, trying to avoid being overheard. "After fucking my best friend – in my own apartment – you deserve two things: Jack and shit."

She laughs, a rich, throaty sound. "Are you still holding onto that?" she asks. "Don't you think it's time you let go and move forward?"

"I have," I say. "You see the dark-haired beauty down there? That's my fiancée. That's me moving forward."

"That silly waif?" she laughs. "That'll be over in six months."

I give her a long, level look, trying to temper my rapidly escalating anger. "You don't know shit, Laurel," I say.

"I know enough to know that she's young. Naive. Idealistic," she says. "I know that she has a real affinity for the poor – whom you disdain."

"Nice, so you stalked her?"

She shrugs. "Googling somebody isn't exactly stalking," she says. "I mean, the information is floating around out there for anybody to see."

"And why would you do that?"

"I wanted to see what I was up against. My competition," she says. "Turns out, I'm not competing against all that much."

"You realize, of course, that game is long over. You lost," I say. "Competition's over, and there's no comeback for you. I'm with Bailey now. End of story."

"Yes, well, I've been known to snatch victory from the jaws of defeat, Colin," she says. "Come on, baby. You know we're good together. We get each other in ways you and the waif never will. You know you should be with me."

I give her a feral grin. "I'd rather stick my cock in a paper shredder."

Taking my plate and glass of wine, I stand up and carry it down to the other end of the table, taking a seat next to Bailey. She gives me a smile and squeezes my thigh beneath the table. I look back at Laurel, who's glowering at us with murderous intent in her eyes.

Just to illustrate the point I was trying to make – or maybe, just to twist the knife a little bit – I lean over and plant a soft kiss on Bailey's cheek. She giggles and returns the favor. Then she gets lost in her conversation with Holly and Paige. It's amazing that the three of them are clicking so well, and are chatting away like long lost friends. It warms my heart to see.

Leaving her mostly full plate behind, Laurel picks up her glass of wine, and stalks out of the room to pout. I just roll my eyes and shake my head. Brayden looks over at me, giving me a shrug. I motion for him to join me in the kitchen that's situated behind the dining room. He stands and follows me through the door. The moment it's closed, I round on him.

"I knew this shit was going to happen," I say.

"What?" he asks. "What happened?"

"Laurel, man," I say. "She's still running around, thinking there's some chance we're going to get together. She sees Bailey as competition."

He whistles low and runs a hand through his hair. "Shit. That's not what she told me, little brother," he says. "I swear it. She said she was in a good place in her life and had zero interest in trying to rekindle anything between you two."

"I told you she's a goddamn liar, man," I say. "An opportunist, and a master manipulator."

"Shit," he says. "This is going to be awkward."

"Yeah, tell me about it," I say. "The best thing we can do is put her back on the plane and fly her ass home."

He sighs and shuffles his feet. "I don't know. I feel bad for her, man," he says. "She's obviously lonely. She's got no one."

"Maybe she would if she wasn't such a rancid bitch," I say.

"Look, I'll play babysitter," he says. "I'll make sure she doesn't get in your hair."

"Why are you so insistent on her staying?"

"I guess I just feel sorry for her," he says. "I mean, I can't imagine what it's like to have nobody. Nobody willing to take you in on Christmas – that's really sad stuff, Colin. I mean, think about it."

"She brought it on herself."

"Damn. When did you become so heartless?" he asks, grinning at me.

I just shake my head. "When did you get to be such a soft touch, Brayden?"

He shrugs. "I blame the wife and kid," he says and chuckles.

"Fine," I say. "But you're responsible for her. Straight up. You keep her far away from me, and you especially keep her away from Bailey."

"Done," he says.

"I'm serious."

"I hear you, Colin," he says. "I promise, I'll keep an eye on her."

I blow out a frustrated sigh and run a hand through my hair. I don't have a good feeling about this. Not at all. I somehow knew this was how it was all going to turn out. Laurel is a snake in the grass. Always has been, always will be. Yeah, I feel bad that nobody is willing to take her in on Christmas, but I also think that shows a hell of a lot about her character, and the kind of person she is.

I take a deep breath and let it out slowly. I can't let her get under my skin. It's Christmas, and my family is here. I have to focus on that, rather than that petty, evil bitch. And I sure as hell won't let her ruin our good time.

"We good?" Brayden asks.

"Yeah," I answer. "We're good."

"Alright, great," he says, clapping me on the shoulder.

We head back into the dining room, and I'm intent on putting this behind us and focusing only on having a good time with my family.

This time of year, family is all that's important.

Chapter Sixteen

Bailey

"Can I just say, I'm really glad that woman didn't come with us," Katie chimes in.

"You and me both," Paige says.

"That makes three of us," Holly agrees.

I sit back in my seat and laugh. I feel a bit bad for Laurel, given the fact that everyone seems to hate her so much. Well – everyone except the boys. I understand where they're coming from, though. She's an old family friend with nowhere to go on Christmas. That has to be one of the loneliest feelings a person can ever experience. But, it forces me to ask myself – why did none of her friends invite her to celebrate Christmas with them? What does that say about who she is?

I always try to give people the benefit of the doubt. I don't know what they've been through or their personal struggles, and I don't know what they're dealing with now. It's not for me to judge. I believe most people can be redeemed, and that at heart, most people are good.

But, less than a day around that woman, and she's really making me reconsider those beliefs.

We're sitting in a spa – the girls all insisted we go out for massages, facials, and mani-pedis. After that, they decided we'd go for lunch. They wanted to make a whole day of it. I've never actually been to a spa, so I'm feeling really out of my comfort zone and awkward.

At the moment, we're all naked, sitting in a pool filled with hot mud. They say it's supposed to be good for the skin, I guess. They picked up on my awkwardness early, and as spa veterans, took me under their wing, so I'm relying on their experience to shepherd me through this bizarre, female-bonding ritual.

"This is one of the perks to being married to a rich guy," Holly says and giggles. "Spa days."

"I'll second that," Paige adds. "I'd never been to a spa before Liam physically picked me up and dropped me off at one for the first time."

"Now, he can't seem to get you out of them," Katie laughs.

Paige throws a bit of mud at her sister-in-law. "Oh, shut up," she says and laughs. "Last I heard, you rack up more frequent flier miles in spas around Savannah than I do."

"Well, that's true," she replies. "But that's only because Aidan forces me to go."

"They love to pamper us," Holly explains to me.

"More like, they like to go out for a beer and a game with their buddies, and keep us busy while they do so," Paige clarifies.

"That too," Holly laughs.

"Hey, I'm happy to go for a spa day whenever my darling husband wants me to," Katie says. "Nothing wrong with pampering ourselves from time to time."

"More like all the time," Paige says.

We all burst into laughter. I can't help it. I love these girls. It's been less than a day, but I feel so at home with them, it feels unbelievable. They seem to accept me for who I am, regardless of my background. They don't judge me for what I have, or what I don't. They aren't criticizing me for how I was raised. They simply talk to me like I'm their equal. Like I'm one of them. And it makes my heart swell with a sense of belonging and joy I've never experienced before.

"So, Bailey, what do you do?" Paige asks.

"Professionally, I'm a paralegal," I say. "I work for a great firm. I do a lot of volunteer work for the poor in Boston. I'm pretty politically active – in fact, that's actually how Colin and I met."

Holly looks at me, with a wry grin on her face. "I have a hard time seeing Colin taking part in a political protest."

"Well, he didn't. Not exactly," I say, feeling my cheeks flush.

"Oh, this sounds good," Katie says. "Do tell."

"Wait. I thought you guys met at an art gallery," Paige says, looking over at Holly. "Isn't that what he told Brayden?"

"Yeah, come to think of it, I thought that's what he said," Holly says.

A lightning bolt of panic shoots through me when I realize I went off-script. I forgot the backstory of this whole fiction. I stammer and start to panic, and suddenly want to dive beneath the mud and never resurface. I just want to leave, run away, and never come back. My heart thumps violently in my chest as I come crashing down from the unbelievable high I've been riding all day.

I'm terrified that if I tell them, they'll tell me I sold out, that I prostituted myself for money and opportunity. I'm terrified they'll tell me I gave my soul as an artist away for access – or harshly judge me for a million other things. I'm so scared that I'm trembling.

Maybe seeing my discomfort, Paige scoots next to me and grips my hand in hers. I don't want this to end. I don't want them to judge or ostracize me from the group for being an outsider. For being a fraud. A phony. For not being who I said I was. I mean, I am, but – I want to punch something so bad right now. Preferably Colin for putting me in this position in the first place.

"Hey, it's okay," Paige says. "Talk to us. You're part of the family. You're our sister now. You can tell us what's going on."

I want to believe every word coming out of her mouth, but I'm afraid to. I screwed up by forgetting the story I was supposed to memorize and remember. I'm afraid that if I tell them, they won't accept me as part of the family, or their sister, any longer. I've never felt as warm and loved for who I am as I have in the presence of these three amazing, strong women. And I've gone and screwed it all up, simply because I couldn't remember a simple white lie.

No, I screwed up in letting Colin talk me into perpetrating this fiction in the first place.

All three women huddle around me, their eyes wide and concerned. Not concerned that I'm a phony but concerned for *me*. Seeing that care in their eyes makes me realize that not only will they *not* judge me, the three of them actually think of me as part of their family – as their sister. I can't explain it, but I know that I don't have to fear their judgment.

I take a deep breath in and let it out slowly. Then, I launch into my story – the real story. I tell them everything from how we met, to our fake engagement, and everything in between. Except for the sex. They don't need to know about that. That's between Colin and me.

"Well, I can't really say I blame him," Holly says with a laugh. "I mean, I hate to say it, but the Anderson boys can be worse than a bunch of old women."

"Yeah, total sewing circle," Paige says, and snickers. "I can totally understand why Colin would want to head that train off before it started."

"I'd like to say that my man wouldn't be party to that," Katie says, "but I'm pretty sure he'd be the loudest one of the bunch."

They all laugh together, and I just watch them, my heart in my throat. I'm still unsure if they really understand what I did or what I'm doing. Paige looks over at me and pulls me to her. Our bodies are slick from the hot mud, and it feels really strange when she hugs me. Not to mention the fact that I've never hugged a naked woman before, which only adds to the awkwardness. Holly and Katie follow suit, each giving me a big hug before settling back into the mud.

As I sit there in silence, I realize that nothing between the four of us has changed. They still see me as one of their own. They aren't judging me or holding it against me. They aren't going to berate me for deceiving them. They just accepted it and moved forward. I'm so overcome with emotion that I almost want to cry. In fact, I feel tears stinging my eyes.

"Whether you've been together for a year, or a few weeks," Holly says, "all that really matters is that he's good to you, and you're good for him."

Katie nods. "There is such a noticeable difference in Colin," she says. "And you're the reason for that, Bailey. All of us can see how happy you've made him."

"There's a light and a fire in his eyes I don't think I've ever seen before," Paige agrees.

"Not in all the time I've known him," Holly says. "I've never actually seen him this happy. Not like this."

"Honestly, I wasn't even sure he knew how to smile," Katie giggles.

We all burst into laughter again, and that overwhelming feeling of camaraderie – of sisterhood – envelops me. It wraps me in its warm, rosy embrace, and squeezes me tight. I've never felt something so good or so pure. I've never felt more accepted or loved for being myself.

"Thank you," I say. "All of you."

"For what, hon?" Paige says.

"For accepting me," I say simply. "For not judging me."

Holly scoffs. "Like any of us have any room to judge," she says. "We've all done things that we're not proud of. All of us."

I look around the mud pool and at the other two women are nodding in agreement.

"It would be incredibly hypocritical for any of us to judge," Paige says. "I mean, what's the big deal? You've been together a few weeks, instead of a few months. So what?"

"I guess, I'm ashamed of the fact that he's paying me to do this," I say. "That I'm using his connections to get a gallery show."

"Sweetie, if that's all you have to be ashamed of, I think you're in pretty good shape," Holly laughs. "I mean, my dad tried to sell me to a Mexican drug cartel."

I stare at her wide-eyed, and she nods. "You're kidding?"

She shakes her head. "Wish I was."

"Liam's ex-wife kidnapped me and then tried to extort him into signing over his company to her," Paige says.

"And my ex tried to sell me into a human trafficking ring," Katie says.

I shift my gaze around the tub, taking in all three of them. Their stories are unbelievable to me. Like something out of a movie – or in this case, three different movies, actually.

"Wow," I say. "Compared to how you all got together, Colin and I seem –"

"Normal?" Holly asks.

I nod. "Yeah," I laugh. "Kind of."

"It's like I told you," Paige says. "The Anderson boys have a thing for taking in the strays."

"That's kind of how I've felt my whole life, to be honest," I say. "Like a stray."

"Well then," Katie says. "You fit right in with the rest of us."

I've never felt such a strong connection or bond to people I've just met in my entire life. It's a nice feeling. A safe feeling. One I could really get used to.

I just hope when this is all over, I get the chance.

Chapter Seventeen

Colin

"What in the hell is she doing here, B?" I ask.

Brayden looks over at Laurel, standing in front of the jukebox as she picks out a new song, swaying to the music. She glances over her shoulder at me, giving me a wolfish smile.

"I'm keeping an eye on her," Brayden says. "Like you told me to do."

"And you had to bring her here?"

He shrugs. "It was either that or send her to the spa with Bailey and the girls," he says. "I figured this was the lesser of two evils."

I sigh. He's got a point. The last thing I want is for Bailey to be trapped somewhere with Laurel. I know how evil she is, and how she'd try and tear Bailey down. It's not an ideal situation, but I guess it's the best we can do.

Turning, I join my other brothers at the bar. They're laughing hysterically about something that happened more than twenty years ago – as if it had just happened.

"You boys need some new material," I say. "Oh wait, don't they say you can't teach an old dog new tricks?"

"Oh, little brother's got jokes," Liam says. "Funny boy."

"Funny looking, maybe," Aidan chimes in.

"I think he looks just fine," Laurel purrs as she saunters over. "Better than fine, actually."

She runs her fingertips across my back as she passes by and slips onto a stool on the other side of Aidan. An awkward silence suddenly descends over the group as everyone decides this is a good time to take a long, hard swallow of beer. *Way to kill a good mood, Laurel.* But then again, she's always been good at that.

"So, anyway," Liam says, trying to break the sudden tension. "What about you and Bailey? How'd you two kids meet?"

"Probably at the organic farmer's market buying patchouli soap," Laurel cracks.

I ignore her and stick to the script I came up with. "At an art gallery opening," I say. "She was exhibiting. I was really struck by her work –"

"Wait, wait, wait," Aidan says, laughing. "When did you become an art aficionado?"

"Not all of us are uncultured heathens like you, dear brother," I say.

"No, not all of us," Brayden says. "But you always were. The closest thing you ever got to art was Japanese anime back in high school."

The three of them break into laughter, howling like it's the funniest thing they've ever heard. I just roll my eyes but can't keep the grin off my face. My brothers are clowns. Always have been, always will be. Life with them was always a three-ring circus. Some things have never changed. Some things, I hope never do.

"How did I know she was an artist?" Laurel says.

"Gee, Laurel," I snap, "I don't know. How did you know?"

She shrugs. "She just gives off that granola hipster vibe, I guess," she says. "So, does she work in finger-paints or paint-by-numbers?"

My face flushed, my temper flaring, I round on her. "What the fuck is your problem?" I nearly shout. "You don't even know her. Who the fuck are you to judge her?"

The bar goes deathly silent, and all eyes turn our way. Brayden steps between us. He grabs Laurel by the arm, practically dragging her out of the bar, and out onto the sidewalk. I can see them arguing through the window.

"Yeah, about that," Liam says. "I'm sorry, little brother. I didn't know –"

I wave him off. "Not your fault," I say. "Not Brayden's fault either. His heart was in the right place. He's right, you know. It's what Dad would have done. He would have told me to suck it up and deal with it for a day. He thought of the Fredericksons as family, and he always taught us to never turn your back on family."

Liam nods. "Unfortunately, that's true," he says.

"I personally can't believe that Dad would have kept a place at the table for her," Aidan says. "Not after what she did."

Liam shrugs. "Yeah, he would've. The Fredericksons were practically family to him," he says. "And you know that when it came to family, Dad was loyal to a fault."

Brayden and a very sulky Laurel come back into the bar. Brayden pats me on the shoulder and murmurs an apology in my ear as he takes his spot next to Liam. Laurel drops down onto the stool beside Aidan again and takes a drink, staring down into her glass, but says nothing. Her silence is a marked improvement from before, at least.

The four of us spend the next couple of hours drinking and catching up, reminiscing about old times, and generally, having a lot of fun. Just like the old days, when we were young and constantly running around together. Good times. The older we get, the more I miss those days.

As brilliant as I think our dad was for dividing the company the way he did, ensuring there would be no fighting amongst the four of us for control, he also did us a huge disservice. By having the four of us run four separate slices of the company, spread out over the continental U.S., he also ensured that we wouldn't be together in the same place all that often.

By trying to save the family, he ended up blowing us all apart.

At least we have times like these where we can get together. Maybe, we even appreciate each other more knowing that our time together is scarce. That scarcity of time together, might be what makes it all the more precious to us.

"How far along is Paige?" I ask.

Liam cocks his head. "Three months, I think," he says. "About that."

"First one married, last one with a kid," Aidan says. "I guess the old man's gun is firing more blanks than live rounds these days, eh?"

Liam cuffs him behind the ear but laughs anyway. "Bunch of damn comedians, all of you," he smirks. "And technically speaking, I'm not the last one with a kid, if you peckerheads stop and think about it."

And just like that, they all turn and stare at me. I feel like a damn bug pinned to a board with the way the four of them are looking at me. Check that, my brothers are looking at me while Laurel is glaring daggers.

"Yeah, you're a bit premature here, fellas," I say. "Hey, isn't that how you ended up with a kid, Brayden?"

"Funny man," he says, laughing as he punches me in the shoulder.

"Seriously, Bailey and I haven't even been together a year," I say, knowing it hasn't even been two months yet. "Let's not rush into anything, okay?"

"That's our baby brother," Liam says. "Always last in everything."

I punch him in the side, which makes him double over, and the rest of us howl with laughter.

"Yeah, yeah, yeah, laugh it up, jackasses," I say, grinning. "I'll be right back."

I set my glass down on the bar and make my way down the long corridor to the bathrooms at the end. I step inside and go to the sink. It's been a while since I've had this much to drink, and I'm feeling the effects. I'm kind of lightheaded and my eyes are glassy. Buzzed. Definitely glad I have my driver waiting out there to cart us around later.

I bend down and am splashing water on my face in. when the door opens behind me. There are a couple of other sinks, so I don't have to worry about monopolizing this one to help me sober up a bit. When I feel a hand on my ass, I jump up quickly and spin around – and find myself face-to-face with Laurel.

"What the fuck do you think you're doing?" I growl.

"Reminiscing," she purrs. "I remember how you felt when you were inside of me. Do you remember that, baby?"

"I try not to," I say. "Because every time I think of you, the only image that pops into my head is my old friend drilling you from behind."

"He meant nothing to me," she says. "He really didn't. I was bored, he was there –"

"He was there for about a year," I say. "Most of the time, when somebody's that bored, they can find a hobby other than fucking their fiancée's best friend."

"I made a mistake, Colin," she pleads. "A terrible mistake. And I've been paying for that mistake all these years. Can't you find it in your heart to forgive me?"

"Sure, I forgive you," I say. "Doesn't mean I want anything to do with you though."

Laurel flashes me a salacious grin before sliding her hand down and clumsily grabbing my dick through my jeans. A grin that I know means she's taking this as a challenge. A game. I grab her hand and yank it off me.

"Don't ever fucking touch me again, Laurel," I snap. "Ever. You got me?"

"Why are you playing so hard to get, Colin?" she whines. "You know how good we were together. You know we belong together. More than you and that short hipster girl ever will."

Listening to her casually dismiss Bailey really pisses me off. The anger inside of me swells to dangerous levels, and I know I need to get out of the bathroom. As if sensing my intentions, Laurel rushes to the door and throws herself in front of it. She reaches behind her and locks it. Not that it will do much good. I'll just move her.

"You put your hand on me again, and I swear to God, I'll start yelling rape," she warns, her voice low.

That's such a low-class move that I have no trouble believing she'd actually do it. I lean back against the sink and fold my arms over my chest.

"What the fuck do you want from me?" I ask.

"You, Colin," she says. "That's all I ever wanted."

"Except for my buddy, and whoever else you were banging at the time."

"I made a mistake," she cries. "I'm not perfect. I fucked up, Colin. I'm sorry."

"Yeah, I heard it all before," I say. "Still not interested. We done here?"

"You know she's not good enough for you," she says. "That ridiculous wannabe, hack artist. You know she can't satisfy you the way I used to."

A cruel grin stretches the corners of my mouth. "You're definitely right about that, Laurel. She can't satisfy me the way you used to."

I see a flicker of hope in her eyes and a smile begins to form upon her lips.

"She satisfies me so much more than you ever did," I say, reveling in watching her face completely fall flat. "She satisfies me in ways you never could have, because unlike you, she's a generous lover. She's not selfish."

"Screw you, Colin," her voice booms, echoing loudly around the small bathroom.

"Not even if you paid me, Laurel."

I slip my phone out of my pocket and call up Brayden's contact on my favorites list. Laurel looks at me with a mixture of pain, rejection, and horror on her face. Brayden picks up on the first ring.

"Hey, B," I say. "You need to come get your girl. She's locked me in the bathroom with her and won't let me out."

I disconnect the call and drop the phone in my pocket, folding my arms across my chest again, as I wait for the cavalry to arrive.

Tears streak down Laurel's cheeks as she looks at me with undisguised contempt.

"What the hell happened to you?" she sneers.

"I grew up," I say. "I moved on. Clearly, you didn't."

"Fuck you, Colin."

All I can do is laugh and shake my head. Brayden knocks on the door, and for a moment, I'm half-convinced that Laurel isn't going to unlock it and let me leave. But, she eventually relents, and unlocks the door. Brayden steps inside, and steps between us. I use the distraction to slip behind the both of them, and head out of the bathroom.

I walk back through the bar, pulling my phone out again. I stop at the bar where Liam and Aidan are still drinking and yakking it up.

"Hey guys," I say. "I'm going to call another car and head home."

"What?" Liam asks. "Why? There's still plenty of daylight left to burn."

Brayden and a very sullen Laurel emerge from the bathroom, and walk over to us. Laurel follows a step or two behind Brayden, looking like a child who's just gotten one hell of a verbal spanking.

"Because I'm not going to spend any more of my free time with her," I say, nodding over at the approaching leggy blonde. "I'd rather spend my time with people who actually deserve it. So, I'll see you back at my place in a bit."

I walk away from my brothers just as Laurel and Brayden reclaim their spots at the bar. More and more people are starting to filter in, so it looks like I picked the right time to bail anyway. I might be going through a lot of changes, but one thing that hasn't changed is that I still detest crowds.

I step out of the bar, and into the cool evening air, doing my best to regain my composure, and push everything that just happened out of my head. For good.

I'm sitting in the kitchen, having a cup of coffee and reading a book, doing my best to enjoy the quiet and solitude of my home while the girls are out on their spa day, the children are with a nanny, and my brothers are still out at the pub. After leaving them, I decided to come home to unwind and relax for a bit. The scene with Laurel in the bathroom really keyed me up.

It sobered me up real quick, and forced me to stop drinking, so at least I'm not going to spend the rest of the day drunk or dealing with a hangover. Silver linings. You have to take them where you can find them sometimes.

A few minutes later, the front door bursts open, and the loud, booming voices of my brothers echo throughout the house. I close the book with a sigh, setting it down on the table. The fact that they're home means Laurel is with them, which means things are going to be tense and awkward all over again.

Honestly, I should just put her back on the jet and send her home, avoiding any possible drama altogether. But then, as I ponder doing just that, I'm stabbed with a renewed sense of guilt all over again. I used to care about Laurel a great deal – I can't deny that. Our relationship eventually became toxic, like poison in my veins. But her family was always there for us growing up, and as much as I'd like to ignore it and send her away, I can't. I have too much of my father in me, apparently.

The click-clack of heels on the hardwood floor draws my attention, and when I look up, I see Laurel standing in the rounded archway of the kitchen. I feel my body tense, and the tide of anger, hot and explosive, begins rising in my body.

"What do you want?" I ask, my voice low and menacing.

Laurel crosses the kitchen, a sheepish, almost remorseful look on her face. I don't ask her to join me, but she sits down at the table across from me anyway, seemingly unable to meet my eyes. I pick up my coffee mug, and take a long swallow of the dark, rich brew, my eyes never leaving hers. She reaches out and drags my book over to her, a faint smile on her face as she reads the title.

Laurel finally looks up at me, and I can see her eyes are rimmed with red. She looks like she's been crying. Though, I've known her long enough, and well enough, to understand that Laurel is a fantastic actress, and can cry on command when she's trying to elicit a little extra sympathy. I wasn't kidding when I said the woman is a master manipulator. I sometimes used to wonder if she was a sociopath, honestly.

"Aren't you gonna offer me a cup of coffee?" she asks, her voice trembling.

"The pot's over there," I say coldly. "Help yourself."

She leans back in her seat and seems to fold in on herself a little bit. I have to say, the expression on her face is one of pure misery. She looks distraught. But then, with Laurel, you never know what's real, and what isn't. That's the problem with being a manipulative bitch – after people see you for what you actually are, they tend to not trust you.

"Listen," she says. "I know you went out on a limb by inviting me here. And I know I've been a little shit since I arrived –"

"Yeah, just a little," I scoff.

She winces as she silently absorbs another verbal blow. Seeing the look of misery on her face – though well-deserved – starts to make me feel a little guilty.

Damn, and I was just getting onto Brayden about being a soft touch.

"At the bar – I had a little too much to drink," she says. "Combine that with being lonely and completely jealous, because even now, after all that's happened, I still want you. Anyway, I know that I acted inappropriately. I crossed the line and I know it. I'm sorry, Colin. I swear to you that it won't happen again."

"It better not, Laurel," I say. "I invited you into my home because of what your family meant to mine for all those years. This isn't about us anymore. Anything romantic between the two of us died a long time ago."

"I know that. In my head, at least," she says weakly. "But, in my heart, I still belong to you, Colin. And you still belong to me. All these years, knowing just how badly I screwed up – it's been slowly killing me. You were the best thing that ever happened to me, and I threw it all away."

"Yes, you did," I say. "But, it's probably for the best anyway. I don't think the two of us would have lasted, Laurel. We're just too different."

She shakes her head. "That's not true, and you know it," she says. "You and I were always good together. We'd still be good together."

"I don't think so," I say. "But, the point is completely moot anyway. It's not going to happen, so there's no use in even thinking about it anymore."

She sniffs and wipes away the tears that roll down her cheeks. "I know," she says. "And that's my fault."

I let out a long breath. "At this point, it doesn't matter whose fault it was. All that matters is that we both carry on with our lives. Move forward and stop dwelling on the past. I have. You can too."

She shakes her head. "I'll never find somebody like you, Colin."

"You haven't even looked," I say. "And besides, I'm just a guy. There are plenty of guys out there who would love to be with you. I know it."

For the life of me, I can't think of a single one. But then, I can't say I know any masochists who like being used, abused, and cheated on. I suppose there might be somebody who fits that bill, though.

She sighs dejectedly, scrubbing a lone tear off her cheek.

"Let's just focus on having a nice Christmas together," I offer. "We'll have some great food, open some gifts – let's have a great time as friends. What do you say?"

"I'd be okay with that," she says. "So – you forgive me?"

I give her a small smile. "Sure," I say. "Now, let's just focus on enjoying ourselves for the rest of the holidays."

"I'd like that."

"Good," I reply. "Well, let's go and see what my brothers are doing, besides drinking all the best liquor in my cabinet."

We're walking across the foyer together when the front door opens, and all of the girls come spilling through in a riot of laughter, their voices echoing all around us.

I turn to the doorway and see Bailey stepping into the house, and when our eyes meet, I can feel the tangible energy, maybe love, even, passing between us. I smile wider and have to resist the impulse to rush over, scoop her up, and keep her right beside me.

I hear a dismissive little snort, and don't need to turn to know that Laurel is walking away in a huff. Guess she wasn't really all that sorry after all.

Chapter Eighteen

Bailey

"What a day," I say.

Finally, in some comfy clothes after a long, but wonderful day, I plop down on the couch in front of the fireplace, letting the roaring fire warm me. With the sun down outside, it's downright bone chilling, and the fire feels nice. Colin hands me a mug of hot cocoa to warm me from the inside, while the fire warms my outside. I grasp the mug in both hands, enjoying the feeling of the warm ceramic. Even though I take a small sip, it still burns my lip and tongue, so I put it down on the table beside me for a minute to cool off.

"So, did you have a good time?" he asks.

"Oh my God, the best," I say. "I absolutely love those girls. They are amazing women."

"Yeah, they are," he says. "They're unique, but all of them are incredible in their own way."

He joins me on the sofa, sitting closer than I was expecting him to. Not that I'm complaining. It's nice to have his big, strong body next to mine.

"What can I say," he goes on. "We Anderson boys know how to pick a woman."

I feel my cheeks flush when he gives me that panty-dropping smile of his. Colin holds his own mug in his hands, cradling it almost protectively. Part of me thinks it's a pity that he's keeping his hands so busy, but I push that thought away. Even though everybody should be asleep upstairs, we probably shouldn't do anything naughty down here.

"I really had the best time with them, Colin," I say. "I mean, I haven't had a whole lot of girlfriends in my life, because honestly, I've met more women like Laurel, than Katie, Holly, or Paige – but those three, seriously, I would hang out with every day. They are super smart and hilarious."

"They seem to have taken to you pretty quickly, too," he says.

"I'm really glad, too," I say. "I was really worried about it. Especially after the horror stories you told me about your overbearing family."

"Well, technically, I only said my brothers are overbearing," he says. "Which, they are."

"And how did things go with them today?"

"It was really great hanging out with them. Made me realize how much I miss them," he says. "Of course, I always say the same exact thing this time of year."

"Doesn't make it any less true."

"No, no it doesn't," he admits wistfully. "Sometimes, I'd really like to have my brothers around more often."

"Only sometimes?"

He nods. "I think if we were in close proximity for more than a few days, we'd eventually kill each other," he says and laughs. "No, seriously, it would be nice to see them more than once a year, though."

I reach over and take his hand, giving it a gentle squeeze. I can see by the faint little smile on his lips, that the memories and nostalgia of his childhood are washing over him. He's thinking about those bygone days of his youth, likely, recalling all of the misadventures he and his hell-raising brothers got themselves into.

A moment later, he gives his head a shake and seems to snap out of it. He looks over at me, and smiles. But, a moment after that, the smile slips a bit, and a frown pulls the corners of his mouth down.

"What is it?" I ask.

"There was an incident with Laurel earlier," he says, and scratches at his beard.

"What kind of an incident?"

He lets out a long breath and tells me what happened in the bathroom at the bar. He didn't really need to tell me every last detail – but, Colin is nothing if not honest and totally transparent with me at all times. It's one thing I really appreciate about him. When he's done with his story, I lean back on the couch and let out a long breath.

"Wow," I say. "She really is something."

"That's one word for it," he grumbles.

"I'm sure it feeds your ego, though," I say. "To know, that all these years later, your ex-fiancée is still carrying a flame for you."

"Hardly."

"So, was it a good day overall?" I ask, trying to navigate the conversation away from Laurel.

He nods. "It really was."

"Then I'm glad," I say. "You deserve some good days. You deserve the best, actually."

"As do you."

We lean toward each other and kiss for a moment. My lips tingle, and I feel fingers of fire racing along my skin, as our tongues touch and swirl together in my mouth. Slowly, we pull back, the energy of that kiss, and the taste of his mouth, fresh on my lips. My heart is racing and my head is spinning. I wish I could have him right here on this couch.

Damn. This man has a *powerful* hold over me.

I clear my throat. "So, would you have let her?" I ask.

"Let her what?"

"Give you a hand job in that bathroom if I weren't around?" I ask.

"You weren't around," he teases. "You were at the spa with the girls.

I giggle and slap him on the chest. "You know what I mean."

"I could have. She was ready to go. I'm pretty sure she would have done anything and everything I asked of her," he says. "But, I didn't. Did I?"

"And why didn't you?"

"Clearly somebody needs her ego stroked somethin' fierce tonight," he says and laughs.

"Damn straight, now get to it," I say and laugh.

"It's because of you," he says. "Because all I could think about – all I can ever seem to think about these days – is you."

My heart feels like it's melting into a puddle of goo in the center of my chest, and all I can do is muster a smile for him. I don't know why, but I'm surprised to hear such honesty from him. His words catch me off guard, but sound like the sweetest music I've ever heard.

"You're good for me," he says.

"The girls all seem to think so," I say.

"Like you said, they're very smart women."

"That they are," I reply. "That they are."

"Do you think if she hadn't been a cheating whore, that you and Laurel would have worked out?" I ask, genuinely curious.

He shakes his head. "I don't know. I'd like to think the answer to that would be no," he says. "But, until I met you, I was a lot different. I put up with a lot more because it was all I knew. Now that you're a part of my life, the answer is most definitely no. In fact, it's a fuck no. All caps."

I laugh but feel my heart stutter in my chest as I listen to him speak.

"For one thing," he continues. "She's the most uptight person on the planet."

I laugh. "I think she came in second in that category."

He gives me a long, unamused expression. "Funny girl."

"I do my best," I say.

Colin smiles a little wider, and we share a look – a moment. And then the thought really solidifies in my mind – that I want to share a lot more of these moments with him. I want to be with Colin. This man fills my heart with joy and gives me pleasure I never dreamed possible. We are good together – we make a perfect team. I can only hope he understands and believes that himself.

I reach for my cocoa, cupping it in my hands to distract myself from the thoughts of his lips pressed to my mouth – or more sensitive spots. He does the same, and we sit there, for a moment, just sitting side-by-side, savoring our warm beverages, and the even warmer fire.

My hands are trembling though, and I don't know why. I guess being this close to him brings out the shy, awkward girl inside me. I bring the warm mug to my lips to take a drink, but thanks to my shaking hands, I spill some down the front of my shirt. It's still pretty hot, and I jump in surprise when it scalds me, making me jump again, and I spill even more on me and the couch.

I am such a hot mess right now, I swear.

"Oh my God, I'm sorry, Colin," I say, putting the cup down on the table again.

"It's alright," he says. "Here, let me grab some napkins."

He rushes off as I examine the damage I wrought. My shirt can be replaced – that I'm not worried about, at all. His furniture can be replaced too, of course, but it's expensive, and it's not mine, so I'm a little more worried about that.

Still reeling from my clumsiness, I don't even notice when Colin comes back into the room. He starts dabbing at the couch, mere inches from me. He hands me a towel, and I start to help clean up as best I can.

"See? That's not so bad," he says.

I notice he's not looking at his sofa when he speaks though. Instead, he's gazing down at me. I swallow the lump forming in my throat, and my heart races as we lock eyes. With him towering over me, I feel so small, and yet, it somehow feels sexy. Or maybe, it's just the look in his eye doing that to me.

He reaches out and touches my cheek, caressing it gently. It sends shivers racing down my spine, and still feels like the most natural thing in the world. I stand up, and he takes my face in his hands, bringing me closer to him. He holds me like that, pressed up against his body, as our mouths meet. I gasp as his tongue parts my lips and touches mine. He steals the breath right out of me, and I can't help but softly moan.

There's a soft rug in front of the fireplace, and he leads me over to it. The warmth of the blaze feels amazing against my skin, as does Colin's touch upon my body. He pulls at my pajama shirt, and I raise my arms as he lifts it off over my head, leaving me in my bra. Never taking his gaze from mine, he reaches around and removes that too. His fingers are nimble and deft, and he has it off in record time.

"Impressive," I say with a giggle.

"I'm a man who knows how to get what he wants."

"Yes, you are," I confirm, my voice a little breathy.

My bra joins my pajama top on the floor beneath us, and his mouth moves down to my breasts. Gently sucking on my nipple, and cupping my breast with his other hand, Colin stares up at me.

I can't deny this feeling any longer. I want him. I need him. God, my body aches for him in ways it's never yearned for another man before.

"Colin," I whimper, as I throw my head back. "Yes, Colin, please —"

I don't even know what I'm asking for, honestly, I just crave his touch, his mouth, his cock, so bad, I want it all at once. But, Colin seems to know exactly what I want. He drops to his knees before me, yanking my pajama bottoms down with him as he goes, panties and all, in one fell swoop. In the blink of an eye, I'm naked and bare in front of him now, fully exposed. Self-consciousness ripples through me, but it ebbs quickly when I see the way he's staring up at me, like I'm the most beautiful woman he's ever seen – something I'll never get tired of seeing.

He moves his hands along the skin of my legs, and his breath is hot against my flesh. He pushes my legs apart, dotting kisses along the sensitive flesh of my inner thighs, making me squirm a bit as he approaches the white-hot center of me. Never taking his eyes off mine, he gently kisses my wet, swollen lips, his tongue darting between the folds. Teasing me. Taunting me. Driving me crazy with desire and need.

I moan quietly, and my knees threaten to give out, but he holds me in place. With the zeal of a ravenous man, he pushes his face forward, diving into me. His tongue circles my clit, and I cry out. I can't keep quiet, even though I'm trying. The sensations are almost overwhelming. When my legs start shaking, Colin pulls his mouth away briefly and looks at me.

"Lay down," he says, his tone gruff and commanding.

I do as he says instantly, laying down on top of the soft rug, and he joins me. A salacious little smile on his face, he parts my thighs, and his mouth goes right back to my pussy. I cry out as he devours my body like it's the sweetest of desserts. His tongue explores the deepest parts of me. And where his tongue can't reach, his fingers make up for it. First one finger, then two, drive me to a state of absolute bliss.

My back arches off the floor as he inserts a third finger, pushing it deep inside of me. He watches my reaction, his face wet with me as my orgasm rocks my body to the core. His fingers rub against the walls of my pussy as he flicks his tongue on my clit.

"Mm, Colin," I whisper. "Oh, my God, yes."

With my hands in his hair, I pull him upward. Still reeling from my orgasm, I already know I need more of him. I need all of him. And he's more than happy to oblige. He kisses me, his mouth and tongue grazing the skin on my stomach as he moves upward. He's taking his time, enjoying my body, not rushing, and it feels amazing. Even though I'm quivering with anticipation, and desperate to feel his glorious, delicious cock deep inside of me, I love feeling his mouth on my body.

I pull on his shirt, and together, we fumble with the buttons. I'm in such a hurry to get him naked, that I mess up and fail to unbutton a single one. He chuckles and helps me, until his shirt slides off onto the floor next to my bra. His chest, bare and beautiful, is a sight to behold. I trace the smooth muscles of his chest with my fingers, admiring the work of art that he is. I'm so engrossed with soaking in every detail of his hard, toned body, that I don't even notice him reaching for his wallet until I see him ripping open the condom package.

But first, his pants need to come off. He makes quick work of those, kicking them onto the floor with the rest of our clothes. His hands move lower, and I watch with wide eyes as he slips the rubber over his shaft, quickly sliding it down. He's so thick and perfect, he makes my body ache. I can't wait to feel him inside of me, to stretch me open fully, as he plunges himself deep inside. Once he's got the condom in place, our bodies come together. He's not inside me, not yet. He's holding himself back, but I feel him rubbing against my opening.

We explore each other's mouths with our tongues, our hands exploring every inch of each other's flesh. His cock continues rubbing against me, the head pressing slightly into me until I groan, begging him.

"Please, Colin," I mewl. "Please, I need you inside me."

My back arches upward at the same moment he thrusts himself into me, and my body opens up to him. Moaning, I dig my nails into his back as he fills me up, stretching me wide open. He stares deep into my eyes as he moves inside of me, and I know, beyond the shadow of a doubt, that this is more than just fucking for him. This is real. There's a connection between us beyond just sex, and it's magical. It makes every movement, every flick of the tongue, every thrust of his cock, that much more vibrant, and intense.

Slowly, he rocks back and forth on his knees, moving in and out of me at a deliberate pace. Each time he enters me, I gasp, surprised at how amazing and erotic it feels to be filled, over and over again. My body tingles with electricity and I never want this to end.

The fire crackles beside us, his skin golden in the flickering light. He continues moving inside of me, a thin sheen of sweat coating his body as he moves with expert precision. I see his jaw clench, and he squeezes his eye shut. I can tell he's trying not to lose control too soon. Each thrust brings him closer and closer to the edge, but I'm right there with him though. Our bodies work together, moving in perfect synchronicity. I feel like we were born to be together like this. Like being together was destined for us.

Colin growls, and his movements suddenly become even more intense, his breathing more desperate.

Colin's mouth explores my neck and chest, kissing me passionately as he continues burying himself deep inside of me. A spasm hits me, hard, making me draw in a sharp breath. Then another. I moan, then cry out.

I dig my nails deeper into his back, raking his flesh, and he lets out a sharp hiss. I wrap my legs around his waist, pulling him down, and holding him even closer to me. We're moving together in perfect unison, and I feel the familiar pressure building up deep within me. And then the dam of my resolve breaks, and I give myself over to a heaving, shuddering orgasm. I bite down hard on my hand to keep from screaming out as my pussy tightens around his cock, milking him as I come.

That sends him over the top. He stares into my eyes, a look of pure bliss etched on his face as he thrusts into me one last time. He grabs hold of my legs, lifting them up and thrusts once more, so he's as deep as he can possibly go. The noise that comes out of him is primal. Animalistic. I can feel his cock swelling within me before it bursts. As I let that wave of sensation wash over me, I cry out his name, and we come together, my body trembling, my breathing ragged.

Totally spent, Colin collapses on top of me before rolling over onto his side. Both of us are staring up at the vaulted ceiling, desperately trying to catch our breath. Slowly, our breathing returns to normal, and when it does, he lifts his head to kiss me, softly, on the lips. When he does though, I see his eyes shift upward, as if he's staring at something behind us.

"What is it?" I ask, turning to look.

"I thought I saw someone. Probably nothing but me being paranoid," he says with a small chuckle as he takes my face in his hands and turns it back to him. "Probably just the light playing tricks on me."

He kisses me again, this time his mouth lingers longer on mine, as he strokes my face. I feel so warm and safe with him, and in that moment, I can't imagine ever having any doubts about us being together when this is all over. When we return to our normal lives. Don't get me wrong, I love my new family, but I'm craving some time alone with him. I'm ready to explore the burgeoning feelings within both of us, free of outside interruption or influence. And free of the fucking drama a psycho ex-fiancée inevitably brings.

I think we've both earned it. I think we both deserve it.

Chapter Nineteen

Bailey

It's Christmas Eve, and everybody is in good spirits – even Laurel, it seems. We've spent a leisurely day eating, playing in the snow, and hanging out. There's been no drama, and no tension. It's been utterly glorious.

I've spent a lot of the day hanging out with Holly, Paige, and Katie – Laurel, though she hasn't been unpleasant or anything, has chosen to remain separate from the four of us. She's been spending most of her time with the boys, drinking, and reminiscing about their shared past. Something I can't share or take part in.

There's some small, obsequious part of me that thinks she keeps dredging up memories of the past to remind Colin how much they all meant to each other. Just another means of trying to drive a wedge between us – a wedge large enough for her tall, blonde, leggy ass. And I hate her more and more with each passing hour because of it.

Yeah, you can call me Tom Petty – or just Petty for short, if you prefer.

"Don't let her get to you," Paige says. "That's what she wants, you know. She wants to make you look like the psycho, unhinged one."

"Classic gaslighting," Katie says. "She excels at it."

"It shouldn't bother me," I say. "I know it shouldn't. But she really gets under my skin."

We're sitting in the kitchen, having a cup of coffee and some pastries out for us. The two small kids are sitting in a playpen set up off the side, entertaining each other. I watch them play for a few moments, a faint smile touching my lips.

"Uh-oh, I know that look," Holly says.

I turn to her and cock my head. "What look is that?"

The three women exchange a look and a laugh. "It's the look that says you hear your biological clock ticking," Holly says.

I laugh. "You're crazy," I say. "I'm only twenty-three. My biological clock is hardly ticking. I'm barely more than a baby myself."

Paige waves me off. "These two weren't much older than you when they got knocked up," she says. "I think you two were both, what, twenty-four?"

Katie and Holly nod in agreement, and Paige looks at me with a bemused little grin.

"I'm the old spinster of the group here," she says. "I didn't get pregnant until after I turned twenty-six."

"Something you need to know is that the Anderson boys have magic sperm," Katie says. "They can impregnate anybody, at any time."

We all burst into laughter, the sudden eruption of mirth making the two kids join in with their goofy grins, and cooing sounds.

"Not to get too personal or anything," Holly says, "but, are you and Colin – you know – sexually active?"

My mind flashes back to the rug in front of the fireplace just last night, and I feel the heat flooding my cheeks.

"I think we know the answer to that," Katie laughs.

"Have you gone to see if you're pregnant yet?" Paige asks.

I laugh. "We always use protection," I say. "I don't think either of us wants any happy little accidents."

Katie and Holly share a look and a laugh between themselves. I look over at Paige, who's grinning like a fool.

"What?" I ask.

"We were always safe too," Holly says. "Yeah, like we said, that magic Anderson sperm – somehow, it finds a way."

A ripple of nervousness passes through me at the thought of being pregnant. Colin and I haven't actually discussed being together – like a real couple – when this weekend is over. Which means, we're nowhere close to discussing having children. I suddenly feel a little lightheaded, and don't want to freak out about the possibility.

"Oh, God," I say.

Paige scoffs. "Don't let them freak you out," she says, a knowing smile still on her lips. "They don't actually have magic sperm –"

"Pretty sure they do," Katie says.

"I'm pretty sure any one of the Anderson boys could impregnate a brick wall."

I giggle and shake my head, but I'm still freaking out on the inside. I'm that duck on the pond all over again, thinking about the possibility of being pregnant. But, what are the odds of two different women, married to two different men of the same family, experiencing condom failure? Astronomical, right?

The thought only freaks me out that much more.

"I haven't had any symptoms," I say. "I mean, I'm not late, I don't have morning sickness –"

"Chances are, you're probably not," Paige says. "These two are some kind of statistical anomaly or something. I mean, look at me. I didn't get pregnant until Liam and I were ready."

"It just freaks me out," I say. "I mean, I don't even know if Colin is going to want to be with me after this. I can't imagine what he'd do if I turned up pregnant."

"Oh, trust me, sweetie," Paige says, "that boy is off the market."

"Head over heels for you," Katie adds. "The fact that he didn't bang that skank in the bathroom should tell you all you need to know."

I was going to ask her how she knew about that, but I answer the question for myself – the brothers. They must share everything. Holly takes my hand in hers and gives me a gentle smile.

"You'll probably want to have the discussion about kids with him at some point," she says. "Because, based on what I see? There's no way he's going to let you go once this is over."

"When what's over?"

We all turn to the sound of Laurel's voice as she enters the kitchen, mimosa in hand.

"Coffee hour, apparently," Katie says. "I should probably change Charlie's diaper."

"Yeah, I think Jace needs to be changed as well," Holly says.

"I'll help," Paige says.

All three women jump up, take the kids, and beat a hasty retreat from the kitchen. I see a flicker of sadness and anger flash across Laurel's face. She silently walks over to the table and sits down across from me. She looks down at the pastries and takes a glazed donut from the platter, setting it down on a plate. She picks at it for a few minutes, tearing off small piece and popping it into her mouth. She chews slowly, her gaze fixed on me.

"Aren't you going to leave too?" she asks. "Make it a clean sweep?"

I shrug, but say nothing, and take a sip of my coffee. I know I should probably leave. Even just sitting here, I can feel the open hostility radiating off of the woman. But, there's a part of me that wants to talk to her. Part of me thinks, if she can see who I am as a person, she couldn't possibly hate me. We've never had a conversation before, so she doesn't know the first thing about me. Maybe, if she knew –

"He deserves better, you know," she says, taking a long swallow of her mimosa.

"Excuse me?"

"Colin. He deserves better than you could ever give him," she replies so casually, I want to slap her across the face.

"You don't even know me," I say.

"Don't need to, and don't want to," she replies. "I know your type."

"Oh? And what type is that?"

"That's a nice dress you have on," Laurel says. "Did you buy that yourself?"

I look down at the vintage-style, cream dress with black polka dots, the sudden detour in the conversation giving me a case of whiplash. It's a cute dress, and one that I fell in love with, the moment I saw it.

"I don't think that's any of your business," I say.

"I think that says it all," she replies, a malicious grin on her face. "Tells me a lot about you. Like the fact that you're low-class, low-rent, poor, white trash. Oh, and that you're a wannabe artist too. Which is so cliché. Honestly, I have no idea how you and Colin hooked up, but he's a good man, with a good, generous heart."

"Yes, he is," I snap. "Which is more than I can say for you."

She shrugs it off casually. "Girls like you see a man like him, and they automatically see dollar signs."

"That is not true!" I object.

She scoffs. "You know it is," she says. "You're using him for his money."

"You're a real bitch."

"The truth hurts," she says. "I can see you trying to worm your way into his life –"

"Yeah, I am, because I care about him," I snap. "And I didn't have to try to do it by offering to suck his dick in the fucking bathroom of some shitty bar. What kind of a slut does that, I wonder?"

She looks for a moment like I slapped her across the face. She didn't expect me to know that, apparently. Laurel quickly recovers though and clears her throat.

"You could never offer him what I can, little girl," she says.

"Little girl? Who in the hell do you think you're talking to?"

"A gold digger," she says flatly. "A low-rent piece of human garbage who's looking for a sugar daddy."

"Fuck you!" I shout.

"Exactly," she says. "You can never be the refined, classy kind of woman he needs. The kind who understands the world he exists in. He doesn't move in the soup kitchen, dumpster diving circles, dear."

"My God, how in the hell did Colin ever get mixed up with a judgmental, evil bitch like you in the first place?"

"Because Colin and I understand each other," she says. "We grew up together. Share a lot of the same views, same morals –"

"Morals?" I scoff. "You really shouldn't be talking about things you have no idea about."

A faint smile touches her lips. "You do realize you're just an amusement to him, don't you?" she says. "That you're merely a play-thing he's using to keep himself entertained for a while? He's never going to marry you."

"That's not true," I say, my voice low, but lacking any sort of real conviction.

"It's very true, actually," she says. "You forget, I know him better than anybody. I know when he's really into somebody, and when he's just getting his rocks off. Sad for you, you're in the latter category. Poor little Bailey."

"You're a liar," I say. "You're nothing but a manipulative, jealous, bitch."

"Perhaps," she says. "But, that doesn't make what I said untrue. If you really stop and think, it kind of gives my words a little more weight. Colin, according to you, hates me. If that's true, he's never going to give me the time of day again. So, why would I tell you that he's just not that into you? It wouldn't benefit me at all."

"Because you play games. That's what you do," I hiss. "You play games and ruin people's lives for fun. And you do it because you live such a sad, pathetic, lonely existence that nobody even wanted to spend Christmas with you, and you had to beg Colin's brothers to bring you along. That's how much of a rancid bitch you are, Laurel. That you had to use somebody's compassion and pity for you, just so you didn't have to spend the holidays all by yourself."

My words seem to hit her a little hard. She winces, and looks away for a moment, and I swear I see a shimmer of tears in her eyes.

Clearly, my words were a direct hit. Good. I want her to hurt. I want her to feel low. Worthless. I want her to feel just how much everybody hates her. She deserves it.

A few silent, tense seconds later, Laurel seems to gather herself. Her face hardens and her eyes narrow, and she clenches that strong jawline of hers. When she looks at me, it's with nothing but contempt and hatred.

"You will only drag him down, you know," she says. "Turn him into something he's not. If you care about him, you should let him go. Let him be with somebody who actually understands his world and can walk with him in it as his equal."

I stand up so quickly, I knock the chair over behind me, not bothering to stop and pick it up. I glare daggers at Laurel, my stomach roiling, the rage inside of me building to a crescendo. It's been a long time since I last threw a punch, but I'm really considering breaking that streak.

No. She's not worth it. It's Christmas Eve. Brawling with Laurel will only cause drama for everybody, and this day is supposed to be about family. About fun. The last thing I want to do is ruin the day for everybody – no matter how much an evil bitch Laurel is. She's just not worth it.

"By the way," she says. "I saw some of your so-called art. It's cute. I guess. But, I'm pretty sure Jace and Charlie in there could probably put together something just as – profound."

I bite my tongue so hard, the coppery taste of blood fills my mouth. I will not cry. I will not let this woman see me cry. She's not worth my tears. She's not worth anything.

I turn and stalk out of the kitchen, my mind whirling a thousand miles a minute, my heart sinking into the bile in my stomach, and my gut churning. Her throaty laughter follows me all the way out, seeming to echo louder in my head with each step I take away from her.

Bounding up a back staircase so nobody can see me, I run to my room, and shut the door. I throw myself down on the bed and let the tears flow.

———

About an hour later, the tears have dried up, and my stomach has stopped doing somersaults. I'm sitting on the daybed, my knees drawn up to my chest, staring out the windows at the winter wonderland beyond the glass. There's part of me that longs to go running out into the snow back there and disappear. Never come back.

I hate to admit it, but Laurel's words got to me. They burrowed deep beneath my skin. I mean, I know I shouldn't let them. On one level, I know she said what she did just to get to me. Just to make me start to doubt myself, and what Colin and I have. I know she's trying to drive a wedge between us.

On the other hand, though, because there's still so much I don't know about Colin, what if there's some small kernel of truth to her words? What if this is all just a game to him. An amusement? What if she's right, and I'm nothing more than a plaything to him?

I know I shouldn't listen to her. I shouldn't give her words one ounce of credence. In my head, and intellectually, I know that.

But, in my heart, I hear something else. All of my own insecurities have come out to play. My own self-doubts. My own fears. I hear them loud and clear, and they're louder than anything else.

I lean my forehead against the glass, and stare out into the backyard, my heart heavy, my mind buzzing. There's a soft knock on the door, and it swings inward. Paige steps in and spots me sitting on the daybed.

"There you are," she says. "We were looking for you."

I give her a weak smile. "Here I am."

She sees I've been crying, and a look of concern flashes across her features. She sits down in front of me and takes my hands in hers.

"What did she do?" she asks, her tone cold.

I shake my head. "Nothing," I say. "It's fine."

"The hell it is," she says. "Look at you."

"It's Christmas Eve," I say. "I'm not going to stir up drama and ruin everybody's holiday."

Paige sighs and lowers her head. She knows I'm right. After a few minutes of silence, she looks back up at me.

"Tell me anyway," she says. "Get the poison out of your system, then we'll figure out how to best deal with it."

I hesitate, but finally tell her everything. With each word I speak, I see her expression growing darker and darker. When I finally finish, she blows out a long, exasperated breath.

"That bitch," she says.

"Tell me about it," I say. "But, this is between us. I don't want to ruin the holidays for anybody. Please."

Paige looks at me, her dark eyes that look so much like my own boring straight into me. I see her mind working, trying to find a way to get rid of Laurel, but not ruin Christmas. Eventually, I see in her eyes, she comes to the same conclusion I did an hour ago – it's impossible to get rid of her without causing all kinds of chaos and drama. And nobody wants that.

"We'll sit on it for now," Paige says. "But you better believe that she's going to get what's coming to her."

I give her a small, wavering smile. "Thank you," I say.

"Nobody screws with my sister like that and lives to tell the tale," she says. "She is going to pay a heavy price for what she did. Just you wait and see."

Leaning forward, Paige pulls me into a tight hug. I wrap my arms around her, letting her embrace me. I draw strength from her touch – I'm just glad it's not a naked, mud-covered hug this time. It's *way* less awkward this way.

She lets me go and sits back, a lopsided little smile on her face. "Come down and join us," she says. "And don't worry, I'll keep that evil whorebag away from you."

"Thank you, Paige," I say. "You and the girls have been so good to me from the start. I just – I can't put into words how much I appreciate that."

"Hey, you're family now," she says. "Nobody screws with family."

Family. Not a word I've heard much in my life. But, one I definitely wouldn't mind getting used to hearing.

Chapter Twenty

Colin

Our traditional Christmas Eve dinner is a huge success. Everybody is drinking, eating, and having a good time. Well, except for Bailey. Oh, she's putting up a good front, laughing and joking along with the girls. But, I can see something hidden in her eyes. There's a masked sadness. A darkness that wasn't there before.

Something happened. I just don't know what. And every time I've tried to talk to her about it, she's blown it off. Earlier, she told me that nothing was wrong, and that she's totally fine. Her words say one thing, but her eyes tell me something else. And I'm sitting here, trying to figure out if it's something I've done – or haven't done – that's upset her.

It's getting late – closing in on one in the morning – and everyone is heading to bed. Tomorrow's the big day, so we won't be sleeping too late. Thankfully, the kids aren't old enough yet to wake us up at the crack of dawn to open gifts. We'll be able to get up at a decent hour, have a nice breakfast, and then spend the rest of the day leisurely opening gifts, and enjoying the day with each other.

At least, that's the plan. I just need to figure out what's wrong with Bailey and see if I can fix it.

I catch her before she heads upstairs, taking her hand, and leading her into the den. I look into her eyes and can see there's something she's struggling with. Whatever it is, it's really weighing on her.

"What is it?" I ask. "And don't tell me nothing's wrong, because I can see right through that bullshit."

A rueful grin touches her lips. "Really, Colin, it's nothing," she says. "It's no big deal. I'll handle it."

"Is it something I've done?" I ask. "Something I didn't do?"

She shakes her head. "No, nothing like that," she says. "It's not you, it's me."

I look at her for a long moment with my eyebrow arched at her. "Really?"

She chuckles and shakes her head. "Sorry, it's just been a long few days. My brain's not working right," she says. "I just need a good night's sleep, that's all."

I stare at her intently, desperately trying to read her thoughts. "You sure?"

She nods. "Absolutely. Scout's Honor."

"I'd feel better about that if you were actually a Scout at some point."

"I dated a Scout once. Is that close enough?"

I scratch my beard. "I suppose so," I say. "You coming to my room tonight?"

She shakes her head. "Not tonight," she says. "I think I need a little sleep tonight."

I pull her to me, longing to feel her body. To be inside of her. My cravings and desire for Bailey only increase with each passing day. Which is both a blessing, and a curse, I think.

"I'd let you sleep with me," I offer.

She laughs softly. "There's a difference between passing out from being physically spent, and actually getting some sleep."

"Okay," I say and plant a soft kiss on the tip of her nose. "Fair enough."

She gives me a grateful little smile, then starts to turn away. I hold her hand and turn her back to me again. Something isn't right. I don't know what it is, but I know it. I can see it plain as day. I just wish she'd talk to me about it.

"You sure it's nothing I did?"

"Positive," she says. "I promise."

I nod and kiss her cheek before letting go of her hand. She stands on her tip-toes and places a soft kiss on my lips before turning away and heading upstairs, leaving me alone in the silence of the house's lower level.

The staff is busy cleaning up from our dinner, and I have nothing to do. Tomorrow's going to be a long day too, so I should probably just go to bed and get some rest.

I head upstairs, and as I walk down the hallway, my eyes linger on the door at the end – Bailey's door. I don't even necessarily need to have sex with her tonight. Just feeling her body snuggled up close to me would be enough. I just wish I knew what was going on with her today.

I step into my room and close the door behind me. Reaching out, I flip on the light and freeze. Posed very seductively, and wearing next-to-nothing, is Laurel. Because, of course, she's laying on my bed half-naked.

Wearing black stilettos, thigh-high stockings, a garter belt, black panties, and a matching bra, Laurel is the picture of seduction. The way she's splayed out on my bed, you'd swear she's doing a photo-shoot for any number of men's magazines.

I can't deny that she's gorgeous. Laurel has always been a knock-out. She's a beautiful woman, no question about it. But, I wouldn't fuck her with somebody else's dick.

"Wow, bringing out the big guns, huh?" I ask.

"I know what you like," she purrs. "I just wanted you to remember that. Remember that I can give you things nobody else can because I know you, Colin."

"That may have been true at one point, but that time has long passed," I say.

She writhes around on the bed, cupping her own breasts, and running her tongue seductively across her lips. Laurel gets to her knees on the bed, her gaze locked on mine, and slides her hand between her thighs. She slips her hand into her panties and starts to touch herself. She moans and gasps softly as she grinds on herself.

She's seriously pulling out all the stops tonight.

I lean against the door and fold my arms over my chest, my expression one of total boredom. If it had been Bailey on my bed doing that, I would have been all over it. In a heartbeat. It's crazy, but all Bailey has to do to make me hard is give me a certain look. If she flashes me a sultry little look or bites her bottom lip, I become rock hard in an instant. If she were there, writhing and grinding on my bed, touching herself like Laurel is doing right now, I actually might die from happiness.

Watching Laurel put on her little show, however, doesn't turn me on – not in the least. In fact, I think it's kind of sad, to be honest. Desperate. She's clinging to something she knows she can't have – I mean, come on, she has to know, on some level, that she's never getting me back, right? – but is desperately trying to hang on to it anyway.

She thinks that by ticking off all the boxes on my arousal check-list, I'm going to lose control of myself and bang her. The problem is – at least, for Laurel, anyway – is that for me to want to sleep with someone, I need more than what I can get from just watching porn. I need that connection. I need that bond and trust.

All three are things Laurel callously threw away, and Bailey and I have in spades.

"Don't you want me, baby?" she moans.

"Not really," I say.

"You know you want me," she says. "I can see how hard you are for me."

"Well, I do want you to get out of my room," I say. "And if you think I'm hard, you better get your eyes checked."

She pouts for a moment, then unhooks her bra, letting it fall, sliding off the bed. Her hips swishing, her breasts bouncing, and her eyes locked onto mine, she crosses the room.

"This is not happening," I say.

"Yes, it is."

"It's really not. Now, get out of my room – in fact, get out of my house – before I call the police," I say. "It was a mistake to let you come here in the first place."

"Don't say that, baby," she says. "I saw you and Bailey in the living room the other night. It didn't look like you were having much fun."

What the hell.

"Don't call me that," I seethe, anger pulsing through my veins. "I knew you were fucking watching us. That's it, Laurel, I'm done with your shit. Get out of my house. Now."

"Where am I going to go?" she pouts.

"Not my problem," I say. "You wore out your welcome here."

"If I say I'm sorry, can I stay?"

"Nope."

"If I say I'm sorry, and I suck your cock, can I stay?"

I look at her for a long moment and shake my head. "What in the hell is wrong with you?" I ask. "What in the hell happened to you? When did you turn into this pathetic, disgusting excuse of a human being?"

I see tears welling in her eyes, but she blinks them back. She's determined to make something out of this – to make her little seduction game work. She doesn't seem to realize, though, that she's already failed. Miserably.

Laurel reaches down, grabbing hold of my cock through my pants and gripping it tightly. I grab her by the wrist, and push her backward, pushing her up against the wall. I pin her arms over her head, my face inches from her. Fury radiates from my every pore, and a thousand thoughts, each darker than the last, float through my mind.

Laurel moans loudly, a small smile touching her lips. I have no idea what she thinks she's doing. This is about the least sexy thing I can think of, but she's acting like she's about to come.

"Yes, baby," she moans. "Give it to me hard and rough. Just like you used to. Just how I like it. Give it to me, baby."

Confusion sweeps over me and I'm starting to think she's lost her mind, until I realize she's not looking at me. She's looking past me. Letting go of her wrists, I turn around and see Bailey standing in my bedroom doorway, her face red and blotchy, tears rolling down her cheeks. A gasping sob bursts from her throat, and she shakes her head.

"Bailey, this is not –"

"Shut up, Colin!" she screams. "Just shut up. You're a liar. You are such a goddamn liar."

I take a step toward her, but she backs up. I stop moving and try to implore her with my eyes.

"This isn't what you're thinking," I say. "It's pretty far –"

"I can't believe I listened to you. I trusted you," she spits. "I can't believe I let myself fall in love with you."

"Didn't I tell you, Bailey?" Laurel croons.

I round on her. "Shut the fuck up, Laurel!"

Laurel just laughs, as Bailey backs away toward the door. Her sweet, innocent face is the picture of absolute heartbreak, and it's tearing me apart inside. I have no idea what Laurel said to her, nor do I care right now. All I know is that it's pushing us apart.

"He's all yours now, Laurel," Bailey says. "You were right. You two *do* belong together."

She throws her engagement ring at me, then turns and runs back out into the hall. I step toward her, but she flees. I hear her footsteps pounding on the hardwood floor as she heads for the front door. A hand grasps my shoulder, trying to hold me tight. I round on Laurel again.

"Get your fucking hand off me," I snap.

"Baby, this is the way it should be, though."

I remove her hand, and give her a gentle shove, just to clear out some space between us. She hits the wall behind her with a muffled curse, and I sprint for the door. Bailey has a lead on me, but as I bound down the stairs, I think I can catch her before she gets to the end of the driveway.

"Bailey," I call to her. "Wait. This is not what you think!"

She reaches the front door ahead of me and throws it open. I reach the door just as Bailey darts across the porch and starts jogging down the short flight of stairs. What happens next feels like it happens in slow motion – and I'm too far away to do anything about it.

I watch as Bailey's feet slide out from under her. She falls backwards, a strangled cry escaping her. Bailey's feet fly up as her head goes down, and the next thing I hear is a sickening crack as she hits the steps headfirst. She slides down the ice-covered stairs, coming to rest at the bottom, where she lays completely motionless and still.

"Oh, God. Oh, shit!" I yell, then turn back and scream into the house. "Somebody call 9-1-1! Anyone! Get some help out here now!"

As I start to cross the porch, I hear feet pounding on the floor inside the house behind me as they bound down the steps. I reach the bottom of the porch steps where Bailey is laying and kneel down beside her. I turn my head and try to listen for her breath. I hear nothing. I put my fingers to her neck, hoping I feel something – but, feel nothing. I know better than to move her, even though she's laying in a pile of snow. She may have suffered spinal cord damage, and if I move her, I run the risk of making it worse – of turning something that she could have recovered from into something horrible and permanent.

Paige and Holly drop into the snow beside me, tears streaming down their cheeks. They look to me for answers, but I'm in too much shock to say a damn word. My brothers are standing on the steps of the porch above us, clearly not knowing what to do with themselves.

"The ambulance is on the way," Aidan says. "I told them to put a rush on it."

I nod, unable to take my eyes off of Bailey. Her lips are turning blue, and I can't tell if she's breathing or not. She's so motionless. So still. I'm afraid that she's dead – it's killing me inside.

Paige puts a gentle hand on my arm, forcing me to look at her.

"What happened, Colin?" she asks. "What was she doing out here in the middle of the night?"

I look up and see Laurel – dressed now – standing in the archway of the front door. She has a sweater pulled tight around her, and a look of faux-concern on her face. The rage in me threatens to boil over.

"Ask her," I say.

All eyes turn to Laurel, and she shrugs. "Bailey, I guess, saw something she didn't like when she walked in on Colin and I having a little fun."

I stand up, glowering at her. "You are such a fucking liar," I say. "She was in my room after dinner, wearing next to nothing, trying to get something going."

"That's not exactly how I remember it happening, Colin," she says. "It's okay to admit it. We're both grown, consenting adults."

"Is that why I heard Colin shouting at you to get out of his room?" Katie asks, stepping out of the doorway behind Laurel. "Because, that didn't sound like a consenting adult to me."

"You need to leave, Laurel," Paige says. "And you need to leave now."

"I don't have anywhere to go," Lauren pouts, as if that ends the debate.

"Not our problem," Holly says. "Get your things and get out. Now."

"This is a misunderstanding," Laurel says. "A total and complete –"

All of the sudden, Brayden's massive frame is looming over her. His eyes are alight with a rage I've seldom seen in him before, and his face is a mask of fury.

"Get your shit and get the fuck out of here!" he roars. "You do it on your own, or I'll pack your shit and drag you out of here myself. You have three seconds to decide. Three..."

Laurel looks around at each of us, her eyes wide with fear. "Are you really going to do this?" she whines. "Are you really going to throw me out in the cold on Christmas?"

"Two..."

"Colin, baby," she says. "Please –"

"One."

Brayden takes a menacing step toward her, but Laurel spins on her heel and runs into the house, bounding up the stairs and to the guest room she's been staying in.

"Somebody needs to make sure she's packing her shit, and I don't trust myself around her right now," Brayden says.

"I'll go," Aidan replies.

The world is suddenly awash in red and blue strobing lights as the ambulance comes roaring down the driveway. I fall to my knees beside Bailey again, feeling my heart shattering at the thought of anything happening to her.

The EMTs force me out of the way as they check her over. I stand to the side, my family around me, offering their support. Paige and Holly each have one of my hands in theirs, and my brothers all have a hand on my shoulder. I knew I cared for Bailey. That was never a question. But, in that moment, as I watch them carefully move her onto the gurney, and then load that into the ambulance, their faces grim, and giving me no signal of hope that she'll be okay, I realize that I love her. I love her so much, I can't bear the thought of living without her.

Chapter Twenty-One

Bailey

The first thing I'm aware of is the harshness of the bright lights overhead, and the stringent, acrid aroma that unmistakably belongs to a hospital. Then, as if I'm suddenly tuning into the right frequency, I start hearing sounds – a series of beeps, and other mechanical sounding noises.

As my senses all start coming back to me, I become keenly aware of the pain radiating throughout my head. I have never felt such agony before, and I almost wish they could cut it off so I don't have to experience it anymore.

I groan before sitting up and opening my eyes – and find myself staring straight at Colin, perched on the edge of the bed. He lets out a relieved sigh and a small smile curls his lips upward.

"Welcome back," he says. "You had us all worried sick."

I look around the room, finding it empty, and have trouble recalling who the "us" is that he's talking about.

"What happened?" I ask.

"You don't remember?"

"If I remembered, would I be asking what happened?"

He grins at me. "I see the fall didn't affect your attitude," he says. "That's a big relief."

"I feel like I'm pissed at you," I say. "Something happened, and I'm pissed at you. What happened?"

He lets out a long breath. "You slipped on the steps a couple of nights ago," he explains. "Went down awkwardly and hit your head really hard."

I nod, but even that movement sends pain radiating through my entire body.

"Why am I pissed at you?" I ask.

"Would you believe me if I said you're not, and it's just a side-effect of your fall?" he asks, grinning.

"There's something there. Something happened," I say. "I remember running out of your room —"

I bite off my words as images start flooding back into my mind. Then, everything starts to come back to me. Bit by bit, the picture in my mind becomes complete, and I remember. And as I do, I feel the anger bubbling up like some toxic stew in a witch's cauldron.

I cut my eyes over to Colin. A look of dismay crosses his face, and he lowers his eyes.

"The doctors said your memory would probably come back in a rush like that," he says.

"Get out of my room," I hiss.

"Not yet," he says. "Not until you hear the real story."

"The real story?" I spit. "The real story is I saw you with that bitch, half-naked, pinned to the wall, fucking her."

"That's not the real story, Bailey," he says.

"Like hell it's not."

I see a dark expression cross his face as he clenches his jaw. He stands up from the bed and slips his hands into his pockets, turning his back to me, and looking out the window. As I look at him, I feel my heart breaking. How could he do that? How could he betray me like that?

It only confirms the thoughts I've secretly harbored in the back of my mind – that Colin is no different from any of the others. That he does what he wants when he wants, without care about who gets hurts along the way. He does things his way, and if you don't like it, you can piss right off.

It kills me to realize that I let myself fall in love with a man who would throw me away like a piece of garbage.

"After you went to your room, I went to mine," Colin starts speaking, his back still to me. "When I went in, Laurel was already there – dressed exactly like you saw her. She tried to seduce me. Tried to get me to sleep with her. She did everything she could think of to get me to sleep with her. And I said no. I said no a thousand times. In fact, right before you came in, I was telling her to get the fuck out of my house."

"Yeah, it sure looked that way with you fucking her up against the wall like that, Colin."

He rounds on me, his face a mask of outrage. "I never fucked her, Bailey," he growls. "My pants never came off. She tried to take them off of me. That's when I grabbed her and pinned her to the wall. To make her stop. I told her I wanted nothing to do with her because I'm in love with you."

Those last few words hit me with a ton of force, leaving me light-headed and gasping for air. Words I longed to hear, I'm suddenly hearing, and I have to wonder if I'm only hearing them because he got caught fucking another woman.

I shake my head, then remember why I'm in the hospital in the first place, as explosions of pain light up my brain. "I want to believe you, Colin," I say. "God, you have no idea how badly I want to believe you. But, I know what I saw."

"No, you know what you think you saw," he says, the frustration in his voice clear. "My pants were never off. There is no way I would have done what you think I did."

"It's true, Bailey."

I groan as I turn my head to see my new visitor. My head is throbbing, and I don't know if I need more drugs or more sleep. Katie is standing in the doorway of the room, looking at me with a concerned smile on her face. She gives me an awkward little wave.

"Hey, girl," she says. "You've looked better."

"Maybe I need a spa day."

"Couldn't hurt."

Colin remains standing at the window as Katie crosses the room and perches on the edge of the bed. She takes my hand in hers and gives it a squeeze. She looks me in the eye, daring me to look deeply and see the truth in her words.

"Colin is telling the truth," she says. "I heard him screaming at Laurel to get out of his house. I heard him telling her it was never going to happen between them, and that they'd been done a long time. She basically confirmed it in front of everybody later on, after they'd taken you to the hospital. Colin never consented, nor did he sleep with her. If you aren't going to take his word for it, I hope you can take mine."

I look deeply into her eyes and see nothing but truth and sincerity. Katie loves Colin, but I know, beyond the shadow of a doubt, that she would never cover for him if he actually betrayed me like that. Katie has far too much integrity to do that. They all do. It's one thing I love about this family, and about Colin.

And now, I feel like a complete asshole for doubting him. Again.

I turn to him and find him still glowering down at me. I don't know what to say to make up for what I've done. Colin has always tried to show me kindness, respect, and compassion. He's never shown me anything but love.

Yet, I keep doubting him. As he said once, I keep thinking the worst of him – and I don't know why I do that.

"I – I'm sorry, Colin," I say miserably. "All of my own doubts and insecurities – I mean, part of me wondered why you'd be with somebody like me, when you could be with a supermodel like her. I let it all eat away at me. I let my baggage impact my trust for you."

He runs a hand through his hair but gives me a small smile. "One, you are more beautiful than Laurel could ever hope to be," he says. "And two, there is so much about you that I love, it would take me days to go through it all. You are the most amazing woman I've ever met, Bailey. You astound me more every single day, and I want to spend my life with you."

My mouth falls open, and I stare at him wide-eyed. Even Katie is caught off-guard and stares at him with a shocked expression on her face. Colin is grinning like a fool, but he takes a small black box out of his coat pocket and looks at it for a long minute.

"This isn't how I wanted to do this," he says. "This isn't exactly my first choice, and it's definitely not my idea of romantic."

"I'm sure there are worse venues out there," I say. "If you want to keep looking for something truly awful."

Katie snickers, but when Colin drops to a knee beside my bed, she covers her mouth with her hands, and I see tears welling in her eyes. At the same time, I must have gotten dust or something in mine because they start to sting and water as well. What a coincidence.

"When I was afraid I might lose you, I knew in my heart, that I couldn't live my life without you, Bailey," Colin says. "I knew then that I had to come clean with my brothers. I told them the truth about everything. And that you bring me more joy than anybody ever has. I feel safe with you, like I can put all of my heart and my trust into you. You make me a better person. More than that, you make me *want* to be a better person, and I want to be with you. Forever. If you'll have me, that is."

Tears are streaming down my face and I look over at Katie, who's crying just as hard as I am. My hand is trembling wildly when I reach out and hold it against Colin's rugged, chiseled face. He leans into it, closes his eyes, and savors it like a man who thought he'd never feel it again.

Slowly, he opens those piercing eyes of his, and they cut a path straight into my heart. I feel the flutter of butterfly wings in my chest, and a surge of adrenaline courses through me.

"Bailey Janson," he says, "I want to be yours, and I want you to be mine. For real this time. Will you marry me?"

"Yes," I answer, my voice barely more than a whisper.

Colin's smile lights up the room as he slips the ring onto my finger. I hold it up and look at it. It's not the size that impresses me – though, it is quite impressive in its own right – it's the fact that it's

Colin Anderson who put it on my finger. My former arch-nemesis is now going to be my husband.

"Life is such a strange, twisty thing," I mutter.

"You can say that again."

"Oh, am I interrupting?"

We all turn to look at the newcomer – a short, Asian woman in a lab coat, holding a clipboard. Obviously, my doctor. I hold up my hand to show off the ring.

"Nothing much," I say. "Just a little impromptu engagement party."

The doctor smiles wide, chuckling to herself. "Well, I'm glad to see you in good spirits, and sounding well," she says. "And also, congratulations. I've seen a lot of things in this hospital before, but an engagement is a first for me."

The door to the room opens again, and the rest of Colin's family – our family – files in. The doctor looks around at them like she's on the verge of kicking them out. Technically, you're only allowed so many visitors at a time. At least, I think.

"Well, I guess I can't really ask any of you to leave in light of the happy news," she says.

"Happy news?" Liam asks.

Katie giggles as I hold up my hand, the light pouring in through the window glinting off the rock. There's a moment of stunned silence, quickly followed by an explosion of cheering, shouted questions, handshakes, hugs, and slaps on the back.

Fearing everything is about to go off the rails, the doctor asserts control again. "I'm willing to overlook the number of people in here," she calls out over everybody, "so long as you keep it down to a dull roar. I do still have a job to do, people."

Everybody lowers their voices to a whisper all at once. It's so perfectly choreographed, that it's hilarious. The doctor flips through my charts, asks me a few questions, and jots down a couple of notes. She closes the chart and slips her pen back into her pocket.

Thankfully, the pain that had racked my body upon waking

seems to be dulling with each passing second. I'm starting to feel better. More like myself.

"Well, we've done all of the bloodwork, and we've analyzed your MRIs, X-rays, and a thousand other things we're going to charge you a lot of money for," she says with a laugh. "Everything came back clean, and you shouldn't have any lingering effects of your fall. We'll prescribe you some painkillers to keep the worst of it at bay until your symptoms disappear completely."

Everybody in the room lets out a relieved sigh. Colin steps closer and takes my hand, giving it a soft squeeze. I look up and he's smiling at me, and I know in that moment – or rather, it's reconfirmed in my mind – that Colin's face is the one I want to see every morning I wake up, and the last I see before I go to sleep at night.

"Also," the doctor says. "The fall didn't harm the baby. There doesn't seem to be any damage, and you should be just fine carrying to term."

As if we'd suddenly been sucked out into the cold vacuum of space, the room falls silent around us, and a strange tension fills the air. I see everybody looking around at each other, I'm sure, with the same question on our minds – did we just hear her correctly?

"Come again?" Colin finally breaks the silence in the room.

The doctor looks up at him, a curious expression on her face. "The baby should be fine," she explains. "Your fiancée's head absorbed most of the blow, and it doesn't seem to have impacted the baby at all."

"Baby?" Colin and I ask in unison.

As if suddenly realizing that we have no clue what she's talking about, a light of understanding dawns in the doctor's eyes. She looks down at her chart and sucks in a breath.

"Well, this is awkward," she says.

We are all still standing – or, in my case laying – in a stunned silence. Nobody's moving. Nobody's speaking.

"As part of our blood panels, we run tests for certain hormones and –" she bites off her words, as if searching for an easier way to explain it to a bunch of laypeople. "Basically, we tested your blood for everything, Bailey. And when we did, we found that you're pregnant. A little more than a month along, but pregnant nonetheless."

Colin's grip on my hand tightens and when I look up at him, I see an expression of fear on his face – an expression I'm sure matches my own. A baby? How in the hell did I get pregnant? We're always so careful. We've always taken the necessary precautions. How in the hell could this have happened?

"I'm going to be a father," Colin mutters under his breath. "Holy shit."

"You're probably going to want to watch that mouth around your child," the doctor admonishes him.

As if somebody pulled the pin out of the dam, the explosion of emotion in the room is overwhelming. Colin's brothers are suddenly hugging him, slapping him on the back, and giving him a lot of ribbing about being the last one again. The girls are all taking turns hugging me, offering words of encouragement and support, and seem genuinely thrilled for me.

Colin and I look at each other, neither of us quite knowing what to make of the news yet. It's shocking, to say the least. And yet, in some strange, perverse way, it fits the rest of our relationship – completely unexpected.

Colin might be scared, but I know he's going to make a great father. He has so much love and compassion to give, and I know that our child's going to feel like the most loved kid on the planet. If anything, I'm going to have to rein Colin in from spoiling the kid too much.

As the news sinks in, for reasons I don't understand, I start to feel better about it. Like our relationship, it kind of just feels – right. It's nothing we planned for, but that seems to be our way, and it's only fitting.

And when I look up at Colin, and see that warm twinkle in his eye, I know for a fact, he's thinking the same thing I am. We simultaneously squeeze each other's hands, both of us looking forward to our future together – as a family of three.

From rock bottom to the top, as long as I have Colin by my side, I know there is no challenge we can't overcome – not even parenthood.

"I told you so," Holly whispers, leaning in close to me. "It's that damn Anderson sperm at work."

I laugh long and hard, embracing her tightly. My friend. My sister. My new family. Nothing in the world has ever felt as good, and as right as this.

Epilogue

Bailey

Fifteen Months Later...

"Are your eyes closed?"

"I have a blindfold on, Colin," I say and laugh. "I can't see anything. Where's Abigail?"

"She's in good hands, I promise," he says.

I let Colin help me out of the car – since I can't see anything, it makes the whole process a bit difficult. He takes my hand in his and guides me along what feels like a sidewalk. It's a cool day in Boston, and we're starting to come out of the grips of a particularly harsh winter. Or maybe it just felt like that since I was cooped up so much.

I wouldn't trade it for anything, though. Not with our sweet little Abigail in our lives. I know Colin was secretly hoping for a boy, but the second he saw Abigail, I watched him fall completely in love with her. He dotes on her, spoils her, and is every bit the amazing father I knew he would be.

He makes sure to take her as often as he can, to give me time to rest and to work on my art. After the show he used his influence to get me booked into a year ago, my work has been in demand. Patrons, both high-end and hipster alike, seem to love my work. Naturally, I have my fair share of haters and critics – it's just the nature of the beast – but I'm beyond thrilled to have finally found success as an artist.

The most gratifying aspect, however, is that my work has prompted discussions on the plight of the impoverished in Boston, and what we can do about it. There have been several public forums on finding ways to assist the underprivileged while leaving them with a sense of dignity and self-worth. I've seen plenty of changes within Boston itself, as well as pieces of state-wide legislation passed aimed at helping the poor.

That, more than anything, has made it all worth it to me.

"Where are we, Colin?" I ask.

"You'll see," he says. "Almost there."

A cool wind tussles my hair, making me shiver. I'm walking slowly and making my way down the sidewalk cautiously, even though Colin is patiently guiding me.

"Are you afraid I'm going to leave you in a ditch or something?" he asks.

"Actually, yeah," I tease. "Kind of."

He laughs. "Well, maybe if you'd bother me about doing the laundry less, you wouldn't have to worry about that."

I laugh along with him and slap his shoulder. "Maybe if you'd do the laundry every now and then, I wouldn't have to nag you."

"True," he says, "But, then you'd just find something else to bother me about."

"That all sounds very true."

We laugh together as we walk together – or rather, as he acts as my guide dog.

"Okay, stop," he instructs.

Colin gets behind me and puts his hands on my shoulders. I can feel a nervous tension coupled with unbridled excitement radiating from him, and I'm now beyond curious. I have no idea what he's doing – or rather, what he's done – that he's so excited about showing me.

"I swear to God, if all you're doing is proposing to me on the Jumbotron at Fenway, I'll kill you," I say.

He scoffs. "Like I'd ever set foot in Fenway. I hate the Sox," he says. "I'm an Angels fan."

"Oh, that's right," I say. "I forgot, you like losing."

He slaps my ass playfully, and we both laugh – though, I can tell his laughter is a little strained, and tight with anticipation. Whatever he's about to do, he's nervous about it. It's then I catch the murmur of whispered voices. There are other people out there. Other people are standing there and staring at me with this stupid blindfold on.

Great.

"Who's out there?" I ask, hesitation coloring my voice.

"Are you ready?" he asks, answering my question with a question – which drives me crazy.

"Yes," I answer. "Yes, I'm ready."

He whips the blindfold off me with a flourish, and I find myself standing in front of a group of people, including all of his brothers, their wives – Paige is holding Abigail for me – Father Gus, Cesar, and a host of other people we know. Our friends, family, and loved ones are all looking at me with barely controlled glee on their faces, like they're waiting for permission to explode.

The trouble is, although I'm ecstatic to see everyone gathered in one place like this, I have no idea what I'm supposed to be looking at.

I scan the crowd again, hoping for a clue. "What, you didn't invite Laurel to this little soiree?"

He laughs and gestures at the buildings behind the crowd. "This has been my passion project for the last year," he says. "What do you think?"

I look at where he's pointing – at a group of clean, modern, state of the art buildings. Colin claps his hands, and the crowd parts, revealing a silver-plated sign etched with the words, "Bailey House."

I stare at it for a long time, still not understanding. I look to Colin, hoping he can clarify it for me.

"Welcome to Bailey House," he announces triumphantly. "I've

been working with some partners and formed a few new alliances over the last year. What we've built, at no cost to the residents, is a large campus to help Boston with our homeless problem. There is a dorm with three hundred beds, a cafeteria, an outreach center, career training center – and a lot more that I can't wait to show you. But this – this is your vision, Bailey. This is what you've inspired me to do."

My heart races with emotion as I look at the buildings, then back to Colin. I put my hands over my mouth, feeling my eyes growing wide with disbelief.

"I – is this for real?" I ask.

"If it wasn't real, would we be standing here?" he laughs.

I smack him playfully in the chest as I feel my eyes welling with tears.

"In time, when we acquire more of the surrounding land, we'll be able to build more dorms, and house more people," he says. "But, I think we're off to a good start."

He hands me a printed brochure for Bailey House. It outlines everything from the mission statement to the available amenities. Tears roll down my face, and I feel my legs grow weak. When they can't support me anymore, I fall to my knees, my entire body shaking with emotion.

It's then that the crowd erupts in applause and cheers. I'm suddenly surrounded by the people I love most in the world. They're hugging me while offering words of congratulations. I don't know why they're congratulating me, though. Ultimately, this is all the doing of one man. My husband. The father of my child.

I turn to Colin and find him beaming at me. I pull him into a tight embrace, burying my face in his chest, and quietly weeping with joy. The level of happiness filling my body is indescribable.

"Thank you," I say. "It's not nearly enough, but thank you."

"I told you before, you changed my entire world, Bailey. That you make me want to be a better man," Colin explains. "This is a culmination of that. If there's anybody who needs to be thanked around here, it's *you*."

I have no words. For the first time in my life, I don't know what to say. I'm absolutely speechless. Stunned.

Surrounded by the people I love most in the world, held by a man who makes me deliriously happy, and standing in front of his creation – dedicated to me – I've never felt happier. More satisfied. I've never felt more loved.

And I've never felt more at home.

THE END

A NOTE FROM THE AUTHOR

Thank you for taking the time to read my novel Just Pretend. I hope you enjoyed reading Colin and Bailey story, as much as I loved writing it.

If you did, I would truly appreciate you taking some time to leave a quick review for this book. Reviews are very important, and they allow me to keep writing.

Thank you again for supporting my work, I am incredibly grateful.

R.R. Banks

ABOUT THE AUTHOR

USA Today Bestselling Author, The Washington Post Bestselling Author, International Bestselling Author, and Author of multiple Amazon Top 20 Bestselling Books.

As a man who is a hopeless romantic, your support is my inspiration. I'm excited to have you read my books so we can go on the hottest romance adventures together! ;)

ALSO BY R.R. BANKS

Accidental Baby

Accidentally In Love

Damaged: A Contemporary Romance Box Set

Saving Emma

Protecting Abigail

Taking Her

Accidentally Married

Accidental Daddies

Claiming Her

Accidental Fiancé

The Wedding Proposal

Rebel

Forbidden

His Property

Redemption

Desire

Damaged

Accidental Daddy

The Christmas Surprise

Becoming Daddy

Saving Her

Major O

Made in the USA
Middletown, DE
27 May 2019